# THE DEVIL'S IN THE NEXT ROOM

# THE DEVIL'S IN THE NEXT ROOM

## JOHN DURGIN

THE DEVIL'S IN THE NEXT ROOM
Copyright © 2025 by John Durgin

Published by Live Free Or Die Press

All rights reserved. This book or parts thereof may not be reproduced in any form, stored in any retrieval system, or transmitted in any form by any means —electronic, mechanical, photocopy, recording, or otherwise—without prior written permission of the publisher.

This is a work of fiction. Names, characters, places, and incidents either are the product of the authors' imagination or are used fictitiously, and any resemblance to actual persons, living or dead, business establishments, events, or locales is entirely coincidental.

Cover Art by Christian Bentulan
Interior and Ebook Formatting by Steven Pajak

Trade Paperback ISBN: XXXXXXXXXXX

*To Montana and Dakota, let's hope none of us go crazy on each other.*

"I tell ya, a guy gets too lonely an' he gets sick."

— John Steinbeck, *Of Mice And Men*

"He had discovered that there was not just one God but many, and some were more than cruel — they were insane, and that changed all. Cruelty, after all, was understandable. With insanity, however, there was no arguing."

— Stephen King, *Misery*

# Prologue

Rebecca Rogers stopped scrolling aimlessly through social media on her phone when she heard a thump from upstairs. She stared at the ceiling, listening for more sounds. Normally, something like this wouldn't scare her. She was used to babysitting kids, dogs, and even the occasional cat. This, however, was the first time she had to care for an elderly person. Mrs. Eggers, an eighty-year-old lady suffering from MS, slept upstairs with the TV blaring some informercial that mumbled from her room above.

That thump couldn't be anything good. Rebecca thought through all the possibilities. Falling out of bed seemed most likely, but there were other, *darker* scenarios that played out in her twisted imagination. After the old lady's son, Roland Eggers, gave her the list of instructions before he left, he had reiterated that she likely wouldn't even need to step foot in his mother's room. Rebecca was there merely for precaution since his mom wasn't allowed to be left alone for long stretches of time due to her condition.

She had almost turned the job down after finding out who

she would be caring for—she had seen enough horror movies to know the things that could happen to a single girl out in the middle of nowhere with a creepy old person tucked away in the home. As soon as Roland had told her how much he was willing to pay her, all those sinister thoughts vanished. She needed money. Fighting to get through college while paying for it herself wasn't easy, even with the partial scholarship she was awarded. Her full-time job at the coffee shop in town simply didn't cut it. So she took the gig, figuring the worst thing she might run into was an old lady who shit herself. Roland said he would be back by midnight, that it was a business meeting he couldn't miss, and he was desperate to have someone look after his mom. Rebecca tried not to pass judgment on what type of "business meeting" could possibly be taking place this late in the evening.

*Thump!*

There it was again, this time louder and from a different location on the ceiling.

*What the hell? Is she crawling around on the floor?*

Rebecca paused the TV, a show she wasn't paying attention to anyway, and listened closely. The illumination from the television screen bathed the otherwise dark room with a faint glow.

"M-Mrs. Eggers?" Rebecca whispered, not realizing her voice was compressed by fear.

A scraping sound moved across the floor upstairs. It was slight, and she likely wouldn't have heard it had she not muted the television, but it was there.

*A cat. It has to be a cat.*

Roland didn't say anything about pets. If he had, she would have felt much more at ease right now. The clawing right above her head stopped. She kept her eyes glued to the ceiling, as if that would somehow keep whatever was responsible for those sounds at bay.

Everything returned to silence, which meant the old lady either got back in bed or died on the floor. Neither of which Rebecca was willing to find out. She would just tell Roland there were no issues and let him discover whatever state his mom was in after she left. She felt awful for letting her mind go there, but she had enough issues on her plate, and seeing a corpse wasn't something she wanted to add.

*I have to check on her. What if it was my gram?*

*I will if it happens again. Otherwise, I'm staying right here.*

After waiting another minute just to be safe, she grabbed the remote to hit <PLAY> when something moved in her peripheral vision. Outside the porch window, in the sliver of light just beneath the mostly closed blind, a flash was there one second, gone the next. Her heart lurched into her throat, and she held back a scream. She looked at her watch, hoping maybe it was close to midnight and Roland had arrived a little early, but she still had a few hours before he'd be home.

At the very least, she would call her roommate, Lacy, to keep her on the phone. She went to her recent texts and dialed her, putting it on speakerphone. The phone rang until the voicemail picked up. *Damn it.*

"Hey, girl, this place is creeping me out. I know, I know, you told me not to take these jobs. Please call me back when you get this," she said, hanging up, then setting the phone on the couch.

She stood, still clutching the remote in one hand as she crept toward the window. The outside light cast a yellow-tinted glow over the porch, but beyond that, a veil of darkness smothered the land. Anything could be out there. Watching her.

"Stop freaking yourself out. You do this all the time. Maybe stop taking these jobs in the middle of nowhere if you're such a wimp."

*Yeah, well, college won't pay for itself. I had no choice.*

As she got closer to the window, she cowered into herself, instinctively trying to hide as she approached. Off in the distance, at the far end of the front yard, Rebecca thought she saw a silhouette. A figure standing perfectly still. She kept her eyes focused on the blurred shape—a lighter shade of black over a darker shade—and leaned closer to the glass. She didn't recall seeing any trees in the yard when she pulled in, but whatever it was, it wasn't moving. The silence was broken up by another foreign sound, a faint whisper tickling her ears. A voice? Multiple voices?

*It's just my imagination, seeing things that aren't really there. Hearing things too.*

Rebecca squinted . . . and the shape moved . . . ever so slightly.

She ducked down below the window. When she did, she accidentally hit a button on the remote. The show resumed on the TV behind her, the sound jolting her upright.

"Fuck!" she said, whirling around. She aggressively pressed the <POWER> button, then tossed the remote onto the couch from where she stood. She closed her eyes and sighed. "This is so damn stupid, Bec. Toughen up," she muttered.

After taking a moment to regain her composure, Rebecca turned and again looked out the window.

The figure was gone.

She instinctively felt around for her cell in her pocket but realized she'd left it on the couch. After one last glance out the window, she turned and marched toward her phone. En route, she noticed the front door cracked open. Only about two feet, but she sure as hell didn't leave it that way. She specifically remembered locking it the moment Roland backed out of the driveway.

*So who the hell opened it? And did someone come into the house?*

It was possible she missed Roland arriving home, but that didn't explain why the door was open, or why Roland didn't announce his arrival. A frigid breeze, far too cold for summer, blew in from the opening, and she pushed away the thought that it was something entering the home with her. Some unseen entity floating inside to take her.

Another thought struck her, and it sent a chill down her spine. *Was the door open when I heard the noises upstairs? Was someone up there with Mrs. Eggers?*

Rebecca ran to the front door and slammed it shut. After re-engaging the lock, she rushed back to the living room window to peek at the driveway for Roland's vehicle. She yanked down the string that pulled up the blinds—and screamed.

A human skull with ancient symbols carved into the forehead stared back at her. No, not a skull, but a man *wearing* a skull over his face. The empty eye sockets burrowing into her were blacker than the night itself.

Rebecca backed up slowly, but the skull-man didn't move, just continued to watch her quietly. She didn't dare go for the front door, knowing he was observing her from the porch, like a rodent in a trap. There had to be a back door that led from the kitchen to the backyard. If she could make it there before he made his way around the home . . . well, she didn't know where she would go. This was the only house within a mile, on land that was surrounded by forest. She would just keep running until she found the closest neighbor and ask the homeowner for help. The partial scholarship she'd received from Keene State wasn't for nothing. Rebecca had been a track superstar in high school, and though she'd put on the "freshman 15" that everyone warned her about, she still thought she could outrun some jackass wearing a Halloween mask.

She ran down the dark hallway, heading toward the kitchen. The whole time, she sensed the skull-man devouring her from the window, his soulless eyes wrapping around her and suffocating any remaining hope she had of escaping. The kitchen overhead light was off, but the one above the sink gave off a beam of a few feet. Sure enough, a back door came into view around the side of the refrigerator.

*Thank God!*

As she grabbed hold of the doorknob, the motion sensor light flashed on in the backyard. Her feet froze in place. The figure marched briskly across the lawn, toward the back door. It wasn't until they got closer that Rebecca realized it was a second intruder, also wearing a skull mask. This person appeared shorter, with a female build and long dreadlocks swaying in the moonlight.

The front door rattled, then cracked, as something repeatedly rammed into the wooden frame. There was nowhere to go; both exits were blocked by intruders. The whispers returned as though they were coming from inside her head.

*How are they doing that?*

Rebecca made sure the back door was locked—not that it would keep these sadistic freaks out—and ran back through the house. Her cell chimed from the couch, reminding her there was hope after all. If she could get to it, call for help, then hide long enough for someone to arrive, there was a chance. When she made it back to the living room, her phone lit up like a beacon, begging her to grab it. She planned to do just that until the front door pulled her attention away.

*Crack!*

There was now an opening splintering down the center of the door, and the skull-man's mask filled the space.

She ran to the couch and snatched up her phone while the intruder continued to work at the door, grunting as he broke through the wood with powerful strikes. She had a missed text from her roommate checking in on her, asking if she still wanted her to call.

Glass shattered in the kitchen, which meant the masked female had breached the home as well. Rebecca ran for the stairs, clutching her phone in one hand as she bolted up them two at a time. When she reached the second floor, she quickly scanned the layout, wondering which room would offer the most protection and give her enough time to call for help. She tried the first door and found it locked. Next came the bathroom, but there was only a standing shower, nothing to hide behind. The third room she came to had a wooden sign hanging on it that read *World's Best Mom*.

Rebecca thought back to the thumping sounds she heard from the living room. The idea of going in there to hide from deadly intruders, only to find the old lady crawling across the floor like Zelda from *Pet Sematary,* didn't exactly sound like the preferable choice, but she was out of options. Carefully, she pushed the door open just as she heard footsteps making their way through the downstairs.

The room was dark and only got darker as she shut the door softly and locked it. She didn't dare turn the light on and give away her location, not that it would take long for them to figure out where she was. Her thoughts went to Mrs. Eggers and how silent the room remained upon her entry. Only the continuous ticking of a clock on the wall broke up the dead air. She could faintly make out shapes in the room, but it was too difficult to see with any clarity. As her eyes adjusted, some of the blotchy objects came into focus. Rebecca spotted the bed against the far wall below a window, but there was no moonlight coming in as the curtains were drawn shut. She squinted, trying to locate the old lady, but all she saw on the surface of the bed was a lump of blankets, or what she assumed were blankets. There were no distinguishable body parts to let her know the lady was even in here. She remembered her phone and quickly dialed *911*.

After one ring, a male dispatcher picked up.

"911, what's your emergency?"

"I need help. Multiple intruders have broken into the home I'm house-sitting. They're wearing skull masks and I think they want to hurt me," Rebecca whispered, choking back tears.

"Okay. Stay calm. Where are you now? Are you somewhere safe?"

"I'm hiding in one of the bedrooms and I can hear them coming up the stairs."

"Okay. Remain quiet. We're sending someone as soon as

we can. Is there anyone else in the home with you besides the intruders?"

Rebecca remembered the old lady sleeping in the bed across the room from her.

"Yes," she whispered.

"Stay quiet, and if they're close by, try to hide with them. If there is more than one of you, the attackers may flee."

It was a thought, but Rebecca doubted the intruders would feel threatened in any way, even if she was able to wake up Mrs. Eggers. She swiped her thumb down the screen to access the flashlight mode, covering the beam with her hand until she got nearer to the bed. Quietly, she inched closer. When she got within a few feet, she uncovered the light and aimed it at Mrs. Eggers.

"Oh my God," she whispered, her trembling hand causing the beam to shake back and forth over the bed.

The old woman was there all right, but she wasn't alive. The bedding was wrapped around her brittle body like a spiderweb, and it was clear by the shape beneath that Mrs. Eggers wasn't in a natural position. Rebecca slowly reached out, pulled the comforter off the old lady, and instinctively threw it to the floor in disgust. Mrs. Eggers's back was arched at an impossible angle, her spine bent in the center, pushing the middle of her torso toward the ceiling. Her hands were withered and worn; the wrinkled skin sapped of any remaining pigment, and her bony digits locked in a curled position on her stomach. The worst part was her face. Her head was snapped back, her glossy eyes staring blankly at the wall behind the headboard of her bed. Her mouth was frozen open, the lower jaw unhinged from the rest of the skull. It looked as if something had sucked the life, her soul, from the cavity of her body. And on her forehead . . . symbols were carved into her skin, blood trickling down into her hairline.

They were the same symbols she had seen on the skull peering in the living room window.

"Ma'am? Is everything okay?" the dispatcher asked, the sound muffled as the phone shook in Rebecca's trembling hand.

The thumping. Something . . . *someone* was in here with—

Rebecca backed up, bumping into a solid mass. Labored breaths fanned across the crown of her hair. As the dispatcher on the phone continued to ask questions, Rebecca ignored them and slowly turned around, staring up at a third intruder, this one much larger than the other two. His skull mask stood out in the dark room like the moon illuminating a pitch-black sky, but his ebony eyes behind the mask drained any hope Rebecca had of getting out alive. He grabbed her by the throat with his massive hand and squeezed. Although his face was covered by a skull, the veins in his neck bulging as he tightened his grip were undisguisable.

Rebecca dropped the phone onto the floor, praying help came before they killed her, but she knew it was a false prayer. The door opened and there stood the other two intruders, the light from the hallway spotlighting their dark attire, foreign symbols in an ancient language adorning their jackets. The brute holding her obviously unlocked the bedroom door for them from the inside while she was staring at Mrs. Eggers.

The large intruder turned to face his cohorts as they entered. The grip on her throat loosened slightly, and Rebecca took a deep breath to fill her deprived lungs. None of them talked. Instead, they stared at each other, communicating through body language. Rebecca gaped at the smaller man, who slowly shook his head. The third member stepped around him, and that's when she realized they weren't dreadlocks dangling from her skull mask . . . they were dead snakes. Actual fucking *snakes*, the smell forcing her to gag as she got closer.

She watched helplessly as the female intruder approached her, tilting her head like a curious dog. The dead snakes moved and for a second, Rebecca could have sworn they weren't dead at all and were moving toward her, ready to strike and inject her with their venom. Then she realized they were just swaying freely like thick strands of hair.

"Please . . ." she forced out.

As she opened her mouth to make a final plea, the woman grabbed hold of her upper and lower jaws with both hands, sticking her fingers inside Rebecca's mouth and holding it open, forcing it wider. She tried to scream, but her jaws were stretched so far that she felt cracks on both sides. The pain was excruciating, shooting up each side of her face. The smaller man approached. Now all three intruders surrounded her, suffocating her space. They leaned down, closer to her hyperextended mouth, then something happened inside her. Deep in the pit of her stomach, it was as if her life force was being pulled, sucked out through her mouth. She clawed at the hand forcing her jaws open. Her strength was depleted; she couldn't even lift her arms anymore. Her vision faded, clouded by a blue haze. And then, her world slid into darkness.

## 3 MONTHS LATER

They say a brother's bond is unbreakable. That through thick and thin, right or wrong, a brother would do anything to protect his sibling. Whether they went years without speaking to one another or communicated every single day of their lives, siblings were supposed to look out for one another. As Brian and Bo Davidson stood silently over their mother's bed while her frail body took in struggling breaths, Brian wondered how true that was.

Their mother was going to die, and she was going to die soon.

Brian wondered if he would be able to care for his brother like Ma always had. He wondered if he could protect him. No matter how bad things got—and as a family they had been through a lot over the years—she always found a way to fix things. A dread filled the pit of his stomach, spreading like the cancer inside Ma. Their world was about to change forever.

His brother's dependence on their mother as a grown man

frustrated Brian. He often thought of how different things could be if it wasn't for Bo's condition. But then Brian would remember that it wasn't Bo's fault. He didn't ask to be this way.

Ma was asleep, her body failing against the cancer eating away at her insides. Her once beautiful blue eyes, now more of a faded gray, rolled behind her sunken eyelids. While Brian was no doctor, he imagined she didn't have long to live. He was bittersweet over her approaching death. It was a relief that her suffering would finally come to an end. After their dad died when they were young boys, it was their mother who raised them alone, teaching them how to become respectful men. Now in their thirties, it wasn't that they *needed* a mother to guide them through adulthood anymore, but they had never gone a day in their lives without her presence. Brian wished he could help. He wished he could take her to a doctor to see if there was any chance of a cure for whatever ailed her. *It's cancer. You know it's cancer.* But as much as he wanted to do that, he knew it wasn't an option.

"Ma . . . Will she sleep forever soon, Brian?" Bo asked.

"Maybe. We should let her sleep in peace, though. Let's go tend to the animals," Brian said, trying to hide the agitation in his voice.

Bo nodded, then turned and left the room. He towered over Brian, a physical freak of nature, but his mind was that of a young child. Brian felt that was somehow more dangerous; whereas he wore his emotions on his sleeve, all the anger had just built up inside Bo over the years, his confused mind unsure how to let it out. Someday, when Brian least expected it, he pictured his stronger brother snapping like a deranged chimpanzee at the zoo ripping off the face of some innocent bystander who was in the wrong place at the wrong time.

After their dad died, they moved out to the middle of nowhere, away from civilization, away from the necessity of day-to-day interactions with other people. Their mother took care of them with her own two hands and prided herself on doing it all without the help of others. They had learned to be self-sustaining, planting their own crops, breeding and raising livestock, and caring for their ten-acre property. On occasion, Ma would send Brian to town to gather supplies, but they had to be careful. Bo would often have one of his episodes when they did anything out of the norm. He had a routine, and he wanted—*needed*—to follow it. Which was part of the reason Brian found himself dreading their mother's death so much. He wasn't sure how Bo would handle it.

"I'm sorry, Ma. For everything."

Brian leaned down and kissed his mother on the forehead, her skin like damp papier-mâché beneath his lips, then left the room to join his brother. Bo was already out the front door, walking toward the barn, which sat close to the farmhouse. Their property was surrounded by acres and acres of forest, secluding them from the outside world. Trees flanked the house on both sides, as far as the eye could see. Only the cleared fields for crops broke up the abundance of maple, pine, and birch. A light breeze swayed the branches, reminding Brian that soon they would need to do their autumn cleanup, as many of the leaves had already begun to fall.

Bo walked across the dirt driveway, his cinder block feet scuffing up dust with each step. The innocence of his brother was something Brian had come to love, but it often made life difficult. After suffering a head injury as a child, it was as though Bo was trapped in time, forever a young boy inside his mind while his body continued to grow into a giant of a man. It had taken years for Brian and Ma to adapt to Bo's new personality, but after much trial and error, they had figured things out. There hadn't been an episode in nearly ten years. Brian thought back to the last time Bo lost control of himself, to the innocent pig that he had beaten to death with a sledgehammer because he thought it was trying to attack him, but all the poor thing wanted was to be fed.

They had enough crops to keep them busy and enough animals to keep food on the table. They had traded their cows with the closest neighbor, Ron Gould, a few years back when the work had become too overwhelming. When they needed beef or dairy, they just bartered with Ron. Ma hated depending on anyone else, especially him, but if they wanted to sustain their lifestyle, it was a necessity. Still, they had plenty of animals and crops to get by. Pigs, chickens, and Brian's favorite, their beautiful Morgan horse, Astra. She often kept Brian company on days when he felt an overwhelming sense of loneliness. Today was one of those days. He decided to head to her stall first while Bo fed the other animals. He passed by the pigpen, ignoring the snorts and pleas for food. They followed him along the fence, squashing the muddy terrain beneath them as they went.

"Sorry, piggies. You'll have to wait for Bo to come feed you."

Astra was chestnut in color with a white blaze traveling down the center of her face, her shimmering hide as soft as silk. Brian entered the barn and walked to her stall. The mare greeted him with a warm whinny. He smiled and stroked her mane.

"Hey, girl. You scaring off the foxes again for your friends?"

Her prominent blue eyes stared back at him, a rarity for her breed. Just one look into them calmed any nerves Brian often felt. In a way, he felt he and Astra were the protectors of the farm. He took care of his mother and brother, while Astra kept watch over all the other farm animals. The familiar scent of manure and urine-soaked wood shavings wafted off the stall floor. Brian placed the halter over Astra's head, then clipped the lead to it and opened the stall door. He led her to the west field, stopping briefly to open the fence gate, then set her free to roam. He watched her in her element for a moment, admiring the beauty of it, then set off to find Bo.

Brian found his brother spreading chicken feed around the henhouse, clucking to them as if they could understand what the hell he was saying. Brian couldn't help but smile as the autumn sun crept over the treetops, bringing a slight warmth to the frigid morning.

"You warm enough, Bo? Maybe grab a jacket, buddy. Still in the low forties," Brian said.

Bo stopped clucking and shrugged. "I like it like this, it feels nice. Can we spend more time with Ma when we're done? She might wake up soon. We haven't talked with her in a long time."

As much as Brian wanted to spend time with their mother, all it did was remind him of the past. What they went through as a family leading up to moving to the farm. He recalled Bo, only a boy, suffering a severe head injury and being lost in a coma for weeks. Standing over a bed was the way Brian had spent a better part of his summer when he was thirteen years old. Those were some of the worst days of his life, and the guilt overwhelmed him whenever he thought back on it.

"We'll see. She needs her rest, and if we keep going in and out, it'll wake her. Let's finish up out here and then I'll make you some breakfast, sound good?"

"Pancakes?" Bo asked with his lips curving up in a child-like smile.

"You got it."

Bo finished feeding the chickens with an extra pep in his step, then they moved on to the pigs.

When they were done, they headed back to the house and Bo took a shower while Brian cooked. He heard the water turn on, followed by his brother humming to himself. This was his chance to check on Ma without worrying about Bo. He turned the burner off and slid the pan to a cool area, then quietly walked down the hall, pushing the door to his mother's room open a few feet to peek in at her. She turned her head and weakly raised her arm, motioning him in.

"Sorry, Ma. I didn't mean to wake you."

"Non—" A violent cough interrupted her, and Brian was thankful that blood didn't come out this time. She wiped the spit from her chin and continued. "Nonsense. I was already awake. Brian, we need to talk. I'm afraid I don't have much time, and there are some things we need to discuss before I'm gone."

"Don't talk like that. We'll get you back to full health before you know it. I need to grab the wheelchair and get you some fresh air."

"Boy, I didn't raise you to be stupid. You know I'm dying, and there's not a damn thing any of us can do about it. I don't want to go outside; I'd probably wither up and blow away in the breeze at this stage. But we need to talk about Bo—about your father and about . . . what happened."

"He knows Dad's dead. Why does he need to know the details? It'll only upset him, Ma."

"I can't leave him knowing he didn't know the full truth. We need him to come in here and sit down. But we need to be delicate about how we say it. Can you do that for me?"

Brian wanted to say no. He saw zero benefit in reliving the past. For Bo, his dad was dead, and it was as simple as that. They had a gravesite on the property that they visited almost daily. If Bo discovered how his dad truly had been and what he did to the family, it would take him a long time to adjust to that, if he ever did. It could also potentially trigger him, and considering Ma wanted to be buried next to her husband's memorial, it would be that much more difficult when they finally had to put her in the ground. Still, he knew he couldn't say no.

"Okay. I'll bring him in after breakfast. Can I get you anything?"

"No, but Brian . . . there are some things I need to tell you, too, before I'm gone. Things you need to know. But I'm going back to sleep for a bit. Love you, son."

Brian nodded as he fought off tears, then shut the door softly and went back to the kitchen.

## 1996

"Boys, let's *go*! The game starts in an hour," Barry Davidson yelled from the living room.

Brian set his book down on his bed and looked over at Bo, who was looping a baseball belt through his pants. They had shared a room their entire lives, and getting dressed in front of one another wasn't something that bothered either of them. What *did* bother Brian was how they had to build their schedule around Bo's athletic events. Baseball was their dad's sport of choice, and Bo was his golden boy.

While Brian was a better student and listened to his parents far more than his brother did—at least to their faces, he *was* a teen after all—Bo often got a free pass for his laziness and lack of effort in school. And if Brian was being honest, the thing that bothered him most about his younger brother, beyond all the shameful jealousy, was that Bo didn't even seem to notice the favorable treatment he got. He was a humble kid who didn't try to brag or show off to his brother.

All that did was make Brian feel even worse, like he was some selfish jerk and Bo was Mr. Innocent, making his parents proud.

Once again, they were off to one of Bo's games, which happened to be the only time the family appeared happy around each other as of late. Brian got up from his bed and exited the room, finding his parents in the kitchen packing a cooler for the day's doubleheader.

"Do I have to go with you guys? Can't I just stay home?"

"It'll do you some good to watch and cheer your brother on. Sitting here on your ass all day reading books or doing whatever it is you do in that room of yours, won't," his dad said, shaking his head before looking over Brian's shoulder toward the boys' bedroom. "Is your brother coming or what? We're going to be late."

Brian sighed and nodded. He wanted to counter his dad's logic—saying that reading books was more likely to benefit him in the future than playing a sport that would, at most, result in a partial scholarship to a tech school and a meager income—but his dad got defensive whenever Brian tried to bring some semblance of realism to the family's pipe dreams of having a kid make it to the big leagues.

Bo entered the living room in full uniform, his baggy jersey untucked and reaching his knees. He carried his duffel bag full of gear as he walked across the linoleum floor, his plastic cleats clacking on the surface. His parents didn't say anything to him—yet another bit of favoritism Brian didn't get. Had he walked through the house with his shoes on, his dad would have forced him to sweep and mop the floor, even if there was no evidence that he trekked a mess through the house.

"Ready, slugger?" Dad asked, his tone changing from agitation to admiration.

Bo smiled and nodded.

There was a time when both boys played baseball together, often setting up in the front yard and playing catch until the sun went down. As they grew older, Brian lost interest when his skills peaked. He was good enough to make the teams, and most coaches understood the brothers came as a package deal, but that didn't mean they had to give Brian playing time. So he'd often waste his summers sitting in the dugout watching his brother and friends with their growing comradery while he scuffed designs in the dirt with his cleats.

The family rushed out of the house, piling into the truck and heading to town, eventually arriving at the field. Brian couldn't wait to get there, not because he wanted to watch the game, but so he didn't have to listen to his dad fawn over his more athletic child and pretend that he wasn't even there. When Dad walked Bo to the dugout, Ma grabbed their cooler from the bed of the truck and came around to Brian's side.

"Hey, kiddo. I know you don't want to spend your summer vacation watching your brother play, but you know how your dad is. I'll talk him into stopping for ice cream on the way home and you can get the peanut butter cup flavor you love. Sound good?"

"Sure, Ma. Thanks."

She playfully messed up his hair and kissed him on the head, then headed toward the bleachers to sit with the other parents. For them, this was their life. Everything revolved around travel schedules to watch their kids play ball all around New Hampshire. As he often did during home games, Brian decided to walk around the outfield fence and enter the trail leading to the forest behind left field. His parents wouldn't even notice he was gone.

He wasn't sure why, but being out of sight, watching from a distance, it just made him feel more comfortable. By the time he got positioned in the woods, the players were on the field. The smell of popcorn made his stomach grumble, and he considered going to the concession stand to get a bag, but he didn't want to leave his place. He watched his brother playing catch with the other outfielders to warm up their arms. Brian really was happy for Bo, but he couldn't shake the jealousy that came while watching him play. He glanced at the stands, which were now far enough away that the crowd was barely distinguishable, and noticed that his dad wasn't sitting with Ma. He scanned along the first base line and found him heading away from the dugout. Brian assumed he was about to go sit with Ma and the other parents. Instead, he walked around right field and back toward the parking lot. Brian forgot all about the baseball game, switching his focus to observing Dad.

As the crowd cheered on the home team with the first batter from the visitors stepping into the batter's box, Brian's dad disappeared behind a vehicle. It wasn't like him to miss any of the game, so whatever he was doing had to be important. Brian decided the risk of getting caught snooping was worth it and made his way through the woods, staying out of sight as he got closer to the parking lot.

The sound of the ball hitting the catcher's mitt snapped like a whip, and the umpire yelled, "*Striiike!*"

When Brian spotted his dad again, he wasn't alone. There was another man there, and though Brian didn't know why, just the sight of the guy sent ice trickling down his spine.

The stranger had the muscular frame of someone fit and healthy, but his face painted a different picture. Dark circles looked permanently carved beneath his eyes, which were such a dark shade of brown they appeared almost black. His long hair was pulled back in a ponytail, and Brian thought if he walked up and squeezed it, a puddle of grease would wring out onto the ground. The forest was silent, as if the bugs and birds knew they were in the presence of something evil.

"*Striiike* two!"

Fans shouted, a mixture of boos and cheers as parents from both teams had something to say about the ump and his calls.

The two men in the parking lot were too far away to hear the conversation, but their facial expressions led Brian to believe it wasn't a happy chat between close friends. His dad appeared on edge just being around the guy. *What are you involved with, Dad?* He thought about how his dad had been acting recently, and he did seem to be more agitated as of late. Brian just assumed Dad was getting annoyed with him, mistreating him because he wasn't the son he was supposed to be. But there were late-night phone calls and random trips to the "store" to grab stuff they didn't even need. How had Ma not picked up on it yet? Or had she?

*Crack!*

An aluminum bat striking the ball jolted Brian upright, snapping a branch beneath his foot right before the fans roared. The strange man turned to see what caused the sound, and Brian dropped down out of sight, hoping the crowd noise helped drown out his location. He was almost certain those unnaturally dark eyes had spotted him. Brian clung to the ground, wishing the soil would absorb him beneath the surface. At least the underbrush blocked him from the parking lot.

He waited, listening for approaching footsteps, but all he heard was the first base coach yelling for the batter to go to second as the crowd cheered on.

When nobody appeared at the edge of the forest, he slowly rose and peered out again. His dad was gone. Brian spotted him climbing the bleachers to sit next to Ma. He took a deep breath, relieved to have escaped Dad finding him and the punishment that would come with it. He glanced back to the parking lot and locked eyes with the strange man.

The guy flashed a sinister smile, revealing yellow teeth and reddened gums. He raised his hand and waved to Brian, causing the hair on his neck to stand on end. That was all Brian needed to send him sprinting through the woods in the opposite direction of the parking lot. When he felt there was a safe distance between them, he stopped to catch his breath. He sat on the trail, hugging his knees, and stayed there for the rest of the game.

## PRESENT DAY

After Bo showered and ate his pancakes, Brian told him that Ma wanted to talk with them. Bo's eyes lit up at the thought of spending time with his mother, but Brian wasn't ready for the conversation that would follow. He led the way, softly knocking on Ma's door. She didn't answer, so he eased the door open and poked his head in. She was sleeping, although her eyes flitted wildly behind her sunken eyelids.

"Maybe we should come back—" Brian started to say when their mother coughed.

"Come, boys. Sit." The words barely made it out, as if they were lodged in the phlegmy blood blocking her airways.

Brian entered the room and motioned Bo in behind him. They both sat in the chairs next to her bed. Because Ma was stubborn and wouldn't let them bring her to the hospital, he had set up her bed the best he could, placing extra pillows beneath her to keep her torso elevated. The room smelled of piss and decay as if it knew its inhabitant was leaving the world behind soon. He made a mental note to get in and clean the place to make it more comfortable for her.

"Ma, can I get you anything?" Brian asked.

"No. Just tell your brother the truth."

She had always been very direct, and with her cancer draining not only her will to live but her patience as well, she didn't mince words when she wanted something done.

Brian cleared his throat. He wasn't ready for this. For years, he'd wondered how to tell Bo what actually happened to him when he was a kid. How he got the head injury. How their dad was involved, and who he really was.

*How I was involved.*

He shook the thought and cleared his voice.

"Bo . . . you know we love you, right?"

"And I love you guys too."

"Ma wants to make sure you know some things before she . . ."

"Before I *die*, son."

Bo's eyebrows furrowed in confusion, and his mouth drooped in a frown.

"But you're getting better, right?"

"Listen to your brother, Bo. I don't know how long I can stay awake."

"You know how we said Dad died? That those men killed him?"

Bo nodded, his eyes glossing over.

"That's not exactly what happened," Brian said.

"What do you mean?"

The confusion overwhelming Bo was heartbreaking, and Brian hadn't even gotten to the worst of it yet.

"We told you that you haven't always been like this. You haven't always had these fears of things, of communication with the outside world. When we were boys, you were just like me. You were a star baseball player, one who Ma and Dad were so proud of, just like we always tell you."

Bo's response reminded Brian of a dog being scolded with no idea what it did wrong. The pieces were trying to come together in his mind, but it was clear he was getting flustered.

"Dad had a lot of anger issues, Bo. Even though he was proud of you, if we did anything wrong to upset him, he sometimes got physical with us. That's . . . that's how you got like this. You did something to upset him, and he attacked you. He caused damage to your brain. I tried to stop him, and he attacked me too. When Ma found him grabbing me . . . she shot him. She did it to protect us."

Bo bolted up from his seat and paced the room, pulling at his hair.

"No . . . no, *no*! Ma would never do that!"

"Bo! Sit down. I did it, okay? Your dad hurt you. I thought he'd killed you and was going to kill your brother. I had no choice. Those men . . . they changed him. He wasn't the same anymore. But not a day goes by that I don't regret what happened. I should have never let it get to that point with him," Ma said, fighting for breath after forcing so many words out.

Bo sat on the floor, hugging his knees. He rocked back and forth, whispering to himself, and all Brian wanted to do was hug his little brother. He carried a lot of regret holding the secret in all those years, but it didn't mean he was ready to share it. Ma was probably right. She said Bo would need to know so there was closure, and that she wanted to be there when he found out in case he had questions. Brian tried to find the right words to help.

"Just because that happened, it doesn't mean we don't love Dad. We can still visit his grave whenever you want. He was a good man that got mixed up with bad people. It changed him. He—"

"No! Ma killed him! You lied to me!"

Bo was hysterical, again getting to his feet and pacing. He flipped over a small table in the corner of the room and screamed. Before they could calm him down, he fled the room, slamming the door shut behind him. Brian felt sick to his stomach.

"It was the right thing to do, Brian. He'll calm down," Ma said.

"Calm down? It's not like we told him Santa Claus is fake, Ma. We told him his mother killed his father! Who knows what this will do to him?"

"You need to be the leader of this family now. That requires doing what needs to be done, even when you don't wanna do it. Sacrifices must be made. We didn't move all the way out here in the middle of nowhere for nothing."

"We did it to keep Bo safe from the world, to make sure he isn't overwhelmed with everything. Right?"

"There's more to it than that. We had to move out here."

"What are you talking about, Ma?"

"I need rest, son. I'm sorry. I want to tell you more . . . About what needs to be done, but I just can't right now. My body's screaming at me. We'll talk in the morning."

He wanted to know what she meant, but he knew he had

to respect her wishes. Without another word, Brian got up and left the room. As bad as he felt for Bo, he felt just as terrible for his mother. She was the one who killed her husband in self-defense. She had this weight on her shoulders all these years. And she carried it without even knowing the actual truth.

# 4

Brian awoke to Bo screaming somewhere in the house. He jumped out of bed, still half asleep, and headed for the door. Daylight bled through the slats in the blinds. Since the head injury, it wasn't uncommon for Bo to have night terrors. The nightmares often got so dark that when Bo explained them, it would make the hair on Brian's arms stand on end. So much death. So much misery.

As Brian blinked away some of the morning grogginess, he sped down the stairs to Bo's room. Only when he opened the door, he was met with a frigid draft seeping in through the cracked window, and his brother wasn't in his room.

"Bo! Bo? Where are you?"

The screams came again, from further in the house.

*Ma's room.*

Brian's heart thrummed in his chest as he sped down the hall toward his mother's bedroom. The door was already open. He knew what awaited him when he walked in, but that didn't make it any easier. Bo was on his knees at her bedside, holding her limp hand. Her eyes stared blankly at the ceiling.

"Ma! You can't die! Please . . ." Bo trailed off, resting his face on the bed as he cried.

Brian stood in shock, still glued to the entryway. He knew this moment was coming, and he knew it would be soon, yet now that the moment had arrived . . . it didn't feel real. Her suffering was over, but theirs was just beginning.

"Bo," Brian whispered.

His brother ignored him, so Brian peeled his feet from the floor and stepped into the room. The smell of death hit him immediately. He rubbed his brother's back, but Bo wouldn't budge. Brian looked at his mother's face, knowing that she was finally at peace after months of excruciating pain. He was the one she looked to for help cleaning up when she was too weak to move. He was the one she confided in when she needed to give instructions on what to do when *the day* finally came. Today was that day. His way of coping had always been to stay busy. Keep his mind off the bad things. If he kept moving, it didn't allow him time to wallow in grief or self-pity.

She told him she wanted to be buried in the south field right next to her husband's grave. She said she wanted to wear her favorite dress that Dad always told her she looked good in. Brian wasn't so sure the dress would fit her anymore—she had lost more than fifty pounds during her sickness—but it didn't matter. He'd do everything she asked of him.

"Bo. She's done suffering, okay? She was in so much pain. Now she can watch over us like she promised." He paused. "We need to bury her. She wants to be next to Dad, okay?"

Brian had prepared over the last few weeks, digging a grave, building a wooden coffin in the barn, and setting it up on a trailer so they wouldn't have to carry her all the way to the gravesite. Not that Bo couldn't do it himself if he wanted to, but Brian wanted to make it as smooth a transition as possible for Ma and her soul.

Eventually, Bo got up from the floor and turned to his brother, hugging him tightly.

"I'll miss her, Brian. What will we do without Ma?"

"We'll do what she wanted us to do. Take care of each other, right? That's what she wanted."

"Okay."

"Why don't you head on out and get some fresh air, bud. I'll take care of this."

"Take care of? No, Brian. We can't move her. Maybe she can be saved. Please!"

Brian fought the urge to start bawling in front of Bo. He had to think of how a child would react to losing a parent. That's what his brother was going through right now. There was a delicate line, and he didn't want to cross it.

"Bo . . . she told me what she wanted from us. I promise. She wants to be buried up by the red maple tree. Her spirit will always be with us, okay?"

Bo pressed his fist against his forehead and squeezed his eyes shut, forcing more tears to spill down his face. Then he gave one last look at his mother and left the room, leaving his brother alone with her corpse. Brian was so worried about Bo's reaction that he hadn't had a chance to take it all in himself yet. He grabbed his mother's lifeless hand and squeezed, shocked to find the skin was already cold. With his free hand, he reached out and closed her eyelids, allowing her to finally be at peace.

"I'm sorry, Ma. For everything. I wish I had the guts to

tell you . . . I'm such a fucking coward." He stared at her lifeless face, half expecting her to respond and tell him it was okay, that we all make mistakes. But he knew she wouldn't do that. Not just because she was dead, but because she didn't know everything.

There was much to do before they could get her to the grave. After sitting beside her for the better part of an hour, with no tears left to shed, Brian got up, went to her closet, and found the white dress she wanted to be buried in. When he slid the other clothes out of the way, he spotted a wooden chest in the dark corner. He stared at it for a minute, wondering what it could be. Curiosity got the better of him and he pulled it out.

He listened for Bo coming back, and when he didn't hear anything, he opened the chest, unsure of what he'd find inside. A musty smell wafted out, temporarily blocking out the scent of death coming from the bed. There were pictures of their family when he and Bo were kids, both parents smiling with the boys in the middle, and pictures of Bo playing baseball. The quality of the photos was nowhere close to modern standards. He placed some of them on the floor next to the chest, planning to show them to his brother later when they were reminiscing. Bo had heard plenty of stories about his childhood from before the injury, but he had never seen actual evidence of it that Brian was aware of.

Beneath the photos was a worn notebook. It looked as if it had survived a flood, the pages wrinkled and delicate to the touch. The first thing Brian noticed when opening it was that the handwriting was his mother's. He carefully skimmed through the pages and realized it was a journal of sorts. Much of the writing was smudged from when it had apparently gotten wet, but he could make out bits and pieces of what it said.

He turned to a page that twisted his insides, and before he got a chance to read the text that went with the accompanying pictures, Bo's thundering footsteps advanced down the hall. Brian shoved the notebook into the chest, closed the lid, then quickly slid it back where he'd found it. Just as he was scooping up the pictures, Bo appeared.

"You ready, brother?" Brian asked.

Bo stared toward the bed, his face drained of color. He nodded without taking his eyes off Ma.

With that, it was time to move their mother.

Brian undressed Ma, trying to avoid staring at her shriveled body. Bed sores infested her translucent skin, sending out a putrid scent that reminded him of spoiled meat. He quickly pulled the white dress up over her exposed ribs, accidentally grazing the rail-thin bones that pressed against the sunken skin and carefully put her arms through the armholes. After he got the dress on, he called Bo back in to help him lift Ma so they could take her to the barn where the coffin sat on the trailer. Even with the strength of his brother and the diminished state of their mother, Brian was shocked at how difficult it was to move her body. Granted, Bo wasn't using all his strength, too caught up in what they were doing and crying throughout the process. When they reached the coffin in the barn, they gently placed her inside, both taking the time to give her one final look before closing the lid.

They pulled the trailer by hand to the south field, careful not to hit any ruts or bumps along the way. Even with the chill in the air, Brian was sweating by the time they reached the plot of land where their family cemetery was located. The sight of his dad's headstone reminded Brian of the notebook he discovered earlier, and he made a mental note to go back to it later when he knew Bo was busy. There were things inside he didn't want his brother seeing. Hell, Ma clearly didn't want either one of them to see it based on where she kept it hidden.

Bo spotted the grave Brian had prepared for their mother, and the hole in the ground triggered more tears. This was it, the last moments they would be with her before she was buried forever. The finality of it all was something Brian wasn't prepared to deal with.

"I promise we'll come out here as much as you want to say hi to her, okay?" Brian assured, fighting back more tears of his own.

"Okay. I'll miss her . . . a lot. Will she be happy here?"

"Well, she's back with Dad, and no matter what he did to us, she still loved him. I know the stuff she made me tell you was upsetting, Bo. Dad didn't want to hurt us, believe me. He got caught up with some bad people and he changed. You get that, right?" Brian asked, although he knew Bo wouldn't understand. He just didn't want Ma's ceremony to be overshadowed because his brother was too distracted by his dad's grave. Bo didn't say anything. Instead, he continued staring at the coffin, biting his lower lip.

The air was heavy, as if it knew the tone of the situation. They lifted the coffin from the trailer and set it down next to the grave. Brian had made sure to dig the hole long enough so they could climb down in and still have room to set the coffin inside. When they had her situated in the hole, they climbed out and Brian read the verse from the Bible that Ma asked him to read. They placed some flowers on top of the coffin, and once they stopped crying enough to function again, they began shoveling in the dirt. They paused a few times, talking to the coffin, telling their mother how much they loved her. Eventually, the hole was filled, with no sign of the coffin beyond the freshly packed dirt. By the time they were done, early evening had crept in. They still had to feed the animals and clean the stalls, all before Brian could make dinner.

"We should get back, it's getting late. I think doing chores will help keep our minds off it. What do you think?" Brian asked, wiping the sweat from his brow.

Bo remained zoned in on the fresh grave, his mind off in some other dimension as he whispered to himself. Brian worried about his brother. He worried that this was an inciting incident to much bigger problems. Ma was the glue that held their dysfunctional family together, and while Brian thought he was prepared to look after his disabled sibling, the weight of doing that alone while also keeping the farm up and running pressed down on him. It was suffocating. Finally, Bo snapped from his daze and walked over to the empty trailer. Without a word, he grabbed the hitch and began to pull it back toward the house on his own. Brian touched the top of his mother's headstone.

"Love you, Ma."

As he went to follow his brother, he took one last glance at his dad's grave. He again thought back to the chest in the closet. Then thought back further to when he and Bo were boys, when he should have seen the signs that could have prevented so much from happening.

## 1996

Brian tossed restlessly. He envied his brother for sleeping peacefully, for having no idea what was going on outside of his own little bubble. Bo snored from his bed and Brian was tempted to get up and shove a sock into his mouth to shut him up. After tossing and turning for the past few hours, the face of that creep staring at him in the woods etched into his brain, Brian got out of bed and grabbed his book. He found his reading light and planned to pull the comforter over his head and read until he got tired enough to fall asleep.

Before he settled in, he overheard his parents arguing about something. Brian set the book and light on his pillow and snuck out to the hall, inching closer to his parents' bedroom.

"What's going on with you lately, Barry? You've never missed a single pitch of Bo's games, yet today something's so important that you had someone come to the field to meet you? Who was that man you were talking to?"

"Jesus Christ, Maggie," Barry muttered.

"It sure as shit wasn't Jesus Christ, Barry. Who was he?"

Brian leaned against the wall outside their bedroom; the door cracked just enough for him to hear clearly.

"A guy from work. Are you really going to give me shit for talking with a friend for five goddamn minutes?"

"It's not just that, and you know it. You were acting strange after. Hell, even *before*. You've been talking in your sleep too. Nightmares like you're a kid again. What were you two talking about today, and why are you getting dressed to go somewhere right now?"

"Stop."

"Don't you tell me to stop. I'm your *wife*. I deserve to know what's going on with you. Are you back into drugs? What the hell is it?"

"Drugs . . . for fuck's sake! I'm not on fucking drugs. I left that shit behind when we started a family. You know that."

"Then why have you been acting so strange lately? I can feel it in the air, Barry. Something evil. You're bringing something evil into this house. Just tell me, *please!*"

"That's enough of this."

Brian heard his dad grunt as he rose off the bed and stomped toward the door. Brian turned and ran down the hall back to his room. He jumped into his bed and lay there, his heart pounding in his chest. His dad moved through the house, but it didn't sound like he was coming toward their bedroom.

*So Ma sees it too. It's not just me. What is he getting involved with?*

"What were you doing?" Bo asked from the darkness.

His brother's voice startled him.

"Nothing."

"Do you think Dad has been acting weird lately?" Bo asked, as if he could read Brian's mind.

"I don't know. He was talking to some guy at your game today. The guy gave me the creeps. Did you see him?"

"No. I heard Dad on the phone the other day with someone, though. He sounded scared. Think he's okay?" Bo asked.

"I hope so. Go back to sleep."

Brian tried to force sleep to come, but it wouldn't. Bo didn't say anything more and eventually started snoring again. The front door to the house opened and shut, followed by muffled voices in the driveway. Brian again climbed out of bed, this time going to the window. Careful not to be seen, he pulled back the curtain a few inches and saw his dad talking to someone standing out of sight. He could only hear some of the words.

"I don't . . . something . . . happening to them," his dad said, pointing toward the house.

Brian adjusted his positioning to get a better view. The driveway was dark, but he spotted a second figure blending with the night.

As his dad continued talking, his hands moving animatedly, the second figure moved closer, the moon now illuminating his face.

It was the man from the baseball game.

"You just do as you're told. Stick to the agreement and all will be fine," the man said in a voice loud enough to hear through the window.

In this lighting, his appearance was even more disturbing. Every crack and wrinkle in his leathered face was amplified, the dark circles resting on the tops of his cheekbones blending with his eyes to give the illusion of two black holes.

They conversed some more before walking around the side of the house toward the garage. Then the truck the man was driving earlier backed out of their driveway. Brian was relieved to see him leaving, until he spotted his dad in the passenger seat as they sped out of sight.

Whatever was going on, it couldn't be good. Confusion commingled with fear to create a strange feeling in the pit of Brian's stomach. This was more than just a quick chat with a co-worker. Not to mention, Brian had met all his dad's friends from work. This strange man wasn't someone he had ever seen before today. After a moment of staring into the empty driveway, Brian climbed back into his bed. Finally, sleep crept in, but not before he heard his mother crying in her bedroom.

# 6

**PRESENT DAY**

Brian finished tending to the animals while Bo slept. At least he *assumed* his brother was still sleeping. He hadn't come out of his room since the night before, and Brian knew he was grieving. Before bed, he had attempted to go into Bo's room to talk with him, but the door was locked, his brother silent. Brian understood grieving was a natural part of life, especially when losing a parent that you were extremely close with. With Bo's condition, Brian was just nervous that the grieving would last longer if he left him alone, that his brother would stay in his room for days.

He scooped horse shit and caked-up shavings into the wheelbarrow with the pitchfork until there was none left, then spread clean shavings around to get the space to Astra's liking. When he was done, Brian wheeled the mess to the compost pile around the back of the barn and dumped it. Then he walked over to where he'd left Astra tied to the outside of the barn while he cleaned and rubbed her neck, scratching the spot he knew she loved.

"What are we going to do about Bo, huh? What do you say, girl? Wanna go for a ride so we can think about it?"

Astra rumbled her lips, sounding like a high-powered motorboat.

"Okay, okay. Let me get the saddle and we'll go for a nice stroll through the fields."

He headed back into the barn to grab tack, then an idea came to him. It wasn't often he got time to himself, as Bo was usually out here with him during the day. Brian quietly entered the home, listening for his brother. When only silence greeted him, he snuck upstairs and into his bedroom, got on his knees, and reached under the bed. He pulled out a small box and set it on his comforter.

Making sure Bo hadn't come into his room, he lifted the lid to reveal a portable radio. Small electronics of any kind in the house had to be hidden from Bo, or he would have a meltdown. After the accident, when they were still boys, Ma would often sneak the radio to Brian while Bo was busy or sleeping. As they grew older, Brian and Ma agreed to limited exposure and to make sure Bo never discovered it. It had been their little secret, and the nostalgia of it sent an unbearable pain through Brian's heart.

It wasn't just fear of certain electronics that came with the head injury. Bo had random episodes where he'd freak out, screaming at the top of his lungs and throwing stuff. There wasn't much that helped in those situations. Talking calmly just went ignored. Raising voices to be heard over the screaming only escalated matters. Touching him led to things getting physical, and getting physical with a man as naturally strong as Bo was not something Brian wanted any part of. And while it had been years since one of his intense episodes, it always felt like one was on the verge of rising to the surface.

Ma was the only one who could get through to Bo in those moments. When Brian was cleaning Astra's stall, he considered what he would do if his brother had one of those episodes. The incidents were often triggered by lack of sleep, by the nightmares that consumed so many of Bo's nights. He could only assume that Bo didn't sleep well last night.

Right now, Brian wanted—*needed*—to clear his mind. Listening to some music while spending time with Astra was just the cure.

He stuck the radio in his pocket and returned to the barn to grab the saddle. When he had it in place, he checked to make sure the cinch was secure and pulled the reins over Astra's head. Then he grabbed the cantle, mounted her, and headed for the trail. The fresh air felt nice, as did the peace and quiet that nature brought with it. He admired the forest, full of lush, green imagery on each side, mixed with the autumn colors of trees turning for the season. As they neared the cemetery, Astra planted her hooves, unwilling to move.

"What's wrong, girl? I know you must miss Ma too. It's okay."

It was odd, almost as if she was scared of the gravesite, which she had been to countless times when he came to visit his dad's memorial. He shook the thought and clicked his tongue, leading Astra away from the headstones.

The trail ascended through rocky terrain, finally coming to an open space with knee-high grass. When he thought he was far enough from the house, Brian pulled out the radio and turned it on, keeping the volume low enough so it couldn't be heard from a distance. He opened his saddlebag and pulled out an apple, taking a few bites before cutting the core out with his pocketknife. He tossed the core into the woods and leaned forward, feeding Astra the rest of it. She loved apples, and Brian couldn't help but smile while watching her chomp down.

"Slow down, girl. I didn't bring much food for our little picnic. What do you feel like listening to today? Some rock music? Country? Let's see what we can find up here."

This had always been one of Brian's favorite things to do, and he appreciated it now more than ever. He scanned through the stations and stopped on one playing classic rock. The song "Free Bird" played, and it brought a tear to Brian's eye. It was one of his mother's favorite tunes, and he couldn't help but feel it was a sign. He listened to Ronnie Van Zant sing about leaving here tomorrow, wondering if he'd be remembered. The lyrics sent gooseflesh across his skin.

He closed his eyes and listened to the song, picturing his mom sitting in her rocking chair on the porch when they were kids, humming the tune. Astra munched on some tall grass, the apple apparently not enough to hold her over until dinner. As the song played, Brian listened to the fall breeze rustling through the forest. He was truly in his element. But then something interrupted the normal sounds of nature. He thought he heard shuffling. He opened his eyes and scanned the area. Brian was shocked to see Bo speeding out of the woods toward him with crazed eyes.

"No! What are you doing, Brian? Stop it!"

"Bo—"

Astra bucked, spooked by the charging giant in her peripheral vision, lifting both of her front legs high. Brian wasn't prepared for it, unable to grab hold of the saddle horn in time. His world turned upside down as he flew from the back of the horse. He flipped over backward, seeing Bo upside down for a split second before hitting the ground, landing on his neck with a sickening *crunch*. Lights flashed in his eyes as the wind was knocked out of him. Brian was now flat on his stomach, lifting his head to find his brother.

"Bo," he managed to mutter before losing his breath again.

He had a second to feel the pain, then he followed Bo's eyes as they were watching something behind Brian. Watching Astra. Brian had just enough time to see her front hooves come crashing down firmly onto the center of his back.

A sudden *crack* emitted from within his body, reverberating from the base of his spine all the way up to his neck. He tasted blood but couldn't think rationally to worry about internal bleeding.

"I'm sorry . . . I'm sorry, no, no, no!" Bo yelled.

Brian tried to respond, but he couldn't speak. He attempted to crawl, but it hurt too damn much. His body was broken. Every breath felt like a jagged blade stabbing into his ribs. Astra continued to whinny, as if she understood she had accidentally crushed her owner. Brian wanted to tell her it was okay, that it wasn't her fault, and that accidents happen. But as he tried to turn over, his eyes closed and everything faded to nothing.

As Brian lost consciousness, the radio continued to play from the tall grass where it had fallen, the song ending and segueing into the local news.

*"Reports are coming in from several rural towns across New Hampshire. Gruesome murders, folks. Victims found with their mouths frozen open, jaws completely unhinged. Ritualistic symbols carved into the victims' foreheads. Law enforcement is stumped, and locals are on edge. If you're out there in these remote areas, lock your doors and keep your loved ones close. Someone or something is out there and leaving a trail of bodies—"*

Bo stomped on the radio, crushing it beneath his massive foot, returning the forest to its natural sounds.

Bo sat on the ground, rocking back and forth as he stared at his brother. Was Brian dead? He wasn't moving. There was blood pooled beneath his mouth. He couldn't stop thinking about that crack. That awful crack. He didn't mean to scare Astra. He didn't mean for Brian to fall off her back.

"This is my fault. So sorry. No, no, no. Brian! Wake up!"

Astra had taken off, roaming the field, leaving Bo alone with his injured brother. All he wanted to do was warn Brian to get away from the radio. It was dangerous, and he assumed Brian would have realized that by now. He couldn't bring himself to think of losing both Ma and his brother. He needed both of them and to have neither would be impossible to live with. He had to get Brian home. He'd feel better in Ma's bed. Ma always made things better.

*I'm still with you, son. I can guide you on how to help your brother.*

## The Devil's in the Next Room

"Ma? Where are you? How can I hear you in my head like that?"

Bo looked around frantically, trying to find his mother. He heard her as clear as day, right there in his ears, yet she was nowhere to be found.

*That's not important right now. What is important, is you getting Brian back to the farm and taking care of him. Just like we took care of you all those years. Can you do that?*

"Y-yes. I'll take care of Brian, just like he took care of me. Yes."

He continued to rock back and forth, wanting Ma to speak again but also fearing her voice. She was supposed to be dead, buried near the red tree. But somehow, her voice was still here. This must have been what she meant when she told him she would never leave him. She had promised. Bo got up and grabbed Brian's feet, then began dragging him toward the trail. His brother started groaning, and Bo realized it must not feel that great after Astra stepped on him. He was already messing up.

"Stupid. You're not smart enough to take care of him!"

He lifted Brian's unconscious body from the ground, then slung him over his shoulder like a bale of hay and marched toward the house. Brian's blood leaked onto his brother's shirt, and Bo remembered how bad the fall really was. Panic set in again—a tightness in his chest that came when he didn't know what to do. He picked up the pace and tried to forget about it, but his thoughts were scattered. He would come back and get Astra later. First, he would get Brian in Ma's bed and take care of him.

"I'm sorry, Brian. I won't let anything happen to you."

# 7

The first thing Brian felt when he woke was a blazing pain spiraling through his back. He attempted to open his eyes only to see blurred shapes and tiny balls of light floating across his field of vision. His head felt as if it had been split down the center with an axe. He tried to blink away the fogginess with no such luck. Once he had come to enough to muster a coherent thought, he recalled falling off Astra and then the horse driving her front hooves down onto his back, like a cement block being tossed off the roof of a building onto an unsuspecting pedestrian below. Astra clearly did it on accident, spooked by . . . Bo, coming through the woods with the intensity of a caged beast set free for the first time. Panic set in and Brian tried to sit up.

Something wasn't right.

His arms wouldn't lift off the bed. He couldn't feel his legs.

*What the fuck is going on? What happened to my legs?*

Brian couldn't keep his thoughts straight, and the headache wasn't helping.

Flashbacks popped through his mind like a set of moving snapshots. His screams that he hadn't even realized he was producing. Bo dragging him along the ground as rocks and roots poked into his crushed back. Ma, standing over Bo's shoulder?

"Bo! Where are you? I can't move!"

The room was dark, the curtains drawn. He squinted, looking for the familiar shapes of his room, but he was somewhere else. He was in his house; he recognized the distinguishable scent that every family had in their home, but there was another unfamiliar smell with it. Like rotten trash, a sweet yet burning smell. Straight ahead, he spotted an open space and realized what he was looking at.

Ma's closet.

Bo had put him in his dead mother's bed. And that wasn't the smell of trash . . . it was decay. The smell of death.

"Bo!"

The room was so damn dark. If he could turn the bedside lamp on, he'd at least be able to see. Being in Ma's bed sent a chill down his fractured spine. Maybe it was a severe concussion messing with his head. Maybe it was the fact that his mother had died in this very spot the day before.

*At least I think it was yesterday. How long have I been out?*

The silence was causing every thought to amplify, every possible scenario to play out. Bo wouldn't know what to do. He wouldn't know how to care for Brian. Did he take off to get help? Highly unlikely. He wouldn't use the phone; they kept it hidden so he wouldn't even *see* it and left the ringer volume muted. And he sure as hell wouldn't drive anywhere. He either went on foot, or he was still somewhere on the farm.

Based on the lack of light coming through the curtains, Brian assumed it was evening, but he wasn't sure how much time had passed. With no clock in the room, it was anyone's guess. He assumed Bo was somewhere in the house, doing God knows what. Brian tried to lift his arms again, but they wouldn't budge. Now that his brain was functioning a bit better, he realized it was because he was strapped down, as though Bo had used the bed as a makeshift stretcher. While Brian felt some relief in that, it was short-lived. He tried to move his legs, assuming they were just strapped down as well, but wasn't met with the same resistance. Instead, they didn't move at all. Brian couldn't feel them.

"Bo! Get in here! Come on, *please!*"

Something shifted in the corner of the room, a tall sheet of darkness moving just a few inches. Then he heard breathing. Heavy, panicked breathing.

"Bo?"

"I'm sorry . . . I'm sorry . . . I'm—"

"Bo? What the hell are you doing in the dark? I need you to help me. Take a deep breath, okay?"

"It's my fault, Brian. I didn't mean to scare Astra."

"Turn the light on, please. I need to see how bad it is."

"I can't. I can't do it. I'm sorry . . . sorry, sorry, sorry . . ." Bo rambled.

Brian knew he had to be careful. His brother was on the verge of a mental breakdown, if he wasn't already having one. Now that Brian knew his brother was in the corner, his shape started to take form. Bo was hugging himself and rocking back and forth. His phobia was an issue, but thankfully, it only applied to certain electronics. There was concern when the doctors first discovered his condition, which they called technophobia, that maybe Bo would fear *all* electronics. The fact that his brother was refusing to turn the light on didn't sit right with Brian because that form of electricity was never an issue before.

"Bo. Buddy. Can you at least get a candle from the kitchen and bring it in? I need to see my injuries," Brian said, talking as calmly as possible. On the inside, he was about to have a mental breakdown himself.

Bo didn't answer for a moment, just continued rocking back and forth in the darkness, moaning. He had listened to Brian's pleas, his shouts for help, and remained silent in the shadows. The idea of his brother handling a lighter in his current state wasn't something Brian wanted to think about, but he needed light. Finally, Bo walked out of the room without saying another word. Brian listened, hoping he'd hear him in the kitchen opening the drawer for the lighter. While he waited, he took in his surroundings some more as his eyes slowly adjusted. His brother had brought him in and set him up in bed, but he clearly hadn't cleaned anything in the room. In the corner, there were still dirty sheets covered in Ma's bodily fluids that leaked out upon her death, their scent poisoning the air. That had to be where the smell of rot was emanating from.

Eventually, Bo reappeared in the doorway with a lit candle in hand. The glow of his face displayed a man who was lost within himself. Pure sadness behind those eyes, yet Brian could do nothing to help ease that pain. As Bo entered the room, Brian's surroundings became clearer. His arms were strapped down with the horse leads. Everything below his waist was covered by one of Ma's blankets, which felt both comforting and disturbing at the same time. This was the blanket covering her when she died. It hadn't been washed and still smelled of death.

Bo set the candle on the dresser and walked up to Brian.

"Why'd you tie me up, Bo?"

"I didn't want you to fall out of the bed when you woke up . . . I can untie you soon, but you need to rest first . . ."

"*No*, Bo. Take these off me now, please. My arms hurt. I know you're scared, and I know you've been through a lot these last few days, but I need to be able to help, okay? Not be tied up like some lunatic at a nuthouse."

A stern tone usually got the point across, but he had to be careful not to yell. Instead of listening, though, Bo backed up, shaking his head.

"Ma always said you're too stubborn . . . That you didn't know when you needed help, Brian . . . I'll take care of you . . . Ma would want that . . ."

Every sentence ended with a long pause, as if Bo was trying to think of what his mother would want him to say. Brian sure as hell knew she wouldn't want Bo to tie him to the bed.

"I think my back's broken, Bo. I need to try and move, then I can get right back in bed, and you can take care of me, okay? Can you do that?"

Bo stopped backing up, staring at Brian in confusion.

"But what if you fall and get hurt worse?"

"You can help me stand, okay? We need to see if I can walk. I might need a doctor—"

"No! Ma didn't trust doctors. You know that!"

"And look where that fucking got her. She's dead because she wouldn't get help, Bo. Now get over here," Brian said, stopping himself from continuing down that path. "I'm sorry.

I don't mean to snap at you or talk badly about Ma. It's just . . . I'm stressed, is all. I promise, if I can't walk, I'll lay right back down, and you can help take care of me."

"Okay."

Bo approached the bed and went to work on the ropes, which were tied so tightly they were digging into Brian's skin, leaving irritated, raw marks. Brian didn't even realize how tight they were until the first one loosened and a sharp pain pumped up through his forearm as circulation found its way back to his limb.

Bo didn't look right. His face was in a permanent snarl, and he was grinding his teeth so hard that Brian heard the molars violently clacking together like two rocks.

"Bud, it's okay. We'll get through this. Take a breath, just like Ma says—"

"Said," Bo responded without looking at Brian.

"What?"

"Like she *said*. She can't say it anymore. She's gone. Gone forever."

Brian's heart broke. Despite how much he himself missed her, his brother *needed* her. Once the feeling came back completely in his free arm, Brian reached over and helped untie the other arm. Bo had tied the knots so tight that it was a wonder they didn't need to cut the ropes off. With both arms free, Brian shook them as one would after their limbs fell asleep, feeling the tingling shooting from his fingers through his forearms and biceps like hundreds of tiny needles.

Bo backed away, waiting for Brian to make the next move. The first thing he needed to do was take the blanket off to get a good look at his lower half. He hesitated but finally reached down and removed it. At first, nothing appeared out of the ordinary. His pants were still on from the fall and for the most part, he looked unscathed. But then Brian noticed his feet, and it wasn't so much that they appeared damaged, it was as if the connection between his brain and toes had a faulty wire. He told his feet to move, and they remained frozen in place.

Panic set in, and he was tempted to try and force his legs out of bed, but he didn't even dare sit up yet.

"What did you see happen, Bo? When I got knocked out, how bad was it?"

"Astra crushed your back . . . just like I crushed the radio. It could have hurt you. I heard your bones break, Brian. Like when I used to hit balls with a wooden bat . . . crack, crack, crack! But Astra, she's okay, she's good. After I carried you back and put you in bed, I went and brought her to the barn."

Brian closed his eyes. It was going to be difficult to talk through this with his brother. He had to remember to ask questions as though he was talking with a child.

"Thank you for helping me, bud. Why did you put me in Ma's bed? It still smells in here. We need to clean it out. I don't know if I can stay in the place . . . where she died."

"I didn't know what to do. But when she was sick, we made sure she was on the bottom floor for the wheelchair. I thought her bed would be comfortable for your legs. And I thought maybe if she was still here with us even though we can't see her, that she could watch over you," Bo said, then put his hands in his hair like he was in trouble.

"Hey, hey. It's okay. You did good. We'll get it cleaned up. What I need right now is to try and get out of this bed and see if I can walk. Can you help me up?"

Bo grimaced and shook his head.

"I don't think you should move. Your back is pretty bad."

Brian knew he was right, but he couldn't handle sitting here another second without doing *something*. He decided to try and swing himself off the bed, but first he needed to sit up. He took a deep breath and attempted to force himself into a sitting position. For the first time, he realized how in pain he truly was. Sure, it hurt while lying in bed, but this newfound pain was like a vise twisting around his spine. His eyes watered and he grunted in agony.

"Don't, Brian. Lay back down!"

He ignored Bo, pushing through the discomfort until he was sitting upright. *That's a good sign.* While his back thrummed with pain, he was at least able to move it, which meant he wasn't paralyzed—at least above the waist.

Bo rocked back and forth on the balls of his feet, too nervous to do anything. Brian rotated his upper body toward the door, wincing as the pain intensified. His legs were dead weight, and he knew before he even tried that they would be useless, but he had to make the effort anyway.

He had to know.

Squeezing the bedsheets that his mother died in, Brian used all the willpower he could, demanding his feet to swing over the side. Whether they actually listened or the momentum of his upper body carried him, his legs slid off the side of the bed. But Brian went with them. He fell face-first, landing hard. The instant his legs met resistance, it was like shards of glass stabbing into everything from the knees down. As the taste of blood filled his mouth, he was pretty sure he chipped a tooth on the hardwood floor.

"Shit. Bo, help me up, please."

He bent down and placed his massive paw beneath his brother's armpit, then lifted him up roughly, unaware of the added pain he was causing. Brian groaned, and for a second, he thought Bo was going to drop him. But his brother set him on the edge of the bed, holding him in a hug so he wouldn't fall over again.

"I can feel them. That's a good sign . . . but there's got to be nerve damage or something. Everything from the knees down tingles. I can't feel my toes, just a constant throbbing pain."

"What about your back? It's all bruised. You need to lay back down, Brian," Bo said in a demanding tone. It was so odd hearing him try to instruct, as he was the one who was usually instructed. Brian and Ma had to tell him to do simple tasks such as taking care of his dishes, making his bed, and even brushing his teeth. He really was like a young child in a grown man's body.

Brian knew his brother was right. Still, he wanted to try and walk. He attempted to push up on Bo's shoulders, but he squeezed Brian's arms and forced him back down onto the bed. His strength was overpowering, leaving Brian completely at his mercy.

"No! You will lay down. You will rest and me and Ma will take care of you."

A knot formed on the inside of Brian's stomach. He didn't know what to say. Not only was Bo forcing him to stay in bed, but what the fuck did he mean by "me and Ma"? Brian submitted to Bo and fell back onto the mattress, which sent an entirely new wave of agony through his body. The look in Bo's eyes told him he had no choice but to comply.

Once Brian was situated, he assumed Bo was going to leave him alone. He felt his heart trying to burst through his chest when Bo picked up the ropes again and approached him.

"Bo . . . you don't need to do that. I'll stay here, okay? You're right. I need rest."

"Ma always said you were too stubborn. That you always thought you were right no matter what. Remember she said you should be a lawyer for always arguing? She was right. I have to *make* you rest."

Brian tried to fight it, but Bo was too strong. He held Brian's arms down, wrapping a rope around each one and tying the knots tight. As much as Brian wanted to resist, his body was exhausted. Attempting to get up was a terrible mistake, but fighting to keep his brother from restraining him took away any remaining strength. Bo stared down at him with glossy eyes. Brian watched as a tear slid down his brother's cheek.

"Please, Bo. Don't do this. I need medical help; you said yourself how bad my back is. It won't heal on its own."

"Rest . . . Go to sleep, Brian. I'll tend to the animals and get you dinner later."

Before Brian could respond, Bo grabbed the candle and headed out of the room, leaving his brother in complete darkness.

## 1996

The months crept by, leaving Brian yearning for the school year to start back up. He never would have thought in a million years that he would want to see summer break come to an end, but here he was. Quitting the baseball team had somehow made it even worse. He was still forced to go to all the games, traveling with his family around the state, but now he was doing it with the added shame of being a quitter. At least when he was on the team, his dad pretended to be okay with one of his kids riding the bench. Now, he was just a loser who sat in the stands with everyone else.

This day was different, however. As his dad slowly transitioned into a different version of himself, he was spending more time with Brian. While Ma began to take on more responsibility, bringing Bo to practice and driving him to games, Dad gradually became less and less of an influence on Bo's baseball development. As strange as he was acting, Brian couldn't help but be thankful he was getting to spend more time with him. Currently, Ma and Bo were at practice, leaving Brian alone with his dad.

They cruised down the windy roads of Sunapee, to where? Brian had no idea. He didn't ask questions. Just the simple fact that his dad took him for the ride to tend to his errands was more than enough to make Brian happy. He watched out the passenger window as trees buzzed by until a body of water came into view. Lake Sunapee was one of Brian and Bo's favorite places to visit when they were younger. His dad had no intentions of a beach day, though; Brian realized that. He turned with a smile on his face to say something—and froze. His dad's eyes . . . something didn't sit right. He looked *scared*.

"What's wrong, Dad?"

"Nothing. Be quiet. I got a lot on my mind, kid. Grown-up stuff."

Brian did as he was told. His dad turned up the radio to drown out the silence. Brian wanted to ask where they were going, and why it was so important that his dad had to miss Bo's practice. While Barry Davidson wasn't a coach, he might as well have been. He was constantly on Bo, pushing him to improve, taking him to tryouts for different travel teams. Much of their free time was spent in the gravel pit behind their home partaking in extra sessions of batting practice. When Brian was younger, he thought it was fun. They even created a makeshift home run derby by setting up a crater in the shape of a baseball field. As they got older, playing for fun became something more serious, and their dad treated them more like clients than sons. As much as he wanted to know what could possibly be so important to miss practice, Brian wasn't about to ruin his one-on-one time with Dad.

Barry slowed down and put on his turn signal, turning down a private access road that led to one of the exclusive sections of the beach. Brian only knew the route existed because they could see the privately owned locations from the main beach, and he often wondered how much money someone needed to own or even rent a house with that type of real estate. Of all the places Brian pictured his dad going, the beach, specifically a private beach, was the last place to come to mind. For one, his dad never went swimming. Any trips here during the summer were with Ma, who took the boys on really hot days and lounged on the sand with one of her thriller novels.

The dirt road was surrounded by trees but up ahead, Brian spotted the water glistening in the sun's rays. His dad drove slowly, scanning the forest on each side as he went.

*Why is he so paranoid?*

When they reached the end, they came to an open space where sunlight blasted the windshield, forcing Brian to shield his eyes. There was a home a few hundred feet to the left, and the owners had their own path to the beach and private dock. This spot was all land, with a boat ramp for town residents to use if they possessed a permit. There was a vehicle parked on the ramp, but the rest of the space was empty. It wasn't until his dad turned the truck and parked that Brian realized who the other vehicle belonged to.

The creepy guy from the baseball game leaned confidently against the side of his truck, smoking a cigarette. He smiled at them through a cloud of smoke, and Brian found himself trying to melt into his seat. This man was the definition of terrifying.

His dad killed the engine and cleared his throat.

"Listen. I need you to stay here, okay? I just have some business to take care of, and then we can go rent a movie or something, sound good?"

Brian wanted to ask who this man was and why he suddenly kept popping up in their lives. Instead, he nodded and remained silent. His dad got out of the truck and shut the door, leaving Brian all alone. He could feel the man's eyes on him, but he looked straight ahead, pretending he was unaware. His window was cracked, and he heard his dad say something quietly as he approached the man.

It killed Brian to not hear what they were saying. An idea came, one he hoped would help hide him from the man while he eavesdropped. He grabbed hold of the sun visor and pushed it against the passenger window to block the top half of the glass, and then he reclined his seat back to be out of sight. They continued talking at the man's truck, so Brian slowly rolled the window down until it reached the bottom of the visor. If the man looked over, he wouldn't see Brian listening to them.

"Barry, Barry. You know what has to be done, fella. Don't make us remind you. You got two lovely boys that wanna see their daddy live a normal life, right?"

"Please don't threaten me. You know I'm going to do what you fucking want me to do. I don't appreciate that kind of shit. You know it won't work on me," Barry said.

"There's the feisty side of you I employed. But let's get one thing clear: I'll fucking threaten whoever the hell I want to threaten, you got that, Jack? Nobody talks to me that way.

You hold up your end of the deal, or things are going to get bad real fast for you *and* your family."

"All right. I got it. When's it need to be done by?"

"Two days. And Barry . . . if you make us happy, we'll fatten the pot for you. That boy of yours is quite the athlete. Let's keep it that way."

"Are you threatening my *kid* now?"

"What if I am? You gonna do something about it? I didn't think so. But no, you know exactly what I'm talking about. Our end of the deal doesn't happen until your end is finished."

"I don't . . . I—"

"Stop talking, Barry. I'm done here. You'll hear from me in two days. And I hope you bring good news."

Footsteps approached the truck, crunching over the compact rocks and dirt of the shoreline. Brian had no idea what to make of what he just heard. It was clear the man wasn't actually a friend at all, but someone threatening his dad—his *family*—if he didn't do something for them. Against his will. But what the hell was that comment about Bo? And what was the man talking about when he said "they" were helping his dad?

Barry walked around the front of the truck, glancing through the windshield and giving Brian a strange look when he noticed him reclined all the way back. Brian brought the seat up as his dad opened the door, and for the first time since they arrived, he dared to look over at the other truck. The man was still leaning against it, smoking a cigarette with a smile, watching Brian. Again he waved and bared his yellowed teeth.

"Hey kid, nice to officially meet ya."

Brian stared straight ahead, trying to control his breath.

When the door slammed shut, he almost screamed. His dad started the truck, muttering under his breath, and made a three-point turn, speeding away from the private road, leaving a cloud of dust behind them.

"I'm sure you heard some of that, Brian. It's nothing for you to be concerned with."

"What . . . Who was that guy, Dad?"

"I told you, none of your business. But I suppose . . . if you start riding with me, it'll be your business. His name's Marcus. I don't want you telling Ma about him, you got that?"

Brian couldn't believe his dad was asking him to keep a secret from Ma. He didn't answer, which prompted his dad to slam his fist against the steering wheel.

"I said, do you understand? Answer me!"

"Y-yes, Dad."

"Okay, good. Because as much as I want to tell her everything, the less she knows about this stuff, the better. The safer she'll be. I got mixed up with some bad people, Brian. People who will make our lives miserable if I don't make them happy. Problem is, it's not just a one-time thing, as much as Marcus makes it sound that way. They won't stop making me be their errand boy," his dad said, his voice trembling in shame.

*Marcus.*

"What does he want you to do?"

Brian wasn't sure he wanted to know the answer.

"Well . . . I'm not sure I'm ready to tell you that yet. It was Marcus's idea to have you tag along. I didn't want you boys anywhere near this stuff. I told him no at first, but he insisted. There's no telling Marcus no. But . . . Ah, hell. This whole damn thing was a mistake. I should've never brought you along."

"What was he saying about Bo? He's not gonna hurt Bo, is he?"

"*No*! If he ever lays a fucking finger on him, I'll kill him," he said, then took a deep breath to calm himself. "I met Marcus on a jobsite. Technically, he doesn't work with me, but he was around one day, just smoking a cancer stick, watching us remodel a home. This was back when you were still playing ball. Every time I'd look up, he was watching, hanging out at the edge of the forest. On my lunch break, I was eating a sandwich, minding my own business, when I felt eyes on me. I knew before I even looked up that it would be him. He was standing over by his truck staring directly at me with that crooked smile of his. I was just going to ignore it, but he called me over. I figured I was either going to get answers as to why he was there or tell him to fuck off, so I went. Marcus said he'd been watching our family. Saw how serious I was about you boys playing ball. He said he could help you two."

Of all the things Brian expected his dad to say, that wasn't one of them. Clearly he spotted the confusion in his son's eyes, so he changed the course of the conversation.

"I'm sure you have plenty of questions, but I'll tell you what you need to know, and that's it. Just like your ma, the less you know, the better. Marcus thought you could help me, and as much as I wanted to keep you out of this, he left me no choice. Tomorrow, I'm going to take you and your brother to the field, let you just be damn kids again. And then, I'll tell you more, okay?"

Brian scoffed. He had no desire to partake in something that would remind his dad of his lack of talent while spotlighting Bo's skills. Gone were the days when they just tossed a ball around for fun. He nodded without saying anything as they drove on. Brian spent the rest of the ride wondering what, exactly, his dad had gotten himself involved in.

## PRESENT DAY

J ay Sager sat in his recliner with the television mumbling in the background, staring at his elderly mother across the room. He was counting down the days until she croaked, and there had been more than one occasion where he wanted to assist her with that. She was an old, miserable bitch. The only reason he stuck around to care for her was because he knew there was a hefty inheritance coming his way once she kicked the bucket. His brother couldn't even handle waiting it out. He skipped town a few years back, telling Jay their mother was his problem and that he could have the fucking money.

Alice Sager, the biggest bitch in New Hampshire, wore that badge with honor when she was coherent enough to do so. These days, she mostly sat in her rocker with her mouth agape, staring off into God knows where as drool trickled down her chin. She was such a miserable person that Jay's dad split town long ago when he and his brother were only in elementary school. Sure, that probably didn't help calm her anger issues any, but it wasn't like she was Mother Teresa *before* he left her to raise two boys herself.

Jay had endless stories of abuse at her hands, both physical and mental. She would often take out her annoyance at being alone on him, wanting him to feel her misery. One time, when he was only six, a snake found its way into the house. He freaked out, screaming at the top of his lungs and backing into the corner. When his mother stormed in and realized what he was crying over, she decided it was a teaching moment. Instead of helping, she locked him in the room with the snake, telling him that only one of them would come out alive. After hours of clinging to the wall, watching the thing slither around on the floor, Jay finally built up enough courage to squash the snake with a book from the desk. He was so proud of himself, but when his mother came back in and noticed that it was her Bible lathered in snake guts, she slapped him across the face and beat the shit out of him with the Good Book.

Not only was the beating horrible, but it led to Jay having a terrible fear of snakes for the rest of his life. The herp in question ended up being a harmless garter snake that she led him to believe was some venomous beast. In a way, he understood what she was trying to do—she was trying to make him stronger. But she didn't have the added softness required to make a great mother.

The living room was dimly lit—only the television and a low-wattage desk lamp provided any sort of light in the large room. From his seat, Jay couldn't tell if his mother was sleeping or dead. Hopefully the latter. He got to his feet, rubbing his handlebar mustache as he approached her.

"Mom, you awake?"

She didn't answer, but once he got close enough, Jay noticed her chest slowly rising and falling with the off-kilter rhythm of old age. She was like an old car, sputtering on the last bit of gas before breaking down for good. Her gnarled hands were hidden beneath a small pillow on her lap. All he had to do was grab it, shove it over her face, and be done with it. But as much as he hated and resented everything about her, he couldn't bring himself to kill his own mother. She beat the ever-living shit out of him growing up, but she also demanded respect. With those beatings, that respect was ingrained into every fiber of his being.

Alice Sager suffered from dementia, and Jay had to admit that some of the best days he'd spent with her were during her episodes. Sometimes she forgot how awful she was, acting like a completely different person: someone who actually *wanted* a relationship with her son. But there were other days that weren't so nice, when she called him by his brother's name, or worse, his dad's. She'd ask him to pleasure her, speaking to him as though he was his father, and that would lead to Jay spending the rest of the night trying to shake that disgusting thought. And then there were the times when she just sat as still as a mannequin behind a department store window, whispering to herself, which led to Jay's skin breaking out in goose bumps.

He decided to let her sleep in her chair and head to bed. He didn't want to deal with one of her less pleasant episodes when he was tired as shit, so he wasn't about to wake her. After turning off the lamp, he placed a blanket over her and turned off the television. With the room now silent and dark, her labored breathing became more obvious. She wouldn't last much longer.

*That heart must be working fucking overtime.*

Jay grabbed a beer from the fridge and made his way up the warped stairs, not worried if the creaking of the old wood was too loud. His mother would sleep through a fireworks display right outside their porch window. He had made sure to crush one of her sleeping pills into her nightly glass of milk, not because he was trying to do any harm—although there were many nights where he considered crushing the whole bottle into her glass—but because she refused to take them herself. She thought they were poison and that he was trying to melt her brain.

He popped the top off the beer and tossed it in his bedroom trash, then sat on the edge of his bed, sipping the glass bottle. It was a lonely life, but he didn't know anything different. As much as his mom didn't seem to want him, she sure as hell did everything she could to keep him isolated with her. Maybe it was a form of tough love.

The moon was large, hogging most of the space in his window, lighting his floor in a bright blue hue. Beyond the window, the trees overtook the land, going as far as the eye could see. His mother didn't have much money when she purchased the place, but she had bought a run-down house in an area that wasn't exactly in high demand at the time. It was pure luck that downtown became a popular destination over the past few years with the new college a few miles away.

A cold draft found its way into the room, sending a shiver through Jay's core. He got to his feet and went to double-check the window, making sure it wasn't open. He often left it cracked a few inches to let the place air out—the old musty smell was overpowering at times. The window was shut and locked. The cold managed to find its way in more with each passing year.

He drank his beer, watching the trees sway in the wind, wondering if he would actually keep this place after his mom died. Jay thought his brother would likely show his face again once news broke of her passing, magically ready to rekindle their relationship and take his half of the inheritance. While their mom didn't have much liquid money, the assets she had tied up in the house and land would bring a hefty sum with the improved economy. The house value alone had increased almost triple from when his mom purchased it. The mortgage was paid off, so anything he sold it for would be straight profit for himself, free and clear.

Jay belched, then chugged the rest of the beer. He was too tired to brush his teeth tonight, which was starting to become more of a regular habit. He rubbed his tongue over his incisors, feeling the layer of sludge from the day's food.

*You're fucking disgusting, Jay. No wonder you can't get attention from any woman who isn't your mother.*

He threw the empty bottle into the trash, wincing at the glass clanking off the metal rim. His bed hadn't been made in days, but it still looked inviting, given his evening buzz settling in. He sloppily kicked his shoes across the floor and took off his jeans, then got in bed and pulled the comforter up to guard against the chill. The house was quiet, but Jay's ears hummed like they always did after a few drinks. Only this time, he could have sworn he heard whispers mixed in. A gust of wind struck the side of the house, creating a whistling noise through the window, drowning out the murmurs burrowing into his head. He felt himself drifting off to sleep.

Jay opened his eyes when he heard floorboards groaning downstairs. He wasn't sure how long he had been asleep, but the moonlight had shifted, no longer providing his room with a natural night-light. He knew he shouldn't have left his mom in the chair. If she woke up, she wouldn't know where she was, and who knew what the hell she would do? Walk out into the front yard naked? Try to cook her cat in the oven? None of it would surprise him after the things he had witnessed her doing over the last few months.

He sat up in bed with his head pounding. There was a glass of water on his nightstand, although he wasn't sure how long it had been there. His mouth was parched, so he grabbed it and took a gulp, tasting the metallic flavor their old well provided.

*Creeeak.*

His mom had to be navigating downstairs by herself in the dark. As much as Jay didn't want to get out of bed, he had no choice. With a deep sigh, he got up and turned on his lamp.

"Jesus . . . Mom, hold on, I'm coming!"

She didn't respond. He knew he heard someone walking around down there. The more he listened, the less it sounded like his mother's gentle steps and more like a heavier set of feet roaming the house. Living out in the woods often messed with him as a kid, all the odd noises and strange shapes taking form in the dark. Now, as a full-grown man, those thoughts didn't come back as often, but they were still there hidden deep inside him.

He walked into the upstairs hall, losing the minimal light his bedside lamp provided. The closest light switch was around the banister, so he continued down the stairs, holding onto the railing to guide him. From the top of the staircase, the downstairs resembled a black hole, ready to suck up anything that got close enough. Each step groaned beneath his weight, hopefully warning his mother that he was coming so she didn't lash out with a steak knife thinking he was some zombie trying to tear her apart.

"Mom?"

Still nothing.

Jay reached the first floor and noticed the front door was cracked open. The same cold draft he felt in his room slapped him in the face, only amplified by the wider gap in front of him. His first concern was that his mother went outside again, something she had done numerous times as her condition deteriorated. Even though the closest neighbor was a good half mile away, he had received a phone call from them two weeks prior saying that his mother was wandering around their backyard. When they confronted her, she said she was searching for her dog, Benny, a small poodle that yipped whenever someone got within five feet of him. But Benny had died when his mother was a little girl.

Jay decided to check her chair first to confirm whether she was still sleeping or not, then he would go search for her if she wasn't there. The lamp in his bedroom shut off, sending the entire house into complete darkness. *Did the power just go out?*

He entered the living room, fully expecting her rocking

chair to be empty, and was shocked to see her still sound asleep. At least he assumed she was asleep; the living room was pitch-black, only displaying the rough outline of her body in the chair.

He walked up to her, and after months of fantasizing about her dying, he wanted anything but that right now. He wasn't sure he could handle finding her dead body in the middle of the night after hearing strange sounds. As he inched closer, her features became clearer, but he still couldn't tell if she was breathing.

"Mom?" he whispered.

She didn't flinch.

Jay reached out to touch her, grabbing hold of her bony wrist. She jolted her head up and hollered in his face, wide-eyed with panic.

"You can't take me!" she said.

"Mom! Settle down, it's just me."

Her eyes wildly bounced around the room, unable to focus on anything of substance. Her vision was bad enough in a fully lit room, so Jay found it highly unlikely she could even see him. He squeezed her wrist, trying to get her composed.

"The skull-man is here," she whispered.

"It's just me, Mom. It's Jay, your son."

She shook her head violently, then looked over his shoulder into the void behind him. Her eyes opened wider, the whites reminding Jay of the moon he had admired out his window earlier in the night.

"No . . . No, no . . . Skull-man is here."

His mother had claimed to see imaginary animals, dead people, even aliens since her diagnosis. This fantasy was a new one. Jay was about to tell her she was just waking up from a bad nightmare when a floorboard creaked behind him. His mother kept her eyes glued to the background, and Jay was reminded of the front door cracked open on his way to the living room. He whirled around, but there was nothing there.

He ran to the front door and slammed it shut, locking the dead bolt. His fucking mother was going to send him to an early grave before she even ended up dying.

"Why'd you open the d—" Jay started, shaking his head and turning back toward the living room to see the shape of his mom standing in the darkness, motionless.

"Mom, what the hell are you doing?"

Jay reached for the light switch and flipped it on, but nothing happened. He flicked it up and down a few times as if that would fix the lack of power. The room remained shrouded in darkness, with his mom a statue in the middle of it. He slowly stepped forward, keeping his eyes locked on her.

"Jaaaay," she said, her voice distant.

"Mom? Are you okay?"

He took another step forward.

She let out a gurgling breath, then reached for her son. Before Jay made it to her, she dropped to the floor, and another figure stood in her place. A skull face stared back at him from the shadows. The eyes had a glint of blue, matching that of the moonlight.

He couldn't speak. His mother's body lay in a heap at his feet, and he assumed she must be dead. The skull face didn't move; it was just . . . there, floating in the darkness. No, the figure was wearing all black, blending in with the room, except there was something attached to the skull. Snakes. Real fucking snakes. Jay's childhood phobia kicked in and he backed away, distancing himself from the sick fuck just standing there watching him in silence.

"What do you want? Get . . . get the fuck away from me!" Jay yelled.

A floorboard shifted behind him, so he spun to look and spotted two more skull-masked figures in the entryway. One of them was massive, well over six feet tall and chiseled like an MMA fighter. The other was no slouch himself, wearing a black jacket with strange symbols decorating the chest. Jay noticed matching symbols carved into the forehead of the skulls they were wearing.

"Afraid of snakes, I see," the smaller man said, then laughed. "They represent our eternal hunger. A symbol of your death . . . and a rebirth of your soul as we take it for our own. One snake for every soul she's taken."

*Eternal hunger? What the fuck?*

They stepped toward him. Surrounded by the intruders, Jay had nowhere to go. He reached for his mother's cane leaning against the couch and swung it at the smaller man. The wood splintered over the skull, and Jay realized it was a real human skull, not some plastic prop mask. The man shook his head without speaking, then looked to the larger freak at his side and nodded toward Jay. Before he understood what that nod meant, the large man charged and grabbed Jay by the throat.

"No, please . . ."

The shorter man laughed, flashing an uneven smile in the mouth of the skull. Jay tried to fight, kicking at the brute, hoping to hit him square in the nuts and make an escape. He was bullied as a boy and learned early on that fighting dirty was often the only solution when you were overpowered or outnumbered. His kick missed the groin and hit the big man's thigh. All that did was piss him off, his grip tightening around Jay's throat.

"Who . . . are you?" Jay grimaced.

"We, are the Hollow Souls. And you . . . you are in the wrong place at the wrong time," the leader said.

Before Jay could respond, the larger man turned him around to face his mother as the third masked figure lifted her body from the floor. She wasn't dead after all, just weakened and beaten. She groaned, mumbling incoherently as the intruder forced her to stand.

"Now you will witness what we want. You will see why we are here," the man said from behind him.

Jay made one last effort to escape, but the tall man kicked the back of his knee, breaking a bone and driving him to the floor. The grip on his neck tightened, and the brute held him in place while the woman with the snakes positioned his mother on her chair, head drooping, gray hair hiding her face. The woman yanked his mother's salt-and-pepper locks until her face was aimed at the ceiling. Jay realized they had already started doing something to his mom before he came downstairs. She was acting almost drunk, slurring her words and moving her limbs lethargically. The lady with the skull mask and snakes for hair gripped his mother's jaws and tore them open, forcing a squeal out of the old lady. Jay had never heard his mother make a sound like that. It was horrifying, and he found himself choking on the fear growing inside him.

His mother's mouth was stuck open like a defective Pez dispenser, her lower jaw dangling from her face. Only the partially torn flesh held the mouth in place. Finally, she opened her eyes fully, staring at her son. In that moment, Jay regretted wishing death upon her. He regretted treating her like shit for the past few years, as though him being stuck at home and making nothing of his life was her fault. And it was all for nothing. He wasn't going to get any inheritance. He wasn't going to sell the house and start over fresh somewhere. Instead, he was going to watch her die, and then the three freaks would move on to him. At least accepting that fate made it easier to sit there. Easier until he watched what they did to her next.

The leader of the Hollow Souls walked around Jay toward his mother, who was trying to speak but the words only came out a jumbled mess with her mouth hanging open in a permanent yawn. The man turned to face Jay, and his lips curved up in a smile. He then focused back on the old woman, placing his hands on each side of her face as though he was going to lean in for a kiss.

What happened next depleted any thoughts of escape. His mother's body began to tremble—first barely noticeable, then increasing, like a tremor becoming a full-blown earthquake. The skin on her face rippled, sucking inward, her chest caving in on itself like a sinkhole swallowing her from within. A strange gargling sound escaped her throat, and then her windpipe snapped. The large man dropped Jay to the floor, but his crushed knee left him unable to move. Not that he would have thought to make a run for it otherwise because he was frozen in fear, watching a hazy cloud with a hint of bright blue coming out of his mother's mouth. Her eyes went wide, the whites going bloodshot as the cerulean cloud swam through the air into the skull faces standing over her. All three of them inhaled, and Jay could have sworn he saw their muscles bulge as though they were being fed strength from his mother.

Her fingers curled into fists, digging at the skin and drawing blood from her palms. Her spine curled into a U-shape, cracking and popping, writhing in pain until the last cloud was extinguished. Her body dropped to the floor, landing on her back, face up. Her dead eyes stared directly at her son, her mouth still in a frozen scream. The female member of the Hollow Souls crouched over her dead body and pulled a blade from her jacket pocket. Jay had no idea what she was doing, then she pressed the blade into his mother's forehead and began to carve. He couldn't see what she was carving in the dark, and he had no desire to. They were mutilating his mother's body. The intruders then turned their attention to Jay. They inched closer, and he screamed for the last time.

## 10

**PRESENT DAY**

A few days had passed, but Brian felt like he'd been in bed for weeks, if not longer. Bo did his best to care for his brother, but he was not even remotely qualified. For meals, he would bring whatever he could find, which often consisted of nuts and bread, but the bread was running low already. Bo had an obsession with peanut butter sandwiches, and with nobody in the house to watch his intake, Brian assumed his brother was having trouble with self-control. He pictured a preteen going through all the junk food while their parents weren't home.

Going to the bathroom was a nightmare. The first time Brian really had to piss, he told Bo to help him get up from the bed and bring him to the bathroom, but Bo refused. He didn't want to risk Brian trying to push himself before he was ready. Instead, he brought a jug for him to urinate in, but Brian couldn't sit up. After trying to get out of bed a few days ago, even the thought of sitting up sent a jolt of pain down his spine. So, Bo had to help him. It was one of the most humiliating moments of Brian's life. His brother had to unzip his pants for him and help guide his penis into the jug.

Eventually, Brian knew he would have to attempt getting out of bed again. This was no way to live, and he needed actual medical help. He wasn't able to drive, and Bo wouldn't attempt it, so he would have to sneak to the phone hidden in the house and call for help. The problem was that he was still tied up, and even if he did break free, there was no telling where Bo would be. Brian had continuously asked if the animals were taken care of, and Bo insisted they were. If there was one thing his brother did really well, it was his chores around the farm. But the food for the animals would only last so long without Brian making his monthly supply run.

The front door opened, and Brian heard Bo trekking through the house, whistling to himself. Brian was starving, having only eaten a handful of cashews for breakfast. It was now well past lunchtime.

"Bo! I'm really hungry. Please bring me something to eat!"

The whistling stopped, insinuating that Bo was going to respond, but instead, the house remained silent. Brian's concern for his brother's mental health increased by the minute. There were signs, albeit minor so far, that Bo was going to crack. He continued to act as if Ma was still alive, carrying out regular conversations with her about how to care for Brian. His eyes had a constant look of instability, as though one wrong sentence would trigger a colossal fit of rage.

After a moment, Bo started whistling again and moving around the house.

*What the fuck . . . He's ignoring me.*

Eventually, Bo entered the room with a glass of water and a bowl of something Brian couldn't see from the bed.

"Thank God. Bo . . . I know it's a lot to remember, but I need to eat more often than this. I'm starving, bud."

"Sorry. I was up at the gravesite visiting Ma. She misses us. She said I'm doing a good job taking care of you, though."

*Lovely.*

"How are the animals doing? How's Astra?"

"Good. I let her out all day and I cleaned the stall. I think she misses you."

"Horses are like giant dogs. She knows when something's wrong. Please make sure she's taken care of, okay? It's killing me not to be out there for her."

"I will."

"How are we doing on food for the animals? It's probably getting low. I usually go get supplies this week to stock up."

"It's . . . fine. I am doing everything right. Ma said so."

*Did Ma tell you to leave me strapped to a fucking bed?*

"I just need to prepare you for the inevitable. We will run out of food, and we can't starve the animals, Bo. I know you won't go to town, so you need to let me try and get help soon."

"Not yet. You can't even pee on your own."

Brian had no rebuttal to that. He sighed and decided it was best to change the subject. He needed to get Bo to remember his place in the family: not a caretaker, but the one who needed to be taken care of.

"Do you wanna hear some more stories about when we were younger?"

Reminiscing about the old days was one of Bo's favorite

things to do. Anytime he was having a breakdown, Ma would tell him stories about when he was a little boy. The smile on her face was infectious while she told the tales, and Bo listened as though it was the first time he had ever heard them.

"Can we talk about a Christmas when we were kids?" Bo asked excitedly.

"Sure. Have a seat. Can you bring that food over for me while we chat?"

Bo slapped himself on the forehead and ran to fetch the tray on the dresser. Brian wasn't sure what his brother had prepared, but when he looked inside the bowl, he almost lost his appetite.

"What is this?"

"It's soup like Ma always made. I put some of the veggies in and everything," Bo said, proud of his work.

Brian bit his tongue. Bo wouldn't use the stove, and they didn't own a microwave because he was scared of them. What sat in front of him was a bowl of cold chicken broth with frozen vegetables that were just starting to show signs of thawing. Suddenly, Brian craved cashews and plain bread again.

"Thanks. You're trying your best."

Bo rolled a stand over next to the bed, the same stand they used to set Ma's food on when she was too weak to come out to the kitchen. He then placed the tray on top of it and sat in his designated seat. The room remained silent for a moment, and Brian realized his brother was waiting for him to eat a spoonful of the soup. He hesitantly grabbed the utensil from the bowl and scooped a small amount of the broth, trying to avoid as many of the frozen vegetables as possible. He held his breath and quickly put the spoon into his mouth, swallowing the cold soup.

"*Mmm.* This is pretty good, brother. Thank you."

Bo smiled and relaxed in his chair, convinced he had done an admirable job with the meal.

"Can you tell a story now?" he asked.

"Yes. Do you remember the Christmas when we both wanted a Mongoose bike because our friends had them, and Ma and Dad got us the knockoffs? We got picked on every day riding to school until we made that jump at the park and all the kids saw us catching so much air. All of a sudden, they wanted *our* bikes . . ." Brian started, knowing Bo didn't truly remember the past, only what he had learned through stories over the years.

"And you made them think our bikes were the coolest thing ever!" Bo shouted. Then his smile slowly morphed into sadness, and Brian realized his brother remembered more of the story than he thought.

"We made them so cool that everyone wanted them . . . including the bullies. Mitch Crenshaw and his crew cornered me in a parking lot, threatening to beat me to death if I didn't give them my bike. Like Ma always said, I was a stubborn bastard. I wasn't letting those assholes walk out of there with my bike, at least without some bloodshed. But they ganged up on me while you were in the store buying candy. You shoulda seen your eyes when you walked out, Bo. You were always one of the nicest kids—too nice if you ask me. I suppose that wasn't a bad thing, considering you were much bigger than most kids, but you wouldn't hurt a fly. It drove me crazy that you wouldn't put people in their place if they picked on you, but that's part of your charm.

"Anyway, I'd never seen rage like that in your eyes before. As much pain as I was in on the ground with them pummeling me, I smiled. I smiled because I knew they were about to pay for what they did to your brother. Funny thing is, if they'd tried to take your bike, I think you would have let them. It wasn't worth it for you to hurt someone over a possession. Your family was a different story, though. You charged at those assholes. When Mitch looked up, I coulda swore he pissed himself right then and there. He tried to get his cronies off me, but they weren't paying attention to Mitch or you. The first punch you threw connected with Mitch's nose, and I heard the crunch from the pavement. So did his crew, but you got one of them while the rest tucked their tails back to their car and sped off. Do you remember breaking that kid's leg?" Brian asked with a sense of pride.

Bo frowned. "Yeah . . . I don't like hurting people, Brian. But they were hurting you, so I had to help."

Brian always wondered how much from before the injury Bo remembered. The story he just told was one he had relived numerous times over the years. Most of the stories he told were like reruns of a sitcom at this point. He hoped that was why Bo remembered, and not that he actually retained the information from before the head injury. There were things leading up to the incident that he didn't want Bo to remember. Brian and Ma had worked hard over the years to paint a different picture of their family's history than what the reality was. They all did things they weren't proud of, including Brian and Ma.

"I know you don't like hurting people, bud. The point of this story isn't to make you feel bad for hurting those bullies . . . it's to make you remember how you saved me from them.

Ma and Dad were proud of you for standing up for the family. And you know what? Those jerks never messed with us again. All thanks to you."

Bo's smile returned, his lips curving up until his crooked teeth were exposed. But behind those eyes, the pain was still evident. Brian wasn't sure if it was the story, or all the trauma of the past few days, or both.

"I didn't feel like no hero that day. The way Ma looked at me when I got home, like I was a monster . . . I never wanted to see that again."

Bo got up and left the room, leaving his brother in silence. Something was eating at Brian's insides, and he spent the next few minutes trying to figure out what it was. Then it clicked. The last thing Bo said before leaving the room was that he remembered the way Ma looked at him when he got home from beating up the bullies. That was something they had never said to him because they didn't want to make Bo feel any worse. Suddenly, Brian wanted to vomit the frozen soup onto the floor.

Bo remembered the past.

## 11

**1996**

With each passing day, Brian found himself traveling more with his dad, which often led to meeting up with Marcus. It was clear that Ma was worried, but she didn't say anything in front of Brian and Bo. In a strange way, she probably felt better knowing one of the kids was with her husband, as if that would somehow keep him in check. What she didn't know was that Brian was left in the truck—sometimes for hours at a time—while his dad ran into places to do whatever it was that Marcus instructed him to do. The easy guess was selling drugs. But Brian didn't think that was right because he had never seen Marcus give his dad anything to deliver.

Brian sat in the truck and scanned through the radio, trying to find some music to keep him occupied while he waited for his dad to come out of the mall. He wasn't even sure why he needed to tag along. Marcus wanted Brian around, but for what? The way his dad looked around nervously when walking into the mall was bad enough, but with each minute that ticked by, it allowed Brian's imagination to run wild.

*What are you doing in there, Dad?*

Either way, he was happy to find their relationship growing, and while he wouldn't admit it, he was also happy to see the relationship between Bo and Dad becoming less and less prevalent. The jealousy he felt toward his brother wasn't something he spoke about with anyone, but it was there buried deep inside of him. Bo, the golden child, could do no wrong. Brian often wondered if Bo felt the same way about him or if he felt pity for his brother. Somehow, that might actually be worse.

Brian skimmed the mall parking lot, watching shoppers scurry in and out. He was pretty sure he'd seen multiple families enter and leave while waiting, yet his dad was still nowhere to be found. It wasn't just how long it was taking that dried Brian's throat with panic. The mall wasn't a place they traveled to very often, and when they did, it was never his dad's idea. They lived an hour away, and Brian could count on one hand how many times they had made the trip. He knew he had to keep it from his mother, and he planned to do just that. He wasn't about to ruin all the time and effort he'd put in over the past few weeks getting on his dad's good side.

Evening approached with the sky a dark gray as a storm brewed in the distance. The clouds reminded Brian of stained cotton balls floating toward the mall. He had been sitting in the truck for at least a few hours when he finally spotted his dad coming out of the exit, but he wasn't alone. With him, a teenage girl laughed at something he said as they got closer to the truck. Brian was perplexed. Who the hell was this girl?

While the girl was laughing, his dad appeared nervous. A sinking feeling entered the pit of Brian's stomach, knowing nothing good could possibly come of this. As they got closer, the girl spotted Brian in the passenger seat and smiled. He forced a smile back, then noticed his dad locking eyes with him. Something was wrong. The girl was beautiful, wearing a white tank top with a glitter design on the chest that read *Bow to the Queen*. Brian felt himself blushing as he read the shirt because when he looked up, she winked. Maybe she thought he was cute, too, although she was too old for him. A pretty girl like this would never give him the time of day anyway, especially being a few years his senior. So why was she with Dad?

His dad knocked on the passenger window, and Brian hesitantly rolled it down.

"Hey, bud. Why don't you hop in the back seat and let Lisa ride up front."

"Lisa? Who is she?"

His dad pursed his lips, flaring his nostrils. The girl didn't notice, but Brian knew that look was the equivalent of "You better fucking listen and don't ask questions, boy."

"We're giving her a ride to the bus station. I was shopping for your mother's birthday and overheard her telling someone she needed a ride. So, I thought I'd do my good deed for the day, right, Lisa?"

"You didn't tell me your son was so cute! Look at this handsome fella. I don't mind riding in the back, little dude. I appreciate your pops doing this for me."

Brian took his eyes off her cleavage and was about to

agree with her when his dad opened the passenger door and motioned for his son to get out.

"Be a gentleman, Brian. Get in the back and let her sit up front, okay?"

Brian nodded and unbuckled his seat belt, climbing out of the truck. Lisa smiled at him as he brushed by her, her perfume tickling his senses. Her beauty, her wonderful scent, none of that mattered. There was no logical reason for his dad to bring some girl into the truck with them or to make Brian get in the back. He did as he was told and slid in behind the driver's side.

"So, Lisa. What brings you to these parts?" his dad asked, pulling out of the mall parking lot.

"Here to see friends. We spend some days at the mall and then I ride back home to my deadbeat parents who don't even care when I come or go."

Was she flirting? Brian felt nauseous.

"Sorry to hear that," Dad said.

They rode in silence for a few minutes before his dad spoke up again, "I just need to make a quick pit stop on the way to the bus station, but you'll be there for departure time. Brian will keep you company, right, Bry?"

*Bry? He's never called me that before. Why is he being so weird?*

Dad took a left turn down a narrow, one-way road. Brian had no idea where they were going, and he had never been on this street before. It looked deserted, full of old homes that were run-down and abandoned. The overcast sky had grown darker to match the mood of the street, and the first few raindrops pattered on the windshield.

"Lovely. Just in time for me to get out," his dad said.

He parked the truck in front of a two-story house with the roof warping inward, clinging to the home as years' worth of water damage ate away at the bones. Torn plastic dangled off the broken windows, revealing what appeared to be an empty room, but Brian couldn't actually see inside the dark space. His dad stared at the residence, then turned back to Brian.

"This shouldn't take long, okay?" He swallowed down something—fear, uncertainty, guilt—whatever it was, it made Brian uneasy.

His dad got out of the truck and jogged up the walkway toward the porch as the rain picked up. Brian watched him knock, the front door opening quickly, then his dad entered the home. Lisa leaned over the center console and smiled at him, stealing his attention.

"I really appreciate you guys doing this for me," she said, chomping on a big wad of gum.

"It's nothing. Happy to help."

"How old are you? I should take you on a date," she said with a wink.

Brian felt his face burning red and hoped it was dark enough in the truck that she couldn't see it.

"I'm—"

Knuckles rapped against the passenger window and Lisa screamed. Brian shifted his attention to the person knocking, expecting it to be his dad.

But it was Marcus.

"Who is this fucking psycho?" Lisa yelled.

Marcus ripped the door open and reached in, grabbing her by the hair with a sadistic grin. He dragged her out of the truck with her legs kicking wildly, her screams echoing down the empty street.

"Shut up, bitch. Nobody can hear you out here."

It didn't stop her from continuing to squall at the top of her lungs. Brian wanted to help her, but he remained frozen in his seat, unable to do anything but watch the horror unfold. Lisa made eye contact with him, reaching for his hand. Brian couldn't help but cry, unsure of what the hell was going on.

"Shut the fuck up!" Marcus yelled, then slapped her. "Fucking help me," he snapped at Brian's dad.

*Please don't help him, Dad, don't do it.*

Before Brian could plead with his dad to stop, Barry marched over and grabbed hold of Lisa's arms, trying to stop her from swinging at Marcus. At least that's what Brian wanted to believe. With her hands restrained, Marcus had an open shot. He punched Lisa in the face. Her eyes rolled back in her head and her body went limp. For a moment, Brian thought that maybe she was dead, but then she moaned—an incoherent, involuntary cry from her unconscious state.

"Hot damn, she's a feisty one, eh?" Marcus asked, suddenly back to his joyful state.

"You said nobody'd get hurt, Marcus. What the fuck is this? What are we doing?" Brian's dad asked.

"What I'm *doing* is none of your goddamn concern now, is it? What you're doing, though . . . is what you promised me you would do. Your end of the deal, right? And you did good, Barry. You did fucking *great*," Marcus said while eyeing Lisa up and down. "Didn't he, boy?"

Brian didn't answer; he was too busy forcing down tears. He had no intention of showing Marcus his weak side.

"Help me get her inside, then we can talk about what's next."

"What's next? I did my part, just like you said. I want to be done with this," Brian's dad insisted.

Marcus scoffed. "You don't get to determine that, Scary Barry. We'll hold up our end of the deal, as we always do. But this isn't a one-and-done situation, my friend. Consider yourself . . . our liaison to them. You will help us get what we need, and we will give you what we promised. And if you don't hold up your end? Let's just not let it come to that."

Barry shook his head, but he didn't say anything. As Brian watched them move Lisa's body around like she was a useless prop, Brian had more questions than before. The men carried Lisa into the house and slammed the door shut. Brian knew he couldn't say anything to his mom or Bo, but what about his dad? Why would he put Brian through all this? Why would he make him sit in the truck and watch as he helped abduct a helpless girl? And what the hell were they going to do with her?

A bout of lightheadedness came on, and Brian had to keep the bile at bay. He tried to force himself to remain upright, but his head felt like dead weight. As he watched the front door, waiting for his dad to come through it, Brian passed out.

Just as he woke up, Dad exited the condemned home—alone. No Lisa. No Marcus. Just Barry, and he looked like a changed man. His clothes were smeared with fresh blood, and Brian knew their lives were changed forever.

## 12

**PRESENT DAY**

Brian awoke and found himself lost in a cloud of agony. It had been days since he had eaten a regular meal. He needed more than food, though. He needed something to relieve the pain. He felt his body begging him for more. More of everything. Pills. Relief. Food. Exercise. But that wasn't possible. With supplies running low, his brother was starting to ration the already small portions of food he brought in a few times a day. There were no set meals. Brian was at the mercy of Bo who would often forget for the better part of each day to care for his brother.

The pain had worsened, not improved, since the accident. As much as Brian wanted to fight his brother to let him see a doctor, he no longer had the energy to do so in any convincing fashion. With each passing day, Brian's thoughts darkened. Sometimes, he wished he had died when he was bucked off Astra. Other times, he considered what it would take to hurt his own brother so he could go for help.

He knew he was losing his grip on reality, seeing things that weren't really there, hearing things in the dark. The isolation slowly ate at his sanity. He wasn't even sure how many days had passed at this point, but he knew it had been at least a few weeks since Ma died. Seeing less of Bo by the day also had him concerned for his mental health. Not only had he taken Ma's death hard, as Brian expected he would, but the burden of caring for his brother and the entire farm couldn't be easy. And now that Brian knew Bo remembered some of the past, he wondered just how *much* he remembered.

Brian attempted to turn onto his side slightly, knowing the longer he remained in one position, the more likely it was that he would add bedsores to his list of maladies. A sharp pain swam from his lower back, up his spine, and to the base of his skull, reminding him that moving wasn't getting any easier.

*I need medicine. It hurts so fucking bad.*

Brian wondered how Astra was doing. Beyond Ma and Bo, there wasn't a thing on the planet he loved as much as he loved that horse. Astra, at least, had plenty of food. The hayloft above the barn was stuffed with bales, but Brian just hoped Bo remembered to feed her. The thought of the animals made Brian realize that he hadn't heard the chickens in a few days. They always clucked around outside, with the rooster waking them up at the crack of dawn.

Having the curtains drawn shut, Brian had no idea what time of day it was. He assumed it was evening, as there wasn't even a sliver of light breaking through. The urge to piss came on strong, and he was tempted to just go, wet himself like the cripple he was. Bo would be sleeping if it was the middle of the night, and at first, he didn't want to bother him. The longer he held it in, the less he cared about waking his brother. As his eyes adjusted to the darkness, he scanned for a bottle nearby to piss in.

"Shit out of luck," he mumbled.

He was about to yell for Bo when he spotted the outline of a shape sitting in the corner in Bo's seat.

"Bo? What are you doing in here?"

The figure didn't move, and he started to doubt that it was even a person. Maybe it was just one of the last few threads of his sanity snapping. The outline didn't so much as twitch, and Brian strained his eyes, forcing them not to blink for as long as possible to catch any slight movement. But he heard breathing. A raspy, phlegmy sound that was barely above a whisper.

"Bo! Stop fucking around! I need to go to the bathroom."

Still, his brother didn't move, as if he was stuffed by a taxidermist, a decoration to go with the furniture. Brian squeezed his bedsheets and clenched his teeth. He was about to lose his damn mind.

The chair creaked beneath Bo's weight.

"Bo, I'm serious! You need to snap out of this and help me! I need painkillers!"

Footsteps marched down the hall, a flicker of candlelight striking the wall outside the door with a dim orange hue. Bo popped his head into the bedroom, the flame dancing to paint his features in shadow.

"I'm sorry, Brian. I was sleeping. What were you yelling about?"

Bo walked in, rubbing his eyes as he began to wake up. Brian wasn't listening to him, though. He was focused on the chair where he thought his brother was just sitting in the dark. Except he wasn't. He was in bed at the other end of the house.

With the candlelight now illuminating the room, Brian found himself speechless.

The chair was empty.

"Brian? You okay?"

He pried his eyes off the chair and met his brother's confused expression.

"Yeah . . . Thought I saw something, is all. I need to go to the bathroom. And I need medicine. Can you get me an empty jug and grab the box of pills in the bathroom, please?"

"Okay."

"And Bo?"

"Yeah?"

"Tomorrow . . . I want to see if I can use Ma's wheelchair. Can you please bring it to me so we can try that? I'm going crazy in here."

Bo hesitated but finally nodded. Brian wasn't sure why his brother was so dead set on caring for him instead of allowing him to try and improve his situation. He had asked for the wheelchair days ago, but Bo wasn't ready to let him try it yet after the incident of falling out of the bed. Hell, it took Brian four days to convince his brother to take the straps off his arms. He had been careful not to trigger Bo since, afraid of being tied back up. It was a positive sign that Bo didn't immediately shoot down the request this time. He returned with an empty plastic jug and handed it to Brian.

"I'm worried about you and the animals. How are you doing with everything, Bo?"

"Fine. Ma reminds me what I have to do so I don't forget."

Brian continued to ignore the mention of his mother in

## The Devil's in the Next Room

present tense, as if she was still out there running the farm and they were one big happy family, but he'd had enough.

"Really? Did she tell you to forget to bring me food all day? Tell you to trap me in a damn room for days on end? Tell you to give me no medicine?"

"Stop yelling at me! I'm trying my best! She isn't always there. Only sometimes. She warns me of things."

"What? What are you talking about, Bo? She warns you about what?"

"I . . . can't talk about it. I don't want to scare you."

"Jesus Christ. Whatever. In these conversations with her, does she have you taking good care of Astra? I swear, Bo, if anything happens to my horse . . ."

"Astra's happy. I feed her every day and do everything you ask me to."

"Do you let her into the south field to graze?"

Bo nodded.

"What about food? If you've been feeding her properly, she should get hay two times a day."

"She eats a lot of the tall grass, and between meals, I give her fruit and stuff I know she likes. She's fine, I promise."

"What about the chickens? I haven't heard them for days."

No response.

"Bo, answer me. What about the chickens?"

"They are so loud. It hurts my ears, Brian. And I don't like the way they follow me."

Brian closed his eyes and sighed. The chickens were a crucial resource for them. If anything happened to them, it would royally screw the farm. He felt helpless, and everything was slowly slipping away from them. Bo was doing the best he could, but he was not fit for this.

"Please go grab the medicine box I asked for."

Bo left the room and came back a moment later with a small kit where they kept painkillers and first aid supplies. Brian wasn't sure which he wanted first: to relieve his bladder or the pain. Hopefully some of Ma's strong pills were still in there. Although he hadn't taken her to the doctor to get an official diagnosis of cancer, he had been able to buy some prescription drugs from an older man who overheard him arguing with a nurse at the hospital during a pit stop there while he was in town getting supplies. He begged them to prescribe something for his mother, but of course, without a proper diagnosis, they wouldn't. They were just doing their job. The man who overheard his pleas was suffering from stage 4 lung cancer and was kind enough to give Brian some of his pills. "I'm not going to be around long enough to need these," he had said.

Brian reached out for the box and Bo brought it over to him. He felt like an addict going through withdrawal; his hands shook as he dug through the assorted meds, seeking out anything that would help the pain. Finally, he found the bottle he was looking for and was relieved to hear a bunch of pills rattling around inside.

"Oh, thank fucking God."

He dumped three into his hand, one more than the prescribed quantity, but he needed a strong dose. He needed to numb this feeling. He dry swallowed them, then let his head fall back on the pillow. With any luck, the capsules would dissolve in his stomach and get to work quickly. Brian licked his lips, realizing how dry and crusty they were from dehydration. He had intentionally forced himself to wait long stretches of time between drinks so he wouldn't have to go to the bathroom as much, but his body needed more fluids.

"Brian, Ma says I have to be careful giving you too many pills. She says you might crave them even when you don't need them. And that pain is a good way to remind you of your sins."

"What? What sins? What the hell are you talking about?"

Brian let his mind wander, thinking of what Bo could be referring to. Could he be talking about the past? Or something recent? He scoffed, realizing he was letting himself accept that his brother was actually talking to his dead mother.

"I think we need to be careful how much medicine we give," Bo whispered, then yanked the box from Brian's grasp and set it out of reach.

"No! Leave it close. You don't know what this feels like, Bo. It hurts so much! And you're gone for hours at a time."

"You'll be okay. You're strong. Here's the jug to use for the bathroom. I'll leave you alone and be back tomorrow."

"Please, Bo!"

His brother left and took the candle with him, returning the bedroom to darkness. Brian cried, unable to hold in the mix of emotions that had been eating away at him over the past few weeks. After going to the bathroom, he put the cap on the jug and dropped it as gently as he could onto the floor at his side. The burning scent of urine filled the room, reminding him of just how dehydrated he truly was. When he was done crying, Brian tried to force himself back to sleep. Eventually, when the medicine kicked in, his body acquiesced. As his eyes closed, he again thought he saw the figure sitting in the chair, frozen in place.

"Ma? Isss that you?" he slurred as the pills took hold. Then he fell asleep.

# 13

Brian knew he was dreaming, but that didn't stop him from feeling like he was really there. He knew he was dreaming because he was a grown man following his dad into a house. He told himself that his dad died when he was just a boy. No, when he was a boy, his dad was *killed* at the hands of his mother. She would do anything to protect her kids. Anything.

Dad entered the dark house, disappearing into the blank void. Brian didn't want to follow, but he did anyway. He needed to know what his dad was doing. As he ran up the porch after him, he realized where they were. It was the abandoned home where they had driven Lisa. The first victim.

Brian pushed the front door open, expecting to see nothing but an abandoned home blanketed in darkness. What he saw instead was a wall of cages. They weren't empty. Each one contained a person—all of them female, some young, some old. He knew Marcus didn't discriminate on age. To him, a soul was a soul—the essence of life and something they used to maintain their powers. Each body was in different stages of decomposition, their lives being drained slowly. Marcus told his dad it worked best when they took their time with the victims, but if need be, they would make it quick.

Some of the prisoners screamed from their cages, begging Brian to help them escape. He wanted to, he really did. But he knew if he let any of them go, his dad was as good as dead.

*He's already dead, asshole. Free them while you can.*

Still, he couldn't bring himself to help the poor victims watching him pass by. It wasn't that he didn't want to, but in this dream, this *nightmare*, his body refused to listen. Instead, he continued through the home, his dad always just turning a corner, disappearing out of sight. Brian picked up the pace, yelling for his dad to stop. The house was a maze, a depraved labyrinth of rot and ruin.

"Dad!"

Brian's voice echoed through the hall, sounding like he was in a hollowed-out cave. The deeper he went, the darker the house became. He had never seen the inside of this home before, but he somehow knew exactly where to go and what it looked like. As he moved through the house, he felt invisible hands reaching for him from the shadows, trying to pull him in.

He came to a set of stairs and stopped. His dad must have come this way, but the steps went so high that Brian couldn't see where they ended. They just went on and on until they vanished into a pit of darkness above. He climbed, yelling to his dad every few steps. It was the whispers of many voices that answered back. Begging him for help. Demanding to be let free. It was the souls of the dead, the past victims of the Hollow Souls. Memories Brian had buried years ago flooded back, reminding him of his part in all of it.

Deformed hands covered in blood pushed through the plaster, stretching the wallpaper until they broke free, reaching for Brian. He swatted them away as he continued to ascend the stairs, seeing the faint outline of his dad's figure nearing the top. He was almost there, just a few more steps . . .

. . . and then he was in the attic, a space darker than the night itself. But his dad wasn't alone. The Hollow Souls were here. They surrounded a victim, blocking the helpless person from Brian's view. His dad hollered, begging them to stop.

One of the figures turned toward the commotion, revealing a skull mask. A blue haze clouded the air around the skull. The man held something that appeared to be a long bone shard, intricate symbols etched on it, giving off a faint glow. A giant appeared between his dad and the victim—the man had to be close to seven feet tall. All Brian could do was watch the scene unfold, like a movie he couldn't turn off. The large figure backhanded his dad's face, sending him soaring through the air and smacking off the wall.

As the skulls circled their victim, Brian got his first glimpse of who it was lying on their back.

It was Bo, but as a child. He wore a baseball uniform, ripped and torn. Brian spotted tears in his brother's eyes, heard him crying for help. But there was another victim behind his brother he couldn't see. The shadows covered most of the second body, all except a small shoe. The tribe of sadistic monsters chanted in a different language, speaking in unison. It all came flooding back to Brian at that moment. What they did to Bo. The deal his dad made with Marcus. With *them*.

Brian charged toward them, but the chanting abruptly

stopped. The room reverted back to darkness, the blue cloud evaporating. Suddenly, Bo was gone. Brian's dad was gone. The second victim was gone.

"Bo? Dad?"

Somewhere in front of him, his brother's whimpering resumed, seemingly a mile away, smothered by a wall of nothingness. Brian blindly reached out, walking slowly toward the sound. His hand landed on a shoulder.

"Bo?"

Only it wasn't Bo. Two dark circles appeared on a cream-colored canvas the shape of a human skull, with ritualistic symbols carved into its forehead. Something moved above the skull—no, on top of the skull. Slithering.

The blue cloud shimmered, giving off a faint glow. Brian froze, too afraid to move. On top of the skull, numerous snakes writhed around, snapping at the air. One of the creatures stiffened, then came face-to-face with him. The snake opened its mouth wide, baring its razor fangs.

"Hello, Brian," a voice said from behind. It was Marcus. Brian would have recognized that voice anywhere. As he went to turn, the snake lashed out, lunging at his face—

Brian awoke to his own screams, drenched in sweat. It had been years since he'd had that nightmare. It had been *years* since he'd thought of the Hollow Souls—the reason his mother moved the family to the middle of nowhere after their dad died. It hadn't just been to protect Bo because of his condition, but also to hide them from the group of sadistic killers. His mind drowned in the horrible memories that he had worked so hard to bury deep in his subconscious. But those memories had resurfaced. And they had to be back for a reason.

The pain pumping through Brian's back became an afterthought. He spent the rest of the night awake in bed, staring at the shadow sitting in the chair.

## 14

**1996**

"I know I owe you an explanation, Brian. You shouldn't have seen any of that, but Marcus insists that I bring you with me. He sees you as an insurance policy. He knows if I have one of my sons with me, I won't do anything stupid, and the girl would be more willing to come if she saw a kid with me," Dad said.

They were sitting in the truck, parked in their driveway as the rain continued to fall. Bo's baseball game had been rained out, so he and Ma were in the house, probably wondering why Brian and Dad weren't coming in yet. Brian wasn't sure he could look his mother or brother in the eye and not burst out crying. While his dad still hadn't told him the fate of Lisa, Brian wasn't so sure he needed, or wanted, to know. The blood was enough to convince him something terrible happened to her. He just kept picturing Marcus's dark eyes devouring Lisa's body with his imagination.

"Dad . . . are we in trouble?"

His dad sighed. "No, this will never track back to us. She was a loner who he selected, knowing it would be easy to cover up. Christ, I can't even believe I'm saying these words." He began to weep, pinching between his eyes.

"I don't mean that. I mean, are we in trouble with Marcus? Is our family in danger?"

His dad swallowed a nervous gulp of air and didn't say anything, but the silence spoke volumes. He didn't know how to answer Brian.

"Dad . . ."

"I-I don't know. There's no turning back at this point. I wish I'd never talked to him that day but I swear, he got in my head. He made me do it, like a fucking vampire, only instead of feeding off my blood, he fed off my desires. I only wanted to help our family, I swear."

"What's this all for?"

Brian didn't expect a response, but his dad sighed and turned to face him.

"Marcus told me he could make Bo special. He said he could make him the best ballplayer this state has ever seen. At first, I thought he meant to train him. But one look at Marcus and I knew he was no athlete, at least in the sporting sense. He said they could give your brother certain abilities, and that all I needed to do was a few favors for them. I know how ridiculous this sounds, like some deal with the Devil or something."

"So what does Lisa have to do with Bo? What did you guys do to her?" Brian asked. He felt the anxiety rising inside him as he stared at the blood on his dad's shirt.

"I didn't do *anything* to her, I swear. It was too late by the time I saw what they were doing. If I had tried to stop them, Marcus would've killed me right there in that house, and you would have been all alone in the truck. He knew what he was doing by making me bring you."

None of it made sense. While Brian was happy not to be in that house when they took Lisa inside, it sure would have helped answer some questions. He wanted answers, but he didn't want to ask his dad the questions to *get* those answers.

*Did you kill her, Dad? Did you help them kill her? Are you lying to me?*

*What are they going to do to Bo?*

*What if we can't stop them from hurting us?*

They both sat in the truck in silence, crying as rain pelted down on the roof like acorns falling from a tree.

"I know it's a lot to ask of you to keep it from our family, I really do. But they can't know about any of this, Brian. There could come a time when Marcus questions them, and he'll know if they're lying or not. Do you understand me?"

Brian nodded, and then a thought came to him. "What about me? He knows I was there. He knows I watched you guys take her into the house, and I saw you come out covered in blood."

His dad punched the steering wheel and hollered, "Fuck! I know that, okay? Whether I took you or not, he wanted you involved. He knew it would make me keep my mouth shut. It couldn't be Bo. Because of what they have to do to him, he can't know who they are."

"'Because of what they have to do to him'? So I'm just some insurance policy, is that it?"

Suddenly, the weeks' worth of spending time with his dad didn't feel so special. Brian understood with a clarity that hadn't been there previously. Dad didn't have him tag along because he wanted to spend more time with him . . . but because he had no choice. It was all for Bo. He was just a pawn to help his dad and Marcus get what they wanted.

Brian opened his door as the storm splashed against the truck's interior. He was done listening to the excuses right now. His dad tried to say something, but the guilt he must have been feeling choked his words. Brian slammed the door shut and ran through the sheets of rain and into the house.

It was obvious that Bo sensed something was wrong with Brian the moment he walked into their bedroom. Brothers had a way of knowing, even if it wasn't obvious to the rest of the world. The glow of their TV lit up the otherwise dark room, and Brian saw Bo staring at him out of the corner of his eye.

"What? Why are you looking at me?" Brian snapped.

"Chill. Just wondering what happened, is all. Did Dad say something to piss you off?"

"No. I don't want to talk about it, okay?"

"Sure. What have you guys been up to anyway? Coach was asking where Dad's been lately. I'm cool with him wanting to spend more time with you and stuff, but it's kinda weird that he just . . . stopped caring about ball, isn't it?"

Brian wanted to just blurt it all out, tell his brother everything that had been happening. He wanted to tell him how evil Marcus was and how their family was in trouble. Yet there was something burrowed deep inside him, forcing him to keep his secret. A false sense of pride came in knowing that he and his dad shared something nobody else knew about. Brian and

Bo told each other everything. This wasn't normal, but he wasn't sure it would do any good to tell Bo. The way his dad spoke, it would put the family in *more* danger if he did. He had to keep reminding himself of that.

"He still talks about you and baseball all the time when I'm with him. I think he just wanted to give you some space, is all. And he just wants to do whatever he can to make you the best player out there on that field. He's obsessed with you and loves you." It was foreign to talk like that with Bo, or anyone in the family. They all loved each other, but they never said it. It was as if Brian was thinking out loud, trying to defend his dad for doing something horrible for the greater good of their family. Every word out of Brian's mouth left a horrible taste.

"I'm worried about Ma too. I see the way she looks at Dad. She doesn't trust him. It's like he's not the same person now," Bo said.

"I promise, he's still Dad. He's just . . . different now. But he cares about us. I know he does," Brian said, knowing he was confusing Bo even more with his cryptic responses.

"If you say so. Do you want to watch a horror movie or something? I can't even remember the last time we did that," Bo said.

"Sure. Let's do it."

Brian couldn't help but feel the real horror movie was about to begin, starring their family.

## 15

**PRESENT DAY**

The nightmare kept Brian awake for most of the night. But just as he really started to let himself go, to submit to a deep sleep, he heard the clanging sound of something banging around down the hall. While his mind wanted him to go to sleep, a cone of daylight rolled in across the threshold. If he allowed himself to pass out now, he knew there was a good chance he'd sleep the day away.

Bo grunted, and Brian was about to shout and see if everything was all right when his brother appeared in the doorway with the wheelchair in front of him and a big shit-eating grin on his face. Brian couldn't help but smile back. It was the first genuine smile he recalled giving since before their mother passed away. The wheelchair was a chance at freedom. A chance at finally getting out of this bed and sitting upright, seeing more than just this damn room and closet.

*And the figure in the corner.*

"Oh, thank you, Jesus. Bo, you made my day," Brian said, trying to force himself up to his elbows.

"Whoa, be careful. Don't fall out of the bed again," Bo said.

Was that a joke? Was Bo finally getting over Ma? Brian could only hope.

"Sorry, I'm just excited. I haven't left this room in days. Bring that thing over here, will ya? And let's go for a walk."

Bo smiled again and wheeled the chair up next to the bed. Brian fought the temptation of jumping out of bed like a kid on Christmas morning. He had worried that even though Bo promised to do this, his brother would change his mind once he saw the chair, remembering back to Ma wheeling herself around until she lost her strength and eventually needed one of the boys to push her. He was glad to see his concerns quelled.

"Let me help you out of bed," Bo said, then placed his giant paws under Brian's armpits and gently lifted him off the mattress.

Pain took his breath away, but he bit down on his lip to hide it from Bo. If his brother saw what simply moving him a few feet was doing to him, he'd likely force him back into bed. He wiped the tears at the corners of his eyes with his shirt as Bo placed him in the chair. Brian couldn't believe this was really happening.

"Where'd you like to go?" Bo asked.

"Take me to see Astra, please. I miss my girl."

Brian would have liked to roll the chair himself, but he wasn't going to be picky right now. He needed to get out of this dark room, the place where Ma took her last breath and left her death fragrance firmly intact. He needed the fresh air as much as he did the daylight.

Bo moved behind the chair and pushed it through the doorway.

The first thing Brian noticed was how messy the house was. While he didn't expect Bo to stay on top of cleaning the place with all the other responsibilities he now had, it was still a shock to see their home in such disarray. The garbage was overflowing, some even piled on the floor surrounding the trash can. The kitchen counter could have been mistaken for a scene out of an apocalypse movie where the group of survivors break into a house to scavenge for leftover supplies.

"I know it's a mess," Bo said, reading his brother's thoughts.

"It's a lot to handle all by yourself. I get that."

As they reached the back door, a sudden sense of dread formed in the center of Brian's stomach. If the inside of the house looked this bad, what were they about to walk out to? Seeing garbage on the floor and old food on the counter was one thing, but discovering half of their animals dead due to neglect would be another.

Bo opened the back door, where they had installed a ramp when Ma was healthy enough to wheel herself around, and pushed the chair outside. The fresh air immediately reinvigorated Brian's senses. He breathed deep, taking in a lungful of nature, happy to smell the farm scents he had grown accustomed to since they were boys. The exposure to daylight was something he didn't plan for after being in a dark room for weeks. He squinted as he scanned the backyard and was pleasantly surprised to see a normal-looking property, apart from the extra-long grass. It didn't match the condemned appearance of the home's interior.

"Thanks a bunch for getting me out of there, Bo. I was going crazy, I tell ya. Awful dreams, seeing things . . . I thought I was losing my damn mind."

Bo continued to wheel him around the side of the house toward the barn in silence, then finally spoke, "What were your dreams about? I've been having bad ones too. I keep wanting to go into Ma's room, but she's not in there anymore. It's you in there now."

Brian had no intention of telling Bo the specifics. The last thing he wanted to do was trigger more memories that they'd worked so hard to get him to forget. He also hated lying to his brother, so he decided to be vague.

"I just dreamed of bad people. The nightmares felt so real, like I was half awake. And then when I did wake up, I thought I saw you in the room with me, but you weren't."

Bo stopped the wheelchair and walked around to face Brian.

"It was Ma in there with you. I told you she was with us."

A chill crawled up Brian's spine at the thought. All this time, he thought his brother was just delusional, unwilling to accept the fact that their mother was dead. There was still a chance that the pills he took had messed with his head, but Brian was finding it harder to deny what he saw. What he heard.

"I . . . Maybe it was her. What was *your* dream about?" Brian asked, deflecting the conversation back to Bo.

"Monsters. Snakes and skeletons. They were coming for us and had evil magic. It was so scary."

If Bo had been looking at Brian's face, he would have seen its color drain.

*What does this mean? Why are we both dreaming about them?*

The way his brother explained it, Brian couldn't help but think Bo sounded like a child describing a nightmare, ready to pull the blankets up over his head to protect himself.

"It's nothing . . . You know you can always come to me if you have one of those dreams, right?"

"Thanks, brother. But if we were really in trouble, I guess it's me who would have to do the running now, huh?" Bo asked, with just a hint of a smile behind it.

"Bo Davidson. Was that a joke you just made? Maybe I can teach you a thing or two yet."

They both laughed as they approached the barn, but Bo's laugh ended abruptly when a chicken crossed their path, clucking away. He stared at the thing like it had three heads and razor-sharp teeth.

"Relax, man. It's just a chicken. Why are you acting like it's going to attack us? You love the chickens."

"Too loud. They keep getting too loud, Brian. They need to stop."

Brian didn't know what to say in response to that. Just when he thought maybe his brother was acting normal, something like this happened. Bo pushed the wheelchair quickly past the chicken, and the sight of the barn door caused Brian's nerves to knot up. If anything was wrong with Astra, he wasn't sure he could forgive Bo, even though that wasn't fair. Astra was more than a horse to Brian, though. When they moved to the farm, his mother asked him what kind of animal he wanted to get. He begged for a horse for the first few years, but she said he wasn't ready for a commitment that big and needed to earn it. They had settled on pigs and chickens and their dog, Alfie, who had passed away when he got into some fox poison. It wasn't until Brian's eighteenth birthday that she surprised him with Astra. They got her when she was just a filly, and it became Brian's responsibility to care for and raise her.

Now Astra was pushing twenty years old, and Brian considered her his best friend. Until recently, not a day had gone by that he didn't talk to her and take her for a ride in the fields. When Ma got sick, he would sit with Astra and cry, telling her stories about growing up as he fed her apple slices. They had been through a lot together, and as Brian approached the barn, he felt a fluttering of nerves like he was about to visit a long-lost friend for the first time in years.

Bo told him the chickens were too loud, but the things barely clucked most of the day. Brian just hoped his brother wasn't growing the same fear of Astra. A whinny from inside the barn filled him with joy as they reached the double sliding doors. Bo stopped the wheelchair and pulled one open. Astra's stall was at the rear corner of the barn, and she had her back to the stall door, eating some of the hay Bo fed her earlier. It took everything inside Brian not to pry the wheelchair away from his brother and speed up to the stall.

"Hey, girl!" he said cheerfully.

Astra turned with a mouth full of hay, the dried grass hanging out each side like uncooked spaghetti. She continued munching on it as she made eye contact with Brian. He felt tears well up in his eyes. She turned and faced the stall door, neighing and rumbling her lips like she always did to communicate. Bo wheeled him right up to the stall so he could pet Astra, and Brian embraced her for the first time in too long.

"I missed you," he said, feeling her warm breath on his cheek. "Is Bo taking good care of you out here?"

"She's okay. I take care of her just like you said to. I think she misses you, though," Bo said.

"Yeah, yeah. I wish I could take you for a ride out in the field, girl. Hell, I hope I can do it again someday. You really launched me, you know that? We'll get some help, though. I promise."

Brian didn't realize Bo had walked to the other end of the barn until he came back with another bale of hay. His giant forearms bulged as he lifted it by the twine. He dropped it next to the wheelchair and Astra nudged Brian's hand in the direction of her food source.

"Okay, okay. Hold your horses. Sorry, bad joke, girl. Here you go," he said, grabbing a handful of hay and holding it up for Astra to eat. She quickly devoured it as if it was her first meal in days, her teeth sliding along his palm as she swallowed it.

For the first time since before the injury, Brian felt pure joy. He needed this in every way. It was something to take his mind off his mother, off the possibility of being paralyzed for the rest of his life.

"Brian, you should go back to bed. You're gonna get tired if you stay up too long," Bo said, breaking up the reunion.

"No . . . I'm fine, Bo. Please give me some more time. I promise I'll tell you if I start to feel sore or tired." Brian was disgusted with himself, hearing the desperation dripping from every word.

"You're stubborn, Brian. Just like Ma says. Come on. Back to bed. I'll take you outside tomorrow, I promise."

Before Brian could protest, his brother pulled him away from Astra.

*No, don't you dare fucking take me back to that room, you bastard!*

*It's not his fault. You know he's doing the right thing. Stop being an asshole.*

"I-I just want more time, is all. You don't know what it's like lying in that bed for hours, day after day. It's really driving me insane, Bo."

"When I got hurt real bad, I was in a bed for a long, long time too. I remember how it felt. You'll be okay, Brian. You just need to listen to Ma and me."

Again, Bo remembering events around the injury was new to Brian. His brother had gone his entire life acting like he had no idea what happened to him. What did he really know? Brian couldn't bring himself to accept that his brother remembered what the Hollow Souls did to him.

Bo pushed him in silence, and the entire trip back, Brian found himself trying to think of ways to get out of the bed himself. The meds made it possible to deal with the pain. He would just have to take the pills and time it when he knew Bo was busy, then he could get out of the room and call for help. If someone showed up to the house, surely Bo would have no choice but to let them check on his brother and get him the medical attention he needed.

He knew the more he fought it, the more Bo would accuse him of just being stubborn and trying to push himself too much, which wasn't exactly wrong. He also knew that he couldn't go another day being bound to that bed. Not after he'd gotten some fresh air and remembered everything he had been missing. A thought came to him, and suddenly he knew exactly what he would do to distract his brother and give himself enough time to get to the phone, call for help, then get under the bedding, all before Bo made it back inside. He just had to make sure he didn't get caught, or Bo would destroy the phone, just like he had the radio.

"I was thinking . . . once all the chores are done, it might be nice if you went out back and picked some flowers, then put them on Ma's grave. She would like that, don't you think?"

"Yes! The purple ones that she loves. I'll do it tonight. Good idea!"

*We'll see about that, brother. We'll see.*

# 16

A few hours passed, and all Brian could think about was getting to the phone. He'd taken more medicine—the supply was dwindling fast—hoping it would kick in by the time he heard his brother leave the house. The phone was hidden in Ma's closet with the ringer turned off. It was one of those cell phones with a certain amount of prepaid minutes on it. Ma said it was the only real way to have one without a monthly bill that they couldn't afford, and even if they could, there would be no way to hide a landline or cell phone bill from Bo. They kept it for emergency use only, and if this situation didn't call for that, Brian didn't know what did.

The sound of the barn door shutting snapped Brian from his thoughts, and he knew it was time. The back door opened and shut, followed by Bo whistling some melody as he walked through the house.

"Bo! Come here for a sec," Brian yelled. He wanted to make sure his brother was headed to the gravesite.

Bo opened the bedroom door and popped his head in, ducking to avoid the doorframe.

"Do you need something?"

"I just wanted to ask you to grab a few extra flowers for me since I can't go up there and all."

"Okay. Do you want to come with me? I can push you."

*Shit.*

"No, no. I don't think that's a good idea. Plus, my body's tired after getting out there today for the first time. I want to rest. But just tell her they're from both of us, will you?" Brian felt awful for using his mother as a distraction to get Bo away from the house.

"Yep. I'll tell her! Anything else you need before I go?"

"Nope. You hang out with her as long as you want and just tell me all about it when you get back, okay?"

Bo nodded excitedly and left the room, then the back door slammed shut again. Brian was tempted to get right out of bed, but he decided to give it a few minutes. He needed to be sure Bo was gone. When he spotted his brother walking by the closest window with a large handful of flowers in hand, he waited just a little longer, until Bo's giant figure shrank in the distance.

"Okay, don't fuck this up, Brian."

He pushed himself up, thankful his brother had stopped tying him down now that he had earned a bit more trust. The pain, though numbed from the pills, was still there. Brian fought through it and spotted the wheelchair in the corner of the room, out of reach. He wouldn't be able to just plop down off the bed into the wheelchair. No, he'd have to crawl like the desperate cripple he was. He was relieved he had started to regain feeling in his toes. It gave him hope that maybe someday, he would walk again. Maybe he could ride Astra and not have the last time be an experience that caused him to lose so much of himself.

*You deserve everything that's happened to you. You know it. Lying to Bo his entire life . . . Lying to Ma . . .*

The floor was only a few feet away, but it might as well have been a two-story drop. There was no soft way to get down, and Brian knew that no matter how many meds he took, when he hit that floor, it was going to hurt like a bitch. He didn't have time to second guess himself, though. He shimmied to the edge of the bed, gritting his teeth with each movement. Then he took a deep breath and swung his legs over the side, bringing on the sensation of needlelike jabs through his feet and up his shins.

He threw the pillows down onto the floor, hoping it would help soften his fall when he landed. With a grunt, he pushed himself off the bed, immediately dropping in a heap. His left knee landed on one of the pillows, but his right smacked on the hardwood floor, sending a shock of pain through his kneecap. Surprisingly, he only felt a slight sensation in his back, which either meant the pills were doing their job, or there was so much nerve damage he was losing feeling.

The closet was less than ten feet ahead so he got to work, turning onto his stomach and army crawling toward the destination. Every so often, he would stop to listen for Bo. On the off chance his brother had turned around and come back, Brian couldn't risk being discovered on the floor. If Bo walked in, he planned to say he just fell out of bed, but he knew that would lead to his brother tying him up again to "prevent" him from getting hurt.

Beads of sweat dripped down his face, stinging his eyes.

Finally, he reached the closet and sighed in relief. The phone was hidden beneath a loose floorboard that he had rigged for Ma to keep any electronics out of sight. As he went to grab the plank, he spotted the chest in the corner of the closet. The one he had opened before his accident and seen . . . so much. Things he tried to push from his mind. Things he didn't know Ma knew anything about. The burden she must have carried all those years, pretending like nothing was wrong.

Brian pried his attention from the wooden chest and refocused it on the floorboard. There wasn't time to dick around right now, and he could go back to it later. He just hoped Bo didn't come in and rummage through Ma's belongings. It wasn't something Brian worried about initially because Bo was such an emotional wreck that he wouldn't even go near her possessions. But after Brian's accident, something changed in his brother. Not only had he placed Brian *in* this room, but he also started talking with an imaginary version of Ma.

*You've seen her too. You know you have.*

*It was the medicine and lack of sleep. She's buried up in the grave plot, she couldn't possibly be here.*

*Yeah, well, stop acting like ghosts existing is impossible. You saw what those monsters could do. What makes ghosts any harder to believe?*

He shook his head and pulled back the floorboard to reveal a small, black cell phone, along with its charger and a set of keys to the truck they kept parked at the bottom of the property. There was important paperwork folded beneath the objects, including Brian and Bo's birth certificates; documentation for the home, which Ma had purchased in her aunt's name to remain hidden from the Hollow Souls; and a folded stack of cash.

He grabbed the phone with its charger and noticed his hand was trembling. This whole plan was half-assed. He didn't even know who to call. The police? They would likely question the whereabouts of their mother. The closest neighbors? That felt like the best option, only Ma didn't exactly have the best relationship with the Goulds. He didn't have time to think of other options.

"Goddamnit."

He plugged the cord into the outlet within reach and flipped the phone open. It wouldn't turn on, so at first, he thought the damn thing was busted. When was the last time he had used it? Must have been years ago. But after a moment, the phone powered on and displayed the home screen. He quickly went to *Contacts*, locating Ron Gould's phone number. Before he could change his mind, he hit the <*CALL*> button and heard the phone ringing. After the second ring, someone picked up.

"Gould Farm, what can we do for ya?"

Brian's words froze in his throat. Hearing the old man on the other end of the line had him doubting the whole idea.

"Hello . . . Anybody there?"

"Mr. Gould, it's Brian Davidson."

"Oh, hello there, Brian! You just caught me about to head out to the fields. Been a while, eh? That mother of yours keeping you boys busy down there?"

"Uh . . . yeah. Listen, Mr. Gould . . . there's been an accident on the farm. I, uh . . . I fell off my horse and I'm pretty banged up. As you know, my mother's been really sick, and well . . . Bo isn't in any shape to drive me to a doctor. I was wondering if maybe you could stop by and take me to the hospital. I know we don't talk much, and it's a lot to ask, but—"

"Good Lord. Course I'll take you. How bad is it?"

"Well, it's not good, that's for sure. I'm starting to regain feeling in my feet, but Astra bucked me off when she got spooked, then planted her hooves in the center of my back. I thought I was paralyzed. Maybe not, but it's definitely broken."

"You're lucky you can still feel those feet. I had a buddy back a few years who didn't fare as well, pisses in a plastic bag now and all—"

The sound of the barn door shutting cracked like a shotgun.

*Bo's back!*

"I don't mean to be rude, Mr. Gould, but I'm in a great deal of pain sitting up to talk right now. If you don't mind, I'd like to get back in bed until you come."

"Oh, you betcha. Sorry, the old lady says I have the gift of gab. Don't feel bad telling me to stop talking. I need to tend to a few things on the farm, but then I'll head down there to grab ya. I'll bring the dually so you can stretch out on the back seat if you'd like."

"Sure. I really appreciate it, Mr. Gould. Thank you so much."

"Not a worry at all. Sorry to hear about your mother not doing well. We haven't always seen eye to eye, but she's a good woman."

*Shut up! Shut up! I need to get off the phone!*

"Thank you for the kind words. I better get back to bed now. Thanks again."

Mr. Gould disconnected the call, and Brian leaned back with a sigh of relief. Help was on the way. Now he just needed to get back into bed before—

"Brian . . . what are you doing?"

He shot around, ignoring the sharp pain the sudden movement caused in his back, and saw Bo standing in the doorway with his eyes masked in rage.

"I-I'm sorry, Bo. I need help. I know you don't—"

"No! You can't have it! It's gonna hurt us. You're gonna hurt us both with it!"

Bo charged into the room and ripped the phone from Brian's hand, throwing it against the wall. The phone shattered into tiny pieces upon impact.

*Just like your hope of getting out of here . . . Shattered.*

"Who were you talking to? Tell me, now!"

For the first time in his life, Brian feared his brother. Sure, he always knew Bo could kick his ass growing up and that with his condition, he was prone to mental breakdowns, but he never thought he had it in him to intentionally harm him. The way Bo was looking at him right now, eyes glossed over with insanity, Brian knew he needed to be careful with his words. There was no telling what his brother would do to him. He was completely unhinged.

"I was talking with Mr. Gould. I asked him to take me to the hospital, Bo. If I don't get help, I may never walk again. Don't you get that?"

Bo shook his head aggressively, panting like an angry dog.

"No . . . No, no, no. I'm taking care of you, just like Ma

wants me to. She didn't trust doctors, and you know it! How could you do this?"

Brian was at a loss for words. Tears trickled down his face, understanding that his brother would do anything and everything to prevent the outside world from penetrating their family bubble.

"Please. I need you to listen to me, Bo. Your mind hasn't been right since . . . since Ma died. You're not thinking logically. Do you want me to be a cripple for the rest of my life? How will you handle the entire farm by yourself? How will you get food for the animals? Or for us? You need me."

Something snapped behind Bo's eyes as if his brain was computing the information, trying to decide what to do. For a second, Brian thought he broke through, had talked some sense into his brother. But then, Bo shook his head again, and Brian could have sworn his brother even raised his upper lip in a snarl as he walked closer.

"No. You didn't listen to us. You put us in danger, Brian. It's time to get back in bed."

Bo grabbed Brian in a bear hug and lifted him in one fluid motion. Pain coursed through his legs as his brother tossed him onto the bed like a ragdoll, no longer concerned about being careful. Brian tried to shake the cobwebs the pain had coated him in, but it was pointless. Bo was too strong. Before he knew it, he'd wrapped the ropes around his brother's arms, pulling them taut. Brian groaned as they cut into his forearms.

"Please . . . don't do this, Bo."

"We'll take care of you like we always have. Just like how you and Ma took care of me when I was hurt. No more letting you free by yourself. I have to be mean about it. It's not my fault, Brian."

He didn't know what to say. Instead, he stared at his brother in stunned silence. This was a side of Bo he had never seen, and it appeared to only be getting worse. He just hoped that when Mr. Gould came, help would arrive with him. Looking into his brother's eyes, he had a feeling things were about to get far worse.

# 17

## 1996

The family sat at the kitchen table, eating breakfast in silence. Brian hadn't been able to stop the images of Lisa getting dragged into the house from poisoning his mind. The last time he saw her, she was reaching for him—as if he would be able to save her from the monsters in that house—and then he blacked out until he awoke to his dad coming out covered in blood. Now, he ate his eggs and toast, staring straight down at his plate, afraid if he made eye contact with Ma or Bo, he would blurt out everything.

"I'm going to take the boys to the field for some batting practice. Why don't you take the day for yourself and relax," Dad said, displaying a strained smile to Ma.

Ma looked up from her newspaper and smiled. "That sounds nice. It's been too long since the three of you did that together. Does that sound fun, Brian?"

The last thing he wanted to do right now was spend more time with his dad. He forced a fake smile and nodded, then glanced at Dad who was watching his every move. Brian wasn't sure why his dad planned to do this today. Maybe he felt guilty for everything that had happened as of late.

*A picnic in the park isn't going to make up for you killing an innocent girl, Dad.*

Bo seemed to know something was up, but he didn't say anything. He just nudged Brian under the table and furrowed his brow. Brian ignored him and kept eating. When they were finished with breakfast, the boys loaded their baseball stuff into the truck and waited for their dad who was still in the house.

"What the hell's going on with Dad?" Bo asked. "He hasn't even been to a practice or game in a few weeks and all of a sudden, he wants to go down to the field with us like old times?"

"I don't know. I think he feels guilty for not being around lately. Maybe he's trying to make up for it?"

Bo saw right through his brother's lie. "Seriously. You know something you're not telling me. What's the deal?"

"Nothing, okay? Why do you always gotta keep going on about stuff? Just let it go."

"You boys ready?" Dad asked as he walked out the front door.

"Yep," Bo answered. Then both boys got into the truck.

As they drove, Brian wondered what his dad's true intentions were. Bo was right. They hadn't done this in a long time, and after the talk with his dad in the driveway the night before, Brian couldn't help but feel there might be other motives than just getting in some batting practice. He hadn't even attempted to get Brian involved in baseball all summer, knowing his son had given up on playing competitively.

Dad drove in silence, but he kept randomly peering in the rearview mirror, making eye contact with Brian. What was he doing right now? Those eyes . . . They were apologetically sad, as if to say, "I'm sorry, Brian. This has to be done." The field was just up ahead, and his dad slowed to turn into the parking lot. Brian's stomach tied into a knot.

The parking lot was empty except for one vehicle.

Marcus's truck.

"Okay, let's get to it. Brian, you start in the batter's box; Bo, you shag the balls in the outfield. Then we'll switch it up."

"Oh, come on! Why does Brian get to bat first?" Bo huffed.

"Stop being a baby. Your brother hasn't come down here with us all summer, so he gets to bat first."

"Fine," Bo said, then got out of the truck and grabbed his bag.

Brian went to get out as well, but his dad reached over the back seat to stop him.

"What?" Brian asked.

"Remember . . . everything that happens is for the family. He won't feel anything. Trust me," he said quietly.

Brian swallowed down his fear. What was his dad talking about? Why was Marcus here? Only Marcus wasn't anywhere to be found, just his empty truck alone in the parking lot like a forgotten relic. Brian got out and approached the dugout while searching for any sign of him. All he saw were endless trees over the outfield fence, where anything could be hiding in wait.

*Dad would never do anything to hurt Bo. I know that.*

*Do I? I've seen a side of Dad that I never knew existed.*

*All this just so Bo can be better at baseball? Is he really that selfish to let someone get hurt . . . or killed as a trade-off?*

He entered the dugout, half expecting Marcus to be absorbed in the shadows. The bench was empty. Only sunflower seed shells and a few empty Gatorade bottles littered the space. It was odd how a place so wide open could feel eerily secluded. Nobody came to the field at this time of day, and the main road wasn't visible with the trees blocking it. As Brian watched his dad carry the L-screen to the pitcher's mound, he grabbed his bat from the bag. Bo jogged to the outfield, hanging back near the fence so he could cover more ground beneath pop flies.

"I doubt Brian can hit them this far!" Bo yelled. He started laughing, and Brian wished he could join in on the brotherly ribbing, but his mind was elsewhere.

His dad set a bucket of balls behind the screen and grabbed his glove. Brian couldn't help but notice his dad scanning the area as well, as if he was waiting for something to happen. Standing in the batter's box, Brian felt eyes on him. Not just his dad's, not just Bo's, but unknown eyes. He couldn't pinpoint where, but it made his skin crawl. And then he heard whispers. Infinite voices buzzing in his brain. He squeezed his eyes shut trying to force them from his head.

"Okay, ready?" Dad asked, lacking any real enthusiasm.

Brian nodded hesitantly, then got in his stance. Even if he could focus on batting, he imagined it would take some time to shake off the rust. He hadn't so much as lifted a bat in months, let alone swung one. His dad threw the first ball, tossing it at a much slower speed than he normally did. Still, Brian swung and missed, feeling the shame that often came with failing in front of his dad.

"Keep your eye on the ball, Brian. It's just like riding a bike."

Cursing under his breath, he stepped back in and waited for the next pitch. The ball sailed at half speed again and this time, Brian skimmed the bottom of the ball and fouled it into the backstop. The voices intensified, and while Brian couldn't make out what they were saying, he knew in his core they were pleading for help. Cries, screams, begging. What was happening to him?

"Keep swinging, the breeze feels nice out here!" Bo yelled.

"Stop antagonizing your brother. He hasn't played in a while."

Somehow, the comment from his dad made it worse, like he was sticking up for a toddler. Brian squeezed the bat tight and stepped back into the batter's box, ignoring the buzzing sensation swarming from ear to ear. His dad threw the ball with a little more heat on it. This time, Brian swung through it, keeping his eyes on the orb, and felt the satisfying sensation of aluminum striking leather. The ball ripped down the third base line, soaring through the air until it reached a few hundred feet into the outfield. Bo sprinted after the ball, and Brian watched with a smirk on his face. For a moment, the concerns that weighed down on him were gone. It was just them again, playing ball like the old days.

But then, as Bo approached the corner of left field, Brian spotted movement in the woods behind the fence. A dark silhouette blocked by the closest copse of trees, moving closer to the field.

"Dad! Someone's out there!" Brian yelled.

Brian knew by the way his dad turned to look that he was already well aware of what was about to happen.

Bo was oblivious, focused on tracking the ball, doing what he loved to do. Did he not hear the voices? The shape drew closer, and then Brian noticed the figure wasn't alone. There were multiple figures, flanking the field as if they were spreading out to make sure Bo couldn't escape.

"Dad! Help him!"

If Bo heard the commotion, he didn't show it. He reached the outfield fence and bent to pick up the baseball.

"Bo! Watch out!" Brian yelled.

His dad stood on the pitcher's mound, staring at the dirt with a numb expression etched across his face.

The first figure came into view, pushing through the last of the branches to reach the fence. Brian wanted to run to the outfield with his bat and attack the figures coming for his brother. But instead, he remained frozen in place, watching it all unfold, the voices increasing in volume and desperation.

*Help us! Save us! Free our souls!*

The figure wore a skull mask with a black hood over the rest of his head, but Brian knew it was Marcus. The posture was unmistakable, walking in a slight hunch—not one of poor posture, but one that carried malicious intent. Bo picked up the ball and turned to see what was moving behind the fence. Before he could react, Marcus's arm shot out and grabbed him by the throat. Even from where he stood, Brian heard his brother struggling to breathe, gasping for air. The other figures closed in, also wearing skull masks. Bo fought to break free, but Marcus was too strong.

"Dad, what are they doing? They're hurting him!"

"No . . . No, son. Don't watch. It's easier that way. He'll be okay, I promise."

"How do you know that?"

The doubt in his dad's voice sounded like even *he* didn't believe what he was saying.

"Help!" Bo finally forced out.

The other two figures picked up the pace as Marcus used his free hand to cover Bo's mouth, muffling his screams. Brian pictured the fear in Lisa's eyes the day before, then the blood on his dad's shirt. He feared for his brother's life, and meanwhile, Dad, their supposed protector, ignored the cries of his own son. The son that he worshiped. What would he let them do to Brian if it came down to it?

One of the approaching figures was a beast of a man, standing well over six feet tall. He reached Marcus first, immediately grabbing Bo by the collar and yanking him up and over the outfield fence. His jersey ripped around the neck, exposing his chest and shoulder. Bo continued to scream for his life, but the decibels lowered in volume as the group dragged Bo into the woods. Eventually, the field returned to silence as Bo, Marcus, and his two followers disappeared deeper into the forest.

With the commotion gone, the voices diminished and Brian now heard his dad crying on the mound. Rage took over. Brian charged at him with the bat in hand.

"Why did you let them take him? What the hell's wrong with you?"

His dad turned to face him, crying. But it was anger in his eyes, not sadness.

"You shut your mouth, Brian. I'm doing what needs to be

done. I will not be talked to that way, do you understand? I told you that he'll be okay. This is all part of the plan."

"What plan? Why do you trust Marcus, Dad? He's a psycho!"

His dad put his hand on Brian's shoulder, then leaned in, touching foreheads. He was now crying uncontrollably.

"I-I have no choice but to trust him. It's too late to turn back, Brian."

# 18

**PRESENT DAY**

It had been a few hours since Bo stormed out after strapping Brian to the bed as though he belonged in the loony bin. The clatter of pots and pans, objects slamming around like a tornado bursting through the front door echoed through the house. The one thing Brian had tried to avoid during this whole ordeal was breaking Bo's trust. If there was ever a chance to get out of here, he just ruined it. Bo had left the room with a wild stare, almost animalistic, full of primal rage.

*He wouldn't do anything to Mr. Gould, would he?*
*I've never seen him this way. He's lost his mind.*

The truth was that Bo had plenty of episodes over the years. Anger wasn't something new to him in those moments, but he had always been self-contained. Ma did everything possible to keep him away from people. Like an untrained dog that would lick a child's face until it was triggered by something unknown, then bite the kid in the face . . . that was Bo right now. Brian had triggered him—broken that trust—and Ma wasn't here to talk Bo off the ledge. If anything happened to poor Mr. Gould, it was Brian's fault.

*You've done worse than get an old man hurt.*

Panic surged through Brian's chest at the thought of what might happen. He wiggled his right arm back and forth, trying to force the rope loose. If Bo had been distracted during all the commotion, maybe he did a sloppy job securing Brian in place. While his arm moved slightly, all it really accomplished was rope burn on his already damaged skin. Each nudge dragged the rope along, digging deeper into the skin. Blood trickled down his forearm as he bit down on his lip to avoid crying out in pain.

Just when he thought there was no hope, he was able to move the arm a few more inches. It was working. With a newfound sense of urgency, Brian aggressively twisted, pulled, and wiggled until the skin beneath turned raw, but he kept going, pushing through it. Eventually, his arm broke free. He rested his head back on the pillow and took deep breaths, trying to ignore the throbbing intensity shooting through his limb.

A vehicle door shut outside. Mr. Gould had arrived.

Brian went to work on his other arm, which, in theory, should have been easier with a hand to loosen the rope, but Bo had tied a tight double knot that had begun to cut off the circulation. He also didn't have full feeling in the fingers on his free hand yet, making it more difficult to grip the knot.

There was a knock at the front door, and Brian wanted to scream out for help, but he knew that would likely end horribly. Either his brother would go to drastic measures to stop Brian from trying to communicate, or he would do something to Mr. Gould. Brian expected Bo to answer the door, but instead, he rushed into the bedroom with crazed eyes.

"Be quiet, Brian. I'll talk with him."

Bo started to leave but then stopped, turning back to his brother.

*Shit. He saw my arm untied.*

"Bo . . . please."

"I'm sorry. This is to help you."

He left the room and shut the door, then Brian heard the click of a lock imprisoning him in his own home. He heard the front door open, and the chatter of Mr. Gould drifted through the wall. The old man's voice was deep but too muffled for Brian to hear what he was saying. It went on that way for a few minutes, the back-and-forth between Bo and their neighbor with fragments of voices, like a radio not quite tuned to a station. At least it appeared to remain civil, no shouting or any sort of commotion. Then the front door shut, and with it, Brian's hopes of leaving the farm. The conversation ceased until Brian heard them rounding the house, still talking with one another, just outside his window now.

"I'm sorry to hear about your mother falling ill. I know we haven't always seen eye to eye, but she means well. And I'm glad to hear you're caring for your brother with her laid up."

"Thanks. Brian always knows what to do. He's smart like Ma was."

"Was?" Ron asked, confused.

"What?"

"You said smart like your ma *was*. Is she okay, Bo?"

Brian's heart cranked into overdrive. Bo wasn't quick-witted enough to come up with something on the fly. He could only imagine his brother on the verge of a breakdown in front of their neighbor. Nobody spoke for a long, uncomfortable minute, and then Ron must have realized Bo's confusion and changed the subject.

"Your brother sure sounded like he was in a great deal of pain on the phone. Just give a holler if you need any help."

"Please . . ." Brian whispered to himself. *Just leave, Ron. Before he hurts you.*

"It's okay! Bye, Mr. Gould! Have a good day!" Bo yelled enthusiastically.

"Oh, one other thing. Not sure how much you boys been following the news, but there's some dangerous tomfoolery going on. Murders and the like. News says that whoever's behind it all's been targeting rural areas just like this. And that there's been old ladies at all the houses where they found victims. Be sure to warn your ma, okay?"

After a moment of silence—likely Bo's mind computing the information he'd just been given—his brother responded, "Thanks for telling me. I better get back to Brian now."

Whatever was said after that was unintelligible as soon as Ron's truck started. Brian was no longer focused on the words anyway. He was lost in his thoughts, repeating what Mr. Gould just said. The dreams, it was like they were warning Brian that this was going to happen. While Mr. Gould, and likely even Bo, didn't know what was going on, Brian knew exactly what was happening. The Hollow Souls were coming, and they were looking for the Davidson farm.

## 1996

Brian and his dad sat quietly in the dugout, waiting for Marcus to bring Bo back to them. Although he'd said Bo wouldn't be harmed, Dad's numb expression conveyed anything but confidence. It was impossible not to be mad at him, but somehow, Brian also felt *bad* for him. Bad because through all these horrible events over the past few weeks, he knew his dad never meant to get this deep into it. He never meant to harm anyone or put his family in danger. If what he'd told Brian was true, it started out innocently enough, just hearing what Marcus had to say when he offered to help, and by the time he realized how truly vile Marcus was, it was too late.

"He'll never let me go, Brian. I'm stuck, and I don't know what to do. I'm scared."

Panic rooted in Brian's stomach, branching out through his body like a burgeoning weed. His dad had never talked like this, usually afraid to show any sort of emotion, holding a stoic presence on the surface. Now, Brian had seen his dad cry *and* admit to being scared. He realized how hard it must be for a parent to put on a front while dealing with the day-to-day stress of money, protection, and care needed to allow their children to flourish.

"Where'd they take him?"

"I-I don't know. Listen, if anything ever happens to me, I want you to tell Ma everything, okay? I want you to tell her and then get the hell away from this town, away from Marcus and the Hollow Souls. This is *my* fuckup, and you guys shouldn't have to suffer for it."

The finality in the admission of those words hit Brian like a closed fist. Was his dad planning on doing something to fix this? Or at least trying to fix it? Was he going to put his life on the line to do so? Regardless of how mad Brian was, he didn't want to lose his dad. He was a good man in a bad place. But then Brian's focus shifted back to his brother—one of the nicest yet most innocent people he'd ever known. Ma often said that Bo wasn't as oblivious as everyone thought, and that he let his issues bottle up inside and didn't show them on the surface. Brian envied that, but he also couldn't imagine carrying that weight every single day. He wore his emotions on his sleeve, both good and bad.

"Do you think they'll do something to you?" Brian asked.

"Well . . . as long as I keep doing what they ask of me, no. I think I'm useful to them. I do their dirty work so they can remain in the background until they're ready. The problem is that I don't want to help them anymore. I can't even sleep at night. Your mother looks at me like I'm a monster, like she knows I'm doing hideous things behind her back. Hell, I wish it was something as simple as staying out late drinking or getting hooked on drugs."

"So just tell her. If she knows your story, she might be willing to forgive you. It doesn't have to be some big secret you keep from her."

"You're wise beyond your years, kid. But it's not that simple. I already told you: the more she knows, the more she's in danger. I only want her to know about it if something happens to me. You got that?"

Brian nodded, hesitant to agree but knowing it was the only answer his dad would accept.

"Okay, good. Now let's be done talking about it."

Brian didn't have anything to add to the conversation anyway. He watched the distant woods, hoping to see his brother coming back from the forest like nothing happened. Hoping to see that trademark Bo Davidson smile. As he let his thoughts go back to his dad, a squealing sound echoed through the trees sending a flock of crows flapping into the overcast sky.

He knew it was Bo, yet it sounded inhuman. It sounded like suffering. The leaves on the branches rustled and swayed, going about their business like nothing sinister was taking place down below. The horrible whispering sounds reemerged, and Brian did all he could not to scream at the top of his lungs. He squeezed the sides of his head, praying for it to go away. Meanwhile, his dad appeared oblivious to not only the whispers but Brian's reaction to them.

Dad started to stand, then didn't move, likely debating whether he should go after Bo or not. Brian wasn't sure what there was to debate, and as terrified as he was, his brother was more important. He jumped up, pushing past his dad, pushing through the buzzing sensation in his head, and ran onto the baseball field toward the outfield fence.

"Brian! No! Get back here, please!"

The pleas were useless. His dad could have been pointing a gun at him, and he still wouldn't have stopped. His feet smacked off the grass as he picked up speed, and just when he reached the fence, he spotted movement through the trees. Then he heard a soft moan, like someone semiconscious trying to come back to reality. Any internal strength he had to confront Marcus evaporated.

He had come too far, though, so he forced himself to jump over the fence and come face-to-face with the all-consuming woodland. His dad continued to yell behind him, now picking up his own pace to try and stop Brian from advancing any farther. Brian didn't give him the chance to catch up, running into the mouth of the forest and onto the trail to find his brother. Following the sounds, it didn't take him long to find the group, who were all on their knees leaning over his brother in the tall grass.

Bo's body thrashed around; his back arched as the muscles in his neck pulsed and strained. His eyes rolled back in his head as the female member of the Hollow Souls held his feet to the ground while the tall man seized his wrists, extending them above his head. The third member was on his knees with his skull mask facing Brian's direction. Only he wasn't looking at him, he was leaning over Bo, chanting something in a different language, holding a long bone shard with a jagged tip that glowed blue. Was he going to stab his brother? Bo cried behind clenched teeth, thrashing his head from side to side. The leaning figure grabbed Bo by the throat but didn't squeeze. He held his head steady, locking it in place. And then the masked man gripped Bo by the mouth, prying it open, releasing his brother's suppressed screams into the wild.

Brian wanted to help, but he knew he wouldn't get five feet before they noticed him coming. The figure holding Bo's face leaned over, getting closer to his open mouth. Everything around them became blurred, shrouded in a cloud of blue smoke. Brian blinked, trying to squint through the haze. Something came out of the skull's mouth, floating through the air and into his brother's body. The bone shard in the masked man's hand pulsated with the chants. Bo spasmed, twitching as if having a full-on seizure. Suddenly, everything went quiet, as though the fog was creating some type of soundproof force field around the group and Brian was trapped on the outside.

He moved back, stepping on a dead twig that snapped beneath his weight.

All three of the Hollow Souls lifted their heads in his direction.

Brian turned and sprinted back along the trail, dodging overgrown bushes and hanging branches, then jumped up and over the fence to the baseball field. He turned and stared toward the woods again just as his dad reached the outfield ten feet behind him.

He watched and waited, ignoring his dad's shouting. Finally, all three of the masked figures appeared in front of him, almost as if they had materialized out of thin air. He knew that wasn't true, yet it did nothing to ease the terror surging through him.

The lead masked figure spotted him standing at the fence and stopped. For a second, Brian thought they were coming for him next. The moaning picked up again, and that's when

Brian realized Bo was with them, being dragged by the other two Hollow Souls. His head drooped, facing the ground so Brian couldn't see how badly he was hurt. It sure as hell sounded like he was in pain. He shifted his focus back to the figure watching him, only it was closer now, just a few feet from the fence. The man stopped and lifted his skull mask. Marcus's deranged face revealed itself with that disgusting smile that made Brian's skin crawl.

"Hey, champ. Good to see ya again. Don't worry about your brother, he's fine. Just a bit foggy, is all. It'll wear off," he said with a smirk. "You might wanna listen to your daddy and get back to him."

Brian squeezed his fists so tightly his fingers hurt. He wanted to kill this man who had ruined their family. He almost shrieked when a hand planted firmly on his shoulder, but he spun around to find his dad standing directly behind him now, his eyes glued on Marcus and the Hollow Souls. He saw the same hatred in Dad's eyes that he felt deep inside himself.

"Hey, Barry. I present to you the new and improved Bo Davidson. Once he comes out of this little hangover, he'll be a new man. You can thank us later. We'll be seeing ya, Barry . . ."

They dropped Bo onto the ground outside the fence, then without another word, they left the way they had come, allowing the forest to swallow them up. Bo lay motionless, and if it wasn't for his low groans, Brian might have feared his brother was dead.

"Help me get Bo to the truck. We need to get him in bed to rest."

Brian was numb. He did as his dad instructed, oblivious to

the rest of the world around him. They walked around the outfield fence, carefully lifting Bo off the ground. Drool pooled at the corner of his lips, sliding down his chin in a thick, goopy mess. His eyes rolled back in his head as he continued to mumble incoherent nonsense. When they got him onto the back seat, Brian and his dad climbed into the front and rode the entire way home in silence.

## 20

## PRESENT DAY

Everything was unraveling and all Brian could do was lie in bed and watch it happen. While Bo had shown signs of remembering more of the past than Brian originally thought, he still didn't think his brother remembered the Hollow Souls and how dangerous they were. He *needed* to know. If the murders Mr. Gould mentioned had occurred in the area, it wouldn't take Marcus much longer to find them. Brian couldn't be strapped to a bed when that happened. Bo needed more than just a story to understand the seriousness of the situation. He needed to see what was inside the wooden chest. The question Brian kept asking himself was, "Why now?" After all these years, how and why was Marcus closing in on them?

The sky had darkened to nightfall, and Bo had yet to bring any candles into the bedroom, leaving Brian with only his thoughts in the inky blackness. He suspected this day would come, he just didn't know it would be this soon, with him partially paralyzed and his mentally unstable brother caring for him.

"Bo! Please . . . come in here."

His brother marched down the hall, a flickering light accompanying his thunderous steps. He appeared in the doorway with a candle in hand, distorting his features and accentuating his bloodshot eyes that had gone feral.

"What?" Bo asked, his voice low and direct.

"I know I've lost some of your trust these past few days, and I'm sorry for that. But I overheard what Mr. Gould was telling you earlier about the murders. Bo, there's a lot I need to tell you, and some of it might be hard to hear."

Bo's expression softened ever so slightly as he entered the room, setting the candle on the dresser. He stood over Brian's bed like a dog awaiting a command. "Worse than what you told me about Dad? What could be worse than that?"

"There's a wooden chest . . . in the closet. I need you to grab it for me, and *before* you open it, let me explain about the past and everything that happened. Can you do that for me?" Brian asked. Bo sighed but didn't say anything, so Brian took that as a sign to continue. "When Ma had me tell you the truth about Dad, there were parts even she didn't know about. At least I *thought* that was the case. What's inside the chest will explain a lot of what you need to know before they get here."

"Who? What are you talking about, Brian?"

"I told you. The murders that Mr. Gould spoke about. I heard him warn you to stay safe. But he doesn't know we're linked to those killers, or that they're looking for us. Please, I need you to trust me right now, Bo."

"'Killers . . . looking for us'? Why would they want *us*?"

"I promise it'll all make sense after you hear what

happened. But first, grab the chest, please. It's in the far left corner of the closet."

Bo walked over hesitantly and kneeled, pulling out the aged wooden chest. Brian's heart pounded at the sight of it. Bo took it to the stand next to Brian and set it down, unable to take his eyes off it as he sat in his chair.

"I love you, brother. The past is one nasty bitch, and I'm so sorry that you have to find out this way. I'll start this story from when the Hollow Souls came for you. Everything they did to you . . . was Dad's fault. But he didn't mean any harm to you or our family. I know for certain if he was able to change how things went down, he would have done just that. And so would I, because I haven't exactly been truthful to you or to Ma. I thought by keeping Dad's secrets all these years that I was protecting the family. But I now realize that Ma was right. You need to know the truth. And you need to know how truly dangerous the Hollow Souls are."

## 1996

A few weeks went by, and Bo seemed to be back to his normal self. *Better* than his normal self. For the first time in months, Brian felt like his family was back to the way things were before. His dad attended all Bo's games, cheering him on from the stands with the rest of the families. Ma even went back to smiling at her husband, joking around with him, and even planting a few kisses on his scruffy cheek. It felt forced, but they were trying, and that's all he could ask for.

Bo's skills showed noticeable improvement as he led his team to a tournament win both at bat and with his play in the outfield. Brian even found himself enjoying the games, eating popcorn from the concession stand and drinking a Coke while his brother became the star of the show. He was happy for Bo. He knew what he'd had gone through to get here, even if Bo didn't.

Marcus and the Hollow Souls were out of the picture, and

a false sense of hope fell over the Davidson family. That all changed after the championship game. Brian was the first to notice him, but his dad spotted Marcus soon after. Brian wasn't sure initially, but then his dad stopped walking while Ma and Bo strolled ahead toward the truck, running through the highlights of the game. Brian squeezed his dad's arm, wondering what it meant to see this evil monster again after weeks of freedom.

*We'll be seeing ya, Barry . . .*

Those words played on repeat in Brian's head for days after the incident with Bo. He had finally allowed himself to relax a bit. And now all the tension, all the anxiety, it came swarming back at once like a horde of angry wasps.

"Go with your mother, Brian. I'll be quick."

"No, Dad. I don't want to leave you."

"I said go. *Now.*"

Brian did as he was told, but he never took his focus off his dad and Marcus. As Ma loaded the baseball gear into the truck, smiling and joking around with Bo and some of the other parents, Brian wished he was close enough to hear what Marcus was whispering in Dad's ear. He was like a slithering snake trying to burrow into its nest. But the defeat in his dad's slouched posture said everything. Just like he'd promised, Marcus wasn't done with him. What could he possibly want from them now? It was as if Dad was an unfortunate link in an evil chain of events that connected this horrible clan of soul-sucking vampires to the rest of the world.

His dad nodded and trudged back toward the family. He wiped at his eyes, and it broke Brian's heart to know the burden he was carrying, even if it was his own fault. There wasn't a day that went by where Brian didn't see his brother thrashing around on the ground, straining so hard that his head might burst like a baked potato in a microwave. Every time he closed his eyes and attempted sleep, it was that mental image that greeted him—only occasionally interrupted by Lisa getting dragged into the dark house by Marcus and Dad.

This image of his dad walking back to the family, knowing he was stuck obeying Marcus for the rest of his life, was another screenshot that planted itself among the nightmarish memories Brian tried so hard to forget.

"Okay, you guys ready?" Dad asked, trying to cover up the dread behind every word.

Brian stared at him as Ma and Bo got into the truck, and for a brief second, they made eye contact. His dad mouthed, "I'm sorry," then hopped in the driver's seat. Brian wouldn't need to wait long to find out exactly what his dad was sorry for.

After dinner, Ma went to her room to watch the evening news while Bo retreated to the boys' bedroom to play some video games. Brian hung around the kitchen, waiting for the chance to get Dad alone to ask what was going on. His dad knew what was coming, and when he noticed the two of them were alone, he advised his son to sit on the couch.

"Okay. Here's the deal, Brian. I'm going to break things off with Marcus. He wants me to get another girl for them. I-I just can't do it anymore. I'm going to have to tell your mother. But before I do that, I need to end this. Here, look at this," he said, pulling something out of his pocket and handing it to Brian.

It was a Polaroid photo of a girl not much older than Brian. She looked similar to Lisa in age and just as beautiful in her own way. Something about the Polaroid quality added to the uncomfortable itch working its way up Brian's arm, as if just holding the picture of the girl infected him.

"Who is she?"

"Her name's Ania. She walks by herself to dance class every Thursday and back home when she's done. They want me to get her on her way home, when it's dark, then bring her to them."

"What do they do to these girls? What did they do to Lisa?"

His dad turned away, unable to keep eye contact with Brian.

"I don't know exactly what they do."

"You were covered in her blood, Dad. What happened?"

"I . . . They did something to her, drained her life from her body or something. The blood was because Marcus attacked her when she clawed his face trying to get away. I tried to stop him from beating her, I really did. By the time he was done, she was barely alive when they . . . did what they did. Somehow, the beating wasn't nearly as bad as watching the life drain from her eyes while they stood over her, sucking out her soul."

"And they took these girls, probably killed them, and then . . . gave power to Bo?"

His dad nodded, still staring at the floor.

"Son. Listen to how you're talking. You sound like a

grown man, but you're just a boy. No kid should be put in this situation. I'm so sorry."

"*Nobody* should be put in this situation, not just kids, Dad. How are you going to end things? When are you supposed to . . . *abduct* this Ania girl?"

"Please don't use that word. I know it's the truth, but I can't think of myself that way. I'm already broken inside, Brian."

*Abduction. That's what it is, Dad. Whether it makes you feel bad or not.*

"They want me to do it tonight. I'll grab her, then I'll—"

"What are you guys talking about? Is all this true, Dad?" Bo asked from behind them.

Brian and Barry turned to see Bo standing in the hallway, all the color drained from his face.

"How long have you been standing there?" Dad asked.

"Long enough. What happened to me? And what is Brian talking about, *killing* girls?" Bo marched ahead on rubber limbs, dropping to the couch to prevent himself from face-planting onto the floor.

"It's not like it sounds, bud. I didn't kill anyone—"

"Girls died because of me?" Bo asked, his voice lost in a distant void as he tried to grasp the situation.

"I'm going to make it right. I promise. I took something important from them that I plan to destroy so they can never do what they did to you, or anyone, ever again."

Brian observed his brother, unsure of what he would do next. After a moment of silence, Bo got to his feet and approached the phone on the wall.

"What are you doing?" Brian asked.

Bo ignored his brother and reached for the landline, then he turned to face his dad.

"I'm calling the cops."

"Please . . ." their dad trailed off, barely above a whisper.

"I'm sorry, Dad. These people need to be stopped," Bo insisted, his voice hitching on the sobs forcing themselves out.

"I *am* going to stop them, Bo! Don't call. It won't do any good."

Bo turned back to the landline, ignoring his dad. Brian was on his feet before he realized what he was doing.

*BAM!*

He rammed his brother into the wall, putting a hole in the Sheetrock, and both boys fell. Bo had already dialed. The phone slid across the floor out of reach, and the faint voice of the operator came from the receiver, just a mumbling chatter but it might as well have been someone screaming at the top of their lungs.

"What are you doing? Get off me! They need to know about this!"

"Stop! He's trying to fix it," Brian said through gritted teeth. He tried to hold his brother down, keep him away from the phone, but he crawled toward it, dragging Brian's weight on top of him with ease. Bo was inches from picking up the phone.

Brian reached out and grabbed it, yanking the cord free and cutting the call short. Bo fought to get his brother off him, and Brian reacted. He didn't realize what he was doing until it was done. He struck Bo in the temple repeatedly until the phone shattered into pieces in his hand. He didn't stop until he felt his dad pull him off, and when he looked down, he realized what he had done. Bo was unconscious, blood pooled beneath his head and spread across the floor.

"What the fuck have you done?"

"I . . ." Brian couldn't finish. Panic set in, and he realized he may have just killed his own brother.

His dad grabbed him by the shirt and slammed him against the wall.

"All of this! All for nothing! I should fucking end you!"

The words struck Brian like a hammer to the skull. He had acted before thinking, but it was to protect his family. To protect his *dad*. How could he say such a thing?

"Barry! Put him down, *now*!"

Ma appeared at the edge of the living room with a gun in hand, taking in the scene. She saw her husband holding Brian against the wall by the collar of his shirt. She saw Brian grimacing at the close proximity of his dad's angry face. She saw Bo on the floor, unconscious, covered in his own blood.

Barry let go of his son and turned to face his wife. He noticed what was in her hand when she raised the gun, aiming it at the love of her life.

"Please . . . it's not what it looks—"

The gunshot was deafening, a cracking thunderbolt that exploded in Brian's eardrums. A dark circle formed on his dad's chest as his hands immediately went to cover the wound. He looked at Ma with a mix of shock and pain. He tried to speak, but only blood came out of his mouth, no words. Then he dropped to his knees, falling onto the floor next to Bo. It was a scene straight out of a horror movie. Brian stood in shock, looking at his dad who was dead, and his brother who could also very well be dead.

The images of Bo staring up at him wide-eyed as the

phone came crashing down on his head, and the crimson hole, the size of a quarter, appearing on his dad's chest played on repeat in Brian's mind. He couldn't move. He didn't realize Ma was screaming until she started shaking him, asking if he was all right.

"ARE YOU OKAY?! DID HE HURT YOU?!"

Brian shook his head, unable to speak.

Distant sirens approached, followed by the flickering red and blue lights strobing through the windows and onto the living room wall, highlighting the hole Bo had made when his shoulder slammed into it.

Ma hugged Brian tight and wept.

"It's okay, baby. I got you."

As the first cruiser pulled into the driveway, Ma ran to Bo's side, checking for a pulse, screaming his name. The front door opened and officers rushed in. One of them grabbed Brian, asking what happened. Before he had a chance to think of a story, Ma answered for him, and he knew he could never tell her the truth. She couldn't know that she'd killed her own husband for something Brian had done.

## 22

**PRESENT DAY**

Bo stared at his brother in disbelief. As soon as Brian was done telling the story, he felt a massive weight lift off his shoulders, but it was quickly replaced by absolute terror when Bo began to snarl, some inhuman growl growing in his chest.

"Bo . . . I'm so, so sorry. I wanted to tell you for years. It was a secret I've lived with, one that's eaten away at me since the day Dad died. I couldn't go anywhere without thinking I was being judged. By Ma, by you. Hell, even the way Astra looked at me sometimes. You mean everything to me."

"You— You did this to me? You're the reason Dad's dead?"

The numb tone he spoke in made the hair on the back of Brian's neck stand on end. It would be difficult for a normal person to comprehend; for someone with Bo's condition, it had to be borderline impossible. If Brian was going to get the point across about just how serious this situation was, he needed to tell the whole story. He must tell Bo who the Hollow Souls are and why they're looking for the farm.

"Yes. There's no other way to put it. It's my fault. Dad's dead because of me. You have your condition . . . because of me." Brian paused, unable to stop the tears from taking over. "The reason you have a phobia of electronics, especially phones, is because of what I did to you. If it wasn't for Ma, I would have killed myself years ago. She helped me through the dark times and did so without even knowing what I'd done. But I need you to understand what the Hollow Souls want. Because I'm stuck in bed, a goddamn cripple, and they'll eventually figure out where we are. When Dad died, the police came, took our stories, and then it was a long, drawn-out court case. Marcus threatened us many times, saying Dad took something that belonged to them, and they wanted it back. Ma said she had no idea who he was or what he was talking about. But because of the media, police, and everyone else who was up our asses after Dad's death, Marcus didn't dare come for us. Then Ma got us out of there as soon as she was proven innocent, as soon as it was deemed self-defense.

"The biggest reason I hid the truth from Ma was because if she knew, you and I both know she wouldn't have been able to lie up on that stand in front of a jury, or to Marcus. She needed to believe she did it to protect us. But poor Dad was just trying to stop me from hurting you."

A single, stubborn tear slid down Bo's cheek, but his glossed eyes remained stoic—evidence of the realization of what happened trying to rip and claw its way into his brain. Brian observed his brother, looking for telltale indicators of the rage Bo was prone to in situations he found confusing.

Those signs were there—his stiff posture, his knuckles turning white as he squeezed the arms of the chair—but Bo didn't act on those urges. He stayed seated, unable to look Brian in the eye.

"Open the chest now, Bo. There's stuff in there I need to show you. I don't expect you to forgive me, but I hope it helps answer some questions you've had all these years."

Bo closed his eyes and took a deep breath. He scratched his forehead as if horrible thoughts were itching inside his cranium. With trembling hands, he grabbed the lid of the chest and lifted it off. From the bed, Brian couldn't see inside it, but he knew what was there.

"What is this stuff?" Bo asked.

"Everything. It's everything you need to know about us. About them. All these years, Ma hid a dark secret of her own. She knew what Dad was up to with them. It's why she didn't trust him, why she thought he had snapped and was beating both of us to death."

Bo lifted a photo from the chest and scrunched his brow. "Who's this girl?"

"Her name was Lisa. She was the first girl—that I know of—who Dad helped them take. I was with him that day. We gave her a ride while you were at a game with Ma. I watched Dad help Marcus drag her into a house."

"What did they do to her?" Bo asked, clearly still confused about what this girl had to do with them.

"They killed her. They sucked the life out of her . . . and they gave you some of her soul. To make you stronger. Dad got in over his head, was stuck helping them. He had to bring them the girls in the photos, and they did things to them and to you, to make you a star. You have to understand . . . It was so hard keeping this from you, but I didn't want you to carry any of the guilt that I do every damn day of my life. It wasn't your fault they did it. And while Dad was no saint, he had no idea what he was getting involved with when Marcus first came to him."

"Marcus . . ."

He said the name with familiarity, as though the mention of it brought back a flood of memories.

"Do you remember him? Do you remember what they did to you?"

Bo shook his head, but the wheels were spinning.

"Keep looking in the chest. There's more."

Bo pulled out a notebook, worn with age but still intact. He could read but not as well as before his injury, due to his cognitive skills being greatly diminished. Brian reached out for it, and his brother handed it to him. Brian was surprised by the contents as he took the time to read the pages. It was a diary of sorts, mentioning many of the events that led to Ma shooting her husband. She questioned who Dad was working with, what he was out doing late at night, and why, all of a sudden, he stopped going to baseball games and remained distant from her and Bo. She wrote about how one night she followed her husband and overheard him talking with Marcus, and how she never confronted him because she was too afraid for her own life. The words oozed with confliction; she clearly still loved the man whom she had children with. She knew deep down that it wasn't him doing all of it, that something had found its way inside him and taken over. She lived with that secret for years and still found a way to forgive her husband. Suddenly, the love he felt for his mother came crashing over him like a tidal wave, and Brian found it difficult to continue reading.

"What? What does it say?" Bo asked.

Brian was so absorbed in the journal that he had forgotten his brother was still sitting next to him. When he looked up at Bo, his brother was as confused as ever.

"Ma knew everything. She did whatever she could to protect us, Bo. I . . . I feel sick—" Brian leaned over and threw up in the trash can next to the bed; a violent shot of pain coursed up his back as his core went to work. When he was done, he wiped his chin and sat back up in bed. "There's more in the notebook. But before we look at it, I need to know . . . what are you feeling right now?"

"Sad. Really sad. I want Ma back. She'd fix everything. Why did Dad have to do bad things?"

"I-I'm sorry, Bo."

"You keep saying that! But it's your fault, Brian! I see things—bad things! I talk to Ma even though she's gone. Why'd you make me so scared? Why'd you do it?" Bo bolted up from his chair, knocking it over. The *crack* when it hit the hardwood startled Brian, reminding him of the gunshot to his dad's chest all those years ago.

Bo threw the chest on the bed and stormed out of the room before Brian could respond. It was heartbreaking, but it needed to happen. Now that he knew more of the story, hopefully Bo would listen to the rest when he was ready. Brian just prayed that time would be sooner rather than later. If what Mr. Gould said was true, and the murders he mentioned had occurred in the area, it meant the Hollow Souls at least had an idea of where to look for the Davidson family. They were running out of time.

Brian scanned the scattered contents of the chest now strewn across the bed. He spotted a folded piece of paper, grabbed it, and carefully opened it. The candle's flame was scant, but it provided just enough light to read by.

*If you boys find this letter, please understand that I loved you both with all my heart. It wasn't easy holding the secrets I did all these years, but I still feel it was for the best. Bo, you are such a passionate and loving human. You wouldn't hurt a fly, even though you could crush anything that got in your way. When I'm gone, I need you to keep your brother in check because he's a stubborn son of a bitch. Brian, I know you read that. Believe me when I say it was written with love. Here's the thing, boys. I hid us as long as I could from those evil monsters. But when I'm dead, that protection will go away. They ruined our family, and they want to finish the job. The deal your daddy had with them was forever binding. There was no breaking it as long as our family was around. Before Marcus was in his life, your dad would spend countless hours trying to find ways to improve our situation. He'd work overtime. A second job on the weekends. As you got older, he only wanted you to succeed. He wanted you to grow up and be in a better position than either of us ever were. So, in a way, I understand why he made the deal with Marcus. That doesn't mean I wasn't pissed off beyond belief with him for doing it. I just regret* never confronting him about it before that awful day, seeing him snap on you boys. Brian got that stubbornness from somewhere, after all. Sorry, Bry. Love ya.

    Brian, remember when we made that grave for Dad after we first moved to the farm? When Bo was still recovering? I wasn't truly honest with you. Yes, I agreed to Bo's request because I wanted a place where we could go to remember your father. That part is true. But we didn't just bury some of his belongings in that hole. We buried what those killers want. Because if they find us, and they don't know where it is, we stand a chance of getting away. We hold the power. A time will come when you boys need to dig up that grave and take it. The power that they gave you is still with you. Whatever sacrificial bullshit they pulled off, it never went away. As I write this, I know I'm dying. I know I don't have much longer to live, and my remaining time is crucial. Look after each other. Take care of the animals. And please, don't cry over me. We've done enough crying over the years. Remember me for the good times because that's what I remember about your dad. I promise it helps ease the suffering. I love you boys. Now get back to work and stop sobbing like a bunch of babies.

    Love,
    Ma


Brian wiped the tears away as he finished reading, feeling

the invisible set of eyes that belonged to his mother watching over him. He smiled, then folded up the letter and put it back in the wooden chest. He recalled digging the grave with Ma. She allowed Brian to add a couple of items—things he thought his dad would like—then on top of those, she placed a box of some of Dad's belongings into the hole before they filled it in. Saying that much of what was inside was private between husband and wife, she didn't let him look at the contents, and he'd never questioned what was inside that box. Now he needed to know. What could possibly be in there that held power over the Hollow Souls? And how could it relate to the strength that Bo received out in the woods?

He picked up all the items off the bed, returned them to the wooden chest, then dropped it onto the floor. When Bo came back, Brian would convince him to bring the wheelchair. They needed to do this together.

Bo stormed out of the house, his head ready to explode. He was so confused. It seemed everything Brian told him made things worse. Dad helped bad people kill girls. Those bad people did something to Bo. Brian hurt Bo's head and made him this way. He wanted—no, *needed*—Ma now more than ever. She would know what to do.

As he marched farther from the house, he glanced over at the barn and considered going inside to feed Astra. He wasn't in the mood to see her, though. She could wait. He passed the pigs who grunted and snorted at him, ignoring their demands.

## The Devil's in the Next Room

And then he came to the chicken coop. His chest tightened at the sight of it. Ever since Ma died, it was like the birds were inside his head. And they were *so* loud. It was like a constant whispering making his brain and ears itch. He wanted to dig inside them and scratch aggressively to get rid of the noise. He had tried everything to make it go away. At first, he started feeding them farther away from the house, allowing them to travel closer to the woods. He hoped a fox would kill them so he didn't have to hear them anymore but so far, only two had been eaten.

It seemed like every space, every corner, had chickens waiting for him. They were asking for help. Begging him to let them free. He didn't understand, and it was driving him crazy.

Now, as he watched them move around, pecking at the ground for scraps, the loud voices returned.

"Why? Get out of my head!"

He needed to relieve the pain, but he didn't know what to do. Bo tried counting the remaining chickens but kept getting stuck at six. He knew how to count, but his mind often got confused and forgot where it left off. And their desperate pleas weren't helping.

"What do you want from me?"

Four or five of the chickens moved to the edge of the fence, clucking in his direction. Bo stepped forward, unsure of what he would do. They wanted help. And he needed help himself. Ma wasn't here right now to talk to him, and he was mad at Brian, so it was up to him to make a decision on his own and do what he thought was right.

"I'll help you."

Bo lifted the twine loop holding the two fence posts

together which kept the chickens contained, then stepped inside. The voices were getting louder, unbearable. He shut the enclosure behind him and turned to see all of them watching him from around his feet, clucking away. Bo bent over and snatched one of them before it escaped. The bird tried to break free and run to safety, but he held it firmly in his grip.

"It's okay. It's okay. I'm going to help you. No more yelling, okay?"

He petted the chicken across the back, just like Ma had taught him. She said they didn't like it when you went against the feathers, ruffling them up. It continued to try and wiggle free, and he could feel a vibrating feeling coming from within the bird as it kept its clucking inside. Eventually, the chicken gave in to his grip and stopped resisting.

"Good chick. I'll help you."

Bo didn't realize he was crying until a tear fell from his chin onto the white feathers. He pulled the chicken in close like he was carrying a football, and with his free hand he grabbed its neck.

That sent the bird back into a panic, but Bo had it firmly in his grasp. He was going to help this chicken, and then he would help the rest. No more yelling. No more screaming.

"I'm sorry."

Bo snapped its neck and after a few seconds of involuntary twitches, felt it go limp. He stared at its lifeless body for a few minutes, continuing to pet it. If he was helping them, why did this feel so bad? He carefully set the chicken on the ground and watched as some of the others walked up to their friend. He wondered if they knew it was dead, wondered if they were happy for it now that he had let it free. Without thinking, Bo grabbed a second bird.

"It's okay. I'll help you. I'll help all of you."

And that's just what he did. One by one, Bo helped all the chickens. He cried the entire time, the sadness overwhelming him. When he was done wiping the feathers off his shirt, he latched the fence shut, then headed toward his mother's grave. He needed Ma. She would know what to do.

## 23

Ron Gould sat on his porch, his straw hat pulled down to his bushy white eyebrows, relaxing with his pipe and watching the smoke drift up into the black sky. He sat in silence, listening to the nightly sounds that came with living in the woods. No matter how hard he tried, he couldn't tear his mind away from the Davidson farm, specifically the way Bo was acting. He knew the kid had suffered a head injury as a young boy and that he wasn't all there, but it was more than that. The way Bo looked at him, his eyes darting around wildly, losing his train of thought mid-sentence.

Ron's wife had long since gone to bed, telling him to let it go, that it was the Davidsons' problem, not theirs. He tried to let it go, he really did. But something kept eating at him. It wasn't just the tall Davidson kid acting stranger than usual . . . It was the call from the older brother. It was the fact that there was no sign of Brian or Maggie. It was the absence of equipment working in the fields and other normal farm sounds. It was as if the place was a ghost town, and the disabled kid its sole survivor.

It was true that Ron and his neighbors hadn't always been on the best of terms. The Davidson clan didn't stand a chance when crossing paths with Mr. Gould's stubborn ways, and it wasn't even their fault. When the previous owners of that farm had lost it to the bank, Ron took it personally seeing a close friend lose everything they had worked so hard for. It didn't help that the new owner who bought the place was a strong-minded woman—Maggie—who didn't put up with Ron's shit, and he wasn't used to being talked to that way by a lady. His wife, Terry, was also a strong woman, but she knew which of Ron's buttons not to push, which resulted in a (mostly) happy marriage that had been going strong for the past forty years.

Regardless of his rocky relationship with the Davidsons, he'd grown to accept them, and they kept to themselves. Mutual tolerance was one thing, but it wasn't like they were on friendly terms. So when Ron got the phone call from Brian earlier, his gut told him it wasn't good. He assumed the mother had finally passed away from whatever sickness she suffered from. His money was on cancer, although the boys never officially told him what was wrong with her, only that she was ill and couldn't come to the door when Ron had stopped by to discuss bartering some of her chickens for some of his butchered meat. He said he'd come back later, and Brian told him the sickness was, unfortunately, long-term.

Ron was surprised to hear Brian's voice when he called, and more surprised that he had suffered an injury severe enough to reach out to the Goulds for help. Ron's parents had raised him a good Christian man, and no matter what history there was between the two families, he didn't hesitate to help the Davidson boy. He should have pressed harder and told Bo he'd feel a lot better if he could just speak with Brian to make sure all was well. He wouldn't admit it, but Bo's impressive size had quashed that thought. Something in those eyes . . . Ron was afraid if he pressed too hard, Bo might snap.

He inhaled deeply, blowing out another cloud of smoke. Terry would protest, but Ron had decided to make another trip to the Davidson farm tomorrow—after he'd taken care of his daily chores, of course. The idea was there as soon as he got back home, then solidified when he attempted to call Brian back, only to have it go straight to a generic voicemail. Maybe the phone died, but his intuition told him there was something odd going on next door.

And then there were the recent murders in the area. While he didn't think Bo would have it in him to kill anyone, nor the smarts to get away with it, Ron would be lying if he said suspicion that Bo might somehow be linked to the murders hadn't crossed his mind.

"You're just letting your thoughts run wild again, Ron. Kid's as dangerous as a cat with no claws."

A cold gust of autumn wind swept up onto his porch, blowing the smoke back in his face. He decided it was about time to get inside where it was warm. He scanned the fields on the dark horizon, looking for any sign of intruders. He might be getting up there in age, but if anyone tried to invade *his* farm, he sure as hell wouldn't go down without a fight. Whoever these killers were, they would regret messing with Ron Gould.

After almost seventy years on this earth, he knew when something was off, and those red flags were waving mightily right now. It was a calm night, but he couldn't help but feel it was the calm before the storm.

Tomorrow, he'd tend to his wife and animals (in that order), then head down to check on Brian Davidson. If his brother, Bo, gave him pushback again, he would just call the local authorities to go and do a wellness check. Ron hoped it didn't come to that, but he'd be damned if he would ignore his intuition.

He got up from his chair, listening to his knees crack like dried timber, then hobbled into his house to get a good night's sleep.

## 24

The familiar scene of a pitch-black bedroom greeted Brian as he woke from another nightmare. Bo hadn't returned with any food after storming out earlier, and Brian's stomach let him know. If he wasn't so hungry, he might actually have laughed at the odd noises coming from his insides, growling like a predatory fisher cat ready to pounce. He really hoped Bo would be willing to talk things out after their interaction earlier, but he seemed more stubborn than usual. He didn't blame him. Since Ma passed, Brian had blindsided his brother with life-altering truths from their past. These revelations would be overwhelming for anyone, let alone someone who had suffered head trauma as a child. The things he had told him had altered Bo's perception of their entire family. He knew he must be reeling from the onslaught of information, feeling confused and overwhelmed.

No matter how many nights passed, the dark space never became comfortable. All the odd shapes that during the day were just his mother's belongings—her coat rack, shirts dangling from hangers in the closet, and the tall mirror staring back at him from the corner—morphed into strange figures watching over him. He could no longer blame it on the meds as he had run out of pills a few days earlier. (Regrettably, his back reminded him of that every time he shifted in bed.) Brian tried yelling for his brother to come and discuss the letter written by their mother, but Bo wasn't having it. He normally got over things pretty quickly, too dependent on others to survive. But now that he was growing this newfound sense of independence, coupled with the fact that everyone he trusted had lied to him, he showed no intention of mending fences.

Brian cleared his throat, preparing to shout again, when the sound of heavy breathing came from somewhere in the darkness. *Not this again.* Since it wasn't the pills, it must be a sign that he was cracking up for real. Losing his fucking marbles. He squinted at the usual spot—Bo's chair in the corner—and sure enough, the shape of someone sitting there presented itself.

"Ma . . . I'm sorry I didn't tell you the whole truth, okay? Please stop messing with me. Bo's—"

The shape moved, and Brian choked on the rest of his sentence.

Initially, he assumed it was the shadow moving, flickering with the candlelight, but then he remembered there *was* no candle. The room was completely dark. There was nothing to move the shadow or even make one, for that matter.

"Ma? Bo?"

The breathing continued, picking up in intensity. The figure stood from the chair, bits and pieces of a body coming into focus as his eyes adjusted. The floorboards groaned beneath the shape—it wasn't in his head.

The figure inched closer, creeping along through the suffocating darkness. It was a female—he made out thin limbs dangling from the body and long hair that covered all her facial features. She was too tall to be Ma.

"Who are you? Booo!" he shouted his brother's name, dragging out the single syllable like a steady dial tone. But there was nobody on the other end of this dial tone. Bo wasn't coming, and Brian wasn't so sure his voice had really escaped his mouth. He was paralyzed with fear.

She took another step closer, which brought her clothing into focus. Brian slapped his hand over his mouth. He would recognize that shirt anywhere.

*Bow to the Queen.*

"Lisa..."

She didn't speak. Instead, she crept closer. Her only visible feature was her mouth, which hung partially open, her lips like dried worms, desperate to burrow back into the earth. Brian tried to lean away from her, practically falling off the other side of the bed. His back sent a stabbing sensation straight up his spine, exploding inside his head like the Hi Striker game at the county fair.

"Please... leave me alone. I'm sorry. I didn't know."

Her labored breathing stopped. She paused her approach. He thought she might accept his apology and go away, but then she leaned over the bed, her matted hair peeling away from her face to display the rest of her features.

"Oh my God."

Her eyes were two smoky marbles, but that wasn't the worst of it. Her right cheek was caved in as though half her expression was attempting to make a fish face except a jagged gash traveled down that side, starting up by her ear and ending at the corner of her lips. She smelled like rotten meat, but a hint of sweetness commingled with the scent of decay, which he immediately recognized as the perfume she was wearing the day she died. That scent lived in the haunted memory of that fateful day.

"What do you want? I said I'm sorry," Brian whispered.

Lisa groaned, a gurgling phlegmy sound that clung to the inside of her throat. He didn't think she was able to talk, but then her mouth opened, revealing a bloody mess with bits of tiny tooth fragments protruding from her putrid gums. Her lower jaw jutted out and continued to open as if she was preparing to let out a big yawn, but then it locked in place.

"*Briiian . . . it's . . . thaaa maaak . . .*"

He had no idea what she was saying, but he wasn't about to ask her for clarification. His heart hitched in his chest, forcing out short, desperate breaths. With her mouth frozen open, her words came out slurred, like someone had injected a gallon of Novocain into her face. Brian wanted to close his eyes, but he couldn't stop staring at her. He kept waiting for her to disappear, for his hallucination to come to an end. Instead, Lisa leaned closer, wrapping her bony hand around his wrist. His skin turned to ice at her touch. He wanted to scream for Bo again, but he couldn't talk.

"*Ehhh eeep iiit inng a MAAK!*"

That last word struck him like a slap to the face, reaching a volume that almost burst his eardrums. Her nails dug into his skin, and finally he was able to scream. He screamed until his throat no longer produced noise. His eyes went blurry, but Lisa's silhouette was still visible. The pain was overtaking his ability to remain conscious. He tried to jerk his arm free, but he was weak, his strength depleted from the screaming. Eventually, Brian blacked out, but Lisa's face was ingrained in his head.

# 25

Bo didn't hear his brother's screams because he wasn't even in the house. No, after the day he'd had, with all the information Brian dumped on him, he needed space. He sat in the moonlight, crying, asking Ma why this was happening. He tried so hard to take care of his brother. All he wanted was to make her proud and to take care of Brian, but no matter what he did, he felt like he was messing it up. Brian pretended not to be upset with him, but Bo knew. He sure did. He could see it in his brother's eyes—undeniable disappointment. With his condition, he struggled to understand things. Everything was so much harder.

And now he knew why he was the way he was. Brian had attacked him and put him in a coma. He had smashed a phone over Bo's head, leaving him with memory loss, cognitive delays, and a lifelong fear of electronics.

"Ma . . . why did this happen?" he asked. "Why would Dad and Brian do all this to us?"

He stared at the grave memorial, which during the day was just a concrete pillar that Brian had forced into the ground as a makeshift headstone, but in the moonlight, it had an almost angelic aspect to it. Bo thought that was fitting. Ma *was* an angel. And she had been watching over him ever since she died, but right now she wasn't answering him. So he kept talking, his breath a mist, blowing into the brisk evening air, wisping through the valley.

"I don't know what to do, Ma. Brian wants me to get him help. Mr. Gould came by today and tried to help. I know you don't much care for that man, but he seemed nice. And he warned us about some bad people. Brian seems like he's mad at me, Ma. I don't like it when he's mad. And I can't keep up with all the chores . . . the whole farm looks like a giant pigpen! Like you used to say about our room when we didn't clean it. We got no food for the animals besides hay and hardly anything left for Brian and me."

He thought back to what his brother had said about how they would run out of food if he couldn't get to town for supplies. Things that Bo never had to worry about because his brother took care of it all. Brian was the one who got the supplies and took care of the crops; Bo tended to the animals. He always liked taking care of the animals, especially the pigs. They reminded him of pink, barely hairy dogs with their floppy ears and curly tails. When Bo was a kid, he would often roll around in the mud with them and snort, and Ma would scream at him to get inside and get cleaned up.

"Hey, Ma. I remembered more of when I was a boy! I used to play in the pigpen, you remember? You got so mad when I came in the house covered in mud, remember?"

Bo didn't understand why she had been talking to him the whole time, giving advice on how to care for Brian, but when he needed her most, she was dead silent. He got to his feet, hoping that moving around would warm his frozen limbs. Beyond his mother's freshly filled grave, his dad's headstone caught his eye. A scowl found its way across his face, and he walked over to it.

"You really messed up, Dad. I'm sorry Ma shot you, but you put us all in danger. Brian said so himself. He lied for you, and now I'm mad at him for it. But it's your fault! Why'd you think I needed help? And those poor girls died . . . because of me. And I know I killed a pig when I was younger, after you were gone, but I never killed nobody. I don't know what to do. Brian says the people who are after us are coming. I think Brian needs rest, still. He's stubborn. That's what Ma always said. But I can't protect the farm myself. And Mr. Gould tried to help but I got scared and told him to leave. I'm *real* scared, Dad."

Even though both his parents were dead, Bo still felt better talking to them, getting it all off his chest. Brian was always the one to look out for him, except for the time with the bullies trying to steal his bike. Maybe these bad people coming were like those bullies. But Bo didn't want to hurt anyone, not ever again. What if they were dangerous, though? No matter what Brian did to him when they were kids, they are, and always will be, brothers—their bond unbreakable. So Bo knew he had to forgive his brother for what happened.

He sat with his back resting against his mother's headstone, digging his fingers into the soil to be closer to her, then closed his eyes to think. That's what Ma always told him to do when there were too many thoughts going through his head. *Close your eyes, like you're shutting the blinds, and block out the rest of the world*, she'd say.

Except this time when he closed his eyes, he drifted off to

sleep, his head bent at an odd angle as he leaned against the concrete pillar. His fingers pushed deeper until the soil touched his third knuckles. It was the closest he'd felt to Ma in weeks, and it felt nice. She would tell him what to do. He just knew it.

## 1996

"What do you boys think of the place?" Ma asked as they exited the vehicle and stared at their new home.

Brian scanned the property, admiring the massive size of the farmhouse and the blanket of trees occupying the surrounding land. The brothers had never lived in a place like this. Instead, they'd spent the majority of their childhood in a double-wide trailer, sharing a bedroom to save space, and their "woods" consisted of four or five trees that leaned over a rusty culvert. Brian wasn't so sure how Ma could afford a place so big by herself, but he wasn't going to question it. He snuck a look at his brother, who had only recently awoken after weeks of being lost in a coma. It was still too early to tell if Bo remembered the accident or what happened before, but so far, he seemed clueless.

"Ma . . . can we get a horse?" Brian asked. The thought of riding through the acres and acres of promised fields that lay beyond the house filled him with happiness. Something he hadn't felt since long before the incident.

"We'll see, buddy. That's a big responsibility that we need to make sure you're ready for. But we'll definitely get some chickens and pigs, maybe a cow or two. How's that sound?"

Brian tried to hide his disappointment, but he knew Ma would see right through it. Bo, however, lit up like a spotlight.

"Yeah! I always wanted pigs," he said, his eyes staring straight ahead, toward the barn but somehow *through* it. The entire drive, Brian had been noticing oddities with his brother. He seemed dazed, slow to respond. He wasn't the jovial, happy-go-lucky boy he had been before the accident. Brian hoped it wasn't permanent.

His mother seemed to notice the change in Bo, too, but she didn't look surprised, only sad. Whatever the doctors told her in private, she hadn't shared with Brian, but maybe they knew Bo wasn't back to his normal self. While Brian wanted his brother back, he couldn't help feeling relieved that Bo didn't seem to remember what had happened.

They headed toward the wraparound porch, leaving their luggage behind. Ma normally wouldn't allow such a thing, but she was just as excited as the kids to see their new home. The house looked like it was three stories, with a mudroom extending out from the side that ended just a few feet from the barn. That alone was bigger than their last home, and it had towering sliding doors with a big *X* on each of them, just like Brian had seen in the movies. Up near the peak of the roof, there was a smaller door. They entered the barn, and his excitement grew at the sight of it. There were already stalls for horses; they wouldn't have to put in any extra effort to prepare the place for one.

Overhead, a ladder rose to a platform that Brian couldn't see from ground level.

"What's up there, Ma?" he asked.

"That's a hayloft, kiddo. Once we get up and running, we'll likely be haying some of the fields and storing the bales up there. We can sell it to locals to make some extra money and keep some of it for ourselves to feed our animals . . . if we decide to get any," she said with a wink.

"Can we check it out?" Brian asked.

She smiled. "Sure. Be careful climbing that ladder, though, boys. That's a far drop if you slip."

Brian heard her but he didn't respond; he was too busy pulling his brother toward the ladder. Bo laughed, but it was different than his usual laugh. It was like he knew he should be having fun but wasn't sure what he was doing. Brian shook it off and grabbed the first rung.

"Okay, I'll go up first, then you follow. This is awesome!"

Brian climbed carefully, reaching the top rung, and poked his head above the floor. The space was wide open, with slits of sunlight poking through the boards on the barn wall shining down on the floor like an orange laser show.

"Come up, Bo. You gotta see this!"

He took the rungs much slower than Brian, but eventually he reached the upper level. His mouth hung open as he admired the loft.

"Ma! This is awesome!" Bo yelled.

"Be careful up there, I mean it!" she said from below.

The brothers investigated the space, quickly deciding it would be their special hangout. They would store their stuff up here—special things that required, at least to them, their own designated spot.

"I think we'll be spending plenty of time up here. How about you, Bo?"

"Uh-huh."

After checking it out for a few minutes, they climbed back down to find Ma admiring the stalls and the rest of the barn.

"We won't ever need to leave this place, Ma. It's so big!" Brian said.

"That's the idea, kiddo. A place like this . . . we can be self-sustaining, rarely needing to leave. You can thank your aunt for signing the paperwork for us. We wouldn't have been able to get approved without your father's income," she said, noticing the confusion on both their faces. "Sorry, you two don't need to worry about that sort of thing at your age. Enjoy. Go have fun and explore the fields. I'll start to bring in some boxes and get dinner ready. When you get back, you can both help me, and we can pick some bedrooms for you. How's that sound?"

"Awesome! Thanks, Ma," Brian said.

Bo just nodded in agreement and smiled. She patted them both on the head and walked back toward the house, leaving them to explore on their own. Brian led the way, following a trail through the tall grass that led to the back of the property. The forest was so dense, he wondered where the fields were that Ma talked about. Eventually, the tight trail opened up and he had his answer. It was clear where the previous owners had planted their crops; there were rows of dirt mounds filling the space, now overgrown with weeds.

After checking out the fields, they walked up a small hill to a lone maple with red leaves that really stood out against the backdrop of green foliage. They decided to take a break and rest, both sitting and leaning against the tree.

"Brian? Can we make a grave for Dad? I miss him," Bo said.

Brian thought carefully about what to say next, inhaling a deep breath of fresh nature air. This place was perfect. Maybe it would help with closure to do something for Dad out here. Brian felt awful not only lying to Ma and Bo, but to the police who had investigated the murder. He had no choice, though. Ma thought she was defending her kids, so if he told them the truth, they would have to arrest her for murder. Brian still feared they would take Ma away for killing Dad. As much as he wanted his older son to tell her everything if something happened to him, Brian decided to take his secret to the grave. What good would come of Bo finding out what really happened to him? Or Ma knowing that Dad didn't harm either of them? It was bad enough that she had to live with the hard fact that she'd murdered her husband.

"I think you're right, Bo. This seems like the perfect spot, doesn't it? We can put a memorial up here for him—a grave, like you said."

Bo smiled and the two of them sat there in silence for a few minutes. Brian watched his brother out of the corner of his eye, wondering what was going on inside his head. What thoughts could possibly be swimming around in that damaged abyss? Bo's eyes wandered, focusing on nothing in particular, and Brian noticed they were glossed over as if his brother was on the verge of tears.

*You did this to him. It's your fault, not Dad's.*

He forced the thought from his head and got to his feet. Bo copied him, imitating his every move.

"We should go help Ma unpack, don't you think? We can do some more exploring later on."

Bo nodded, and they walked back toward the house.

Ma, or as anyone besides her boys would call her, Maggie, sat at the dinner table with just enough space cleared for her to set the plates of food down for the family to eat. She continued to contemplate what the boys had asked her earlier. They wanted to create a memorial for Barry. Although she was pissed off, hurt, and still in shock over everything that happened, she agreed it was a good idea. Not just because no matter what went down, she still loved her husband with all her heart, but also because she knew there were things that had caused Barry to change. Things far beyond her understanding. And when she had finally uncovered what he was up to with that scumbag, Marcus, she realized Barry was in over his head. He was being forced to do awful, depraved things for this man and his group of followers.

When she decided to follow her husband, she had no idea what secrets she would discover, but what she saw was beyond anything she could have ever imagined. She had planned to confront him, threatening to leave with the kids if he didn't stop, but then the incident happened. She shot her husband. Without ever getting the chance to ask him why. Why did he put his family in danger? Why did he allow himself to deliver innocent girls to these monsters? And was she any better a person than her husband for not immediately reporting it to the authorities?

It didn't matter now. It was too late. She had two children to care for, and she couldn't allow herself to be so self-righteous as to confess everything to the police, landing her kids in the foster system. She'd allow herself to go to hell before putting them in that situation. Instead, she decided she would lock those secrets inside, willing to carry the weight of doing so for the rest of her life if it meant Brian and Bo could live out their days with the worst of the trauma behind them.

The boys had asked to bury some of their father's belongings at the memorial site since there were no remains on the property. His body was six feet under at Newberry Cemetery, and she told them they couldn't risk going to visit the grave in case Marcus was watching. Right now, Brian and Bo were picking out some things to put in the hole that they had spent the better part of the afternoon digging. She had a few things of her own already placed safely in a box, intending for it to never be opened again. Things she wanted buried with him, even though his body wasn't there and it was just a memorial to his loss.

When the kids were ready, they all walked up to the site the boys had handpicked, and Maggie immediately found herself overcome with emotion. She wiped the tears away before the boys realized she was crying. The location was perfect. Serene. An image straight out of a painting, and she could see herself and her kids coming here regularly to talk to Barry. They gathered around the grave and held hands.

"Your daddy was a great man, boys. I know you know that. I loved him with all my heart, and it's a shame what those men did to him," she said, eyeing Brian to see if he would hold up his end of their secret. Maggie did not want Bo knowing she was the one who killed his father. At least not yet. There would come a day when they would tell him, but not now when the trauma was still so fresh.

"Brian, do you have anything you'd like to say to him?"

He nodded and walked toward the open grave with the belongings he'd brought: a few baseball cards and his favorite shirt he wanted his dad to have, hoping that if there was a spirit, it would make him feel less alone.

"I know we didn't say it, but I love you, Dad. I'm sorry I didn't try harder to be what you wanted me to be; I know you only wanted us to make you proud. I was too selfish, only cared about myself. I promise to look after Ma and Bo for you . . ." He couldn't continue as tears choked down the rest of his words. Instead, he gently placed the items in the hole and walked back to Ma.

She found it difficult to look Brian in the eye, heartbroken that he truly felt he wasn't good enough for Barry. Bo walked up next, but he didn't say anything. Instead, he dropped a few flowers into the hole with his baseball cap and mouthed, "Bye."

The boys walked back to the tree and waited for Maggie to say her goodbyes and set the box she had packed into the grave. She opened it and looked, making sure the kids couldn't see. The contents were far too complicated for them to understand the meaning of. And they were safer if they didn't know what was inside, at least until they absolutely needed to.

She closed the lid and placed the box on top of the items already in the hole, then brushed her hands off on her pants.

"Barry, I'm so sorry about what happened to you. You were a great husband, a great dad, and a great man. I know if you could change the day you met those monsters, you would go back in time and be sure to fix it. I wish . . . I wish it didn't end this way." She took a deep breath, trying to stop herself from completely losing it in front of her kids. They needed her to remain strong right now. "The boys will make you proud. We love you."

Nobody spoke for a few minutes, and eventually Maggie began to fill in the hole using the shovel planted upright in the dirt mound. Brian came to her and put his hand on her shoulder, reaching for the shovel. And that did it. She couldn't hold the tears in anymore, handed the shovel to her oldest boy, and walked back to the trail hoping they didn't see her grief. As she continued toward the house, she focused on the sound of the shovel dumping dirt into the hole, burying the last connection to the Hollow Souls.

## 27

**PRESENT DAY**

Brian opened his eyes to the morning sun lighting up his room. The curtains remained shut, but the bedroom door was open. It was closed when he went to bed; Bo had slammed it on his way out. He suddenly remembered Lisa lurking over him, leering with her hazy orbs. *It must have been a terrible nightmare, right?* Only when he glanced at his forearm, he spotted four gouge marks of equal size—as if fingers had squeezed so tight around his wrist, they'd pierced through the skin.

*She was really here.*

The floorboards creaked in the hallway, and Brian prepared himself for Lisa's decaying corpse to shuffle through the entryway. He was relieved when Bo appeared, and even more relieved when Bo smiled—a far cry from his state of mind when he'd stormed out of the bedroom the night before.

"Bo, how you doing, buddy?"

"I'm sorry, Brian. I didn't want to be mean to you last night. I was really mad. It's not your fault."

"Apology accepted, little brother. And I'm sorry too. How are you today?"

"Better. Ma talked to me last night. She said I should help you more. She said you need me."

"Yes. She's right. We may not have much time, and there's still so much I need to tell you. How 'bout this? If you get the wheelchair, I'll cook breakfast, just like old times. Think about how long it's been since you had those pancakes you love so much."

Bo smiled.

"Okay. Chocolate chip?"

"Sure. While we're eating, I want to talk about what Ma wrote in the notebook. Promise me you'll try not to get too upset this time. You need to know what we're dealing with here, Bo."

"I promise. Pinky swear." He walked up and held out his hand, which Brian noticed was caked in dirt.

The brothers wrapped pinkies and smiled.

"I shoulda told you all this a long time ago," Brian said. "And if we're going to stop what's happening, we need to be honest with each other. No more secrets . . . Deal?"

Bo frowned, then nodded. Brian realized he still needed to earn back his brother's trust. He also realized the same applied to his trust in Bo. With the way his brother looked last night, it wouldn't surprise him if he lost his cool at even the slightest change from the norm—and there were likely to be many uncomfortable situations in the coming days. "Okay, Bo. Grab that wheelchair and get me the hell out of this room. Those pancakes aren't going to make themselves."

## The Devil's in the Next Room

After getting Brian situated in the chair, they went to the kitchen. He couldn't help but notice, it looked even worse than the last time Bo let him out of the bedroom. He wasn't going to say anything, though . . . given his brother's current state. Bo sat at the table while Brian wheeled himself around the kitchen, grabbing what ingredients he could find. He checked the refrigerator, happy to see that his brother had at least restocked the eggs. They appeared fine, so he got to work, adding everything to a giant mixing bowl, then spooning the batter into a hot pan on the stove. Sitting in the wheelchair, his face was close to the burner giving off a warm radiance that felt relaxing in the chilly home.

"Bo, when's the last time you put wood in the fireplace? It's freezing in here, man."

"Um, last night. Want me to get some now?"

"No, no. It's fine. I was just wondering. It can't be easy trying to remember all the tasks that need tending to, huh? Again, I'm sorry if I've been hard on you since the injury."

Bo lowered his head, ashamed of his failures. "It's okay. I know I keep messing up."

"You know, you just need your brother's famous pancakes, is all. Once you eat these, you'll be a new man," he said, smiling. Then spun one of his wheels to rotate around and see Bo's reaction. It dawned on Brian that he was trying extra hard to cheer his brother up, and it was probably obvious.

The fresh smell of batter cooking to a light brown filled the kitchen, and Brian's stomach rumbled in response. It seemed so long since he'd eaten a real meal. He wouldn't be shocked to learn he'd lost at least ten pounds, if not more. He flipped the first batch of pancakes with a spatula, and when they were done, piled them onto a plate and set it on the counter.

"I got it," Bo said, jumping to his feet, excited to help. He grabbed the plate and carried it to the table, then grabbed silverware while the next batch cooked. For a moment, Brian was almost fooled into thinking life was back to normal. Until he remembered he was wheeling around the house instead of walking. Until he remembered there was a group of soul-sucking killers trying to find them.

Finally, they both sat at the table and ate, too busy chewing to do any talking. Brian reached for the pitcher of water, his brain firing off a warning that his back might not appreciate it, but the pain didn't come. At least not to the same extent that it had been for weeks now. There was no way he was healing without proper healthcare, was there? As much as he wanted to attempt getting out of the chair and walking, he couldn't risk it in front of Bo. The last thing he wanted was to be strapped down to Ma's bed again and spend another night in solitude. Instead, he pushed the thought into the back of his mind and told himself to test his legs out later, when his brother wasn't around.

"Listen. There's no other way to put this, Bo. Bad people are coming for us. They've been looking for us ever since Dad died, and now it seems they're getting close. We don't have many options. I can't drive, and you wouldn't ride with me if I could. We could get Mr. Gould to call the police and get them involved, only we have no idea if or when these monsters could show up on our doorstep. Plus, what would we even tell the cops? That we have ties to this group of killers going around the state murdering people? That could just dig up past secrets that Ma worked real hard to hide. And then there's the fact that Ma's dead. We don't own this place, she did. Well, technically, our aunt did. And while I don't know the laws around this type of thing, I assume us not reporting her death could get us in trouble.

"So, our other option is to defend the farm. If we're prepared for them, maybe we stand a shot at taking them down."

Bo frowned, the wrinkles in his face conveying the fear he must have felt.

"I don't want to hurt nobody, Brian."

"Remember my Christmas story from the other day? I know you don't like hurting people. But when it comes to defending your family, that's when you gotta do what you gotta do, Bo. These people are far more dangerous than those bullies who tried to steal our bikes."

"I don't know . . . Can't we turn all the lights off and hide? Maybe they'll think nobody is home and go away."

"Jesus, Bo. You're too innocent for your own good. No, that wouldn't work. If they find out we live here, they'll wait as long as they need to. And there's another thing I wanted to tell you about. The box Ma put in Dad's grave . . . it has something in it they want. I read her notebook last night. She didn't want us to know unless it was absolutely necessary."

"What's in the box?" Bo asked, confused as ever.

"She didn't say. I think it was another way of protecting us from knowing. What I know so far is . . . we need to dig it up. We need to have an advantage over them when they come. Obviously, I can't shovel dirt, but I want to be there. Do you think you can push me up the hill?"

Bo shook his head. This came as a surprise to Brian because his brother had volunteered to push him up the hill when he picked flowers for Ma's gravesite. There must be another reason Bo didn't want to take him.

"What is it? There's nothing to be scared of, bud. It's an empty grave, remember? Just some belongings that we wanted buried to remember him by."

"No . . . No, no. I promised Ma I wouldn't go back up there. I promised her."

"What? What are you talking about?"

"Ma said I'd get in trouble for digging."

Brian closed his eyes and shook his head, trying to hide his annoyance.

"Please, Bo. Not right now with that. This is important. We *need* to dig. She'll forgive you. You know she wants us to protect each other and the farm, right? This is how we do it."

Bo sighed, then paused . . . thinking. "Okay."

After breakfast, they went outside and were greeted by a brisk breeze that sent a shiver through Brian's core. He worried the ground might be too frozen, or at least starting to freeze, which would make digging deep enough to retrieve the box a pain in the ass. He wheeled himself toward the barn while Bo grabbed a shovel. An abnormal stench filled the air as Brian closed in on the doors, his eyes immediately blurring as they started watering. He stopped wheeling and wiped them on his sleeve, then scanned the barn interior for the source of the smell.

"Bo! What the hell is that stench, man? It's putrid!"

He was used to the smells of the farm, scents that would cause most people to lift their upper lip in disgust: the pigpen, with goopy mud and flies; the henhouse; and Astra's stall, which, even though it was cleaned daily always had an odor of piss-covered shavings. But this was different. It smelled like . . . death.

Bo came running over to him, eyes flitting left and right, then looking nervously at Brian.

"The chickens . . . I stopped them from screaming in my head, Brian. I'm sorry. I don't want you to look in the coop. I don't think you want to."

*Actually*, he did. He wanted to know what kind of mess the farm was left in while he was out of commission. What did Bo mean when he said he 'stopped them from screaming in my head'? The chickens were crucial to them. Now wasn't the time for that, though. Instead, he wheeled forward into the barn and stopped at Astra's stall. She ignored him, and it broke his heart. Bo had left her tied to the wall, so all Brian saw was her backside. She was looking into the corner.

"Hey, girl . . . you okay? I know you miss riding."

She turned slightly and snorted. Brian had heard of horses getting depressed if they were taken out of their normal routine. It appeared Astra was headed down that path, if she wasn't already full-blown depressed. It crushed him to see her this way. But at least she was still here. As much as Brian wanted to spend time with her, they had to get moving. Bo was strong and wouldn't have any issues pushing the wheelchair through the tall grass, but it would still take some time to reach Dad's grave.

Brian gave one last look around the barn, trying to figure out where the smell was coming from. If Bo had killed all the chickens, would they really smell this bad? Especially this fast? He shook his head and wheeled back out to the yard.

"Okay, we better get a move on. You ready?" he asked Bo.

"No . . . but I know we have to do it."

With that, they headed up the hill.

# 28

Ron Gould parked the tractor beneath the lean-to on the side of the barn and killed the engine. He'd been up since five a.m. working in the fields to harvest what remaining crops he could before they rotted from the impending frost. There were slim pickings left, but he had learned over the years not to let any good produce go to waste. He pulled his pipe out of his chest pocket, filled it with tobacco, then lit it and inhaled deeply.

Normally, while he was out working, he would enjoy the fresh air, listening to the sounds of nature that surrounded him out in the middle of nowhere. But today, he found himself too distracted. He kept picturing Bo and his strange behaviors. He kept thinking of the call from Brian, the sound of desperation in his voice. Ron knew he should have been more insistent when he was there. He should have pushed to speak with Brian before he left.

Now that he was done with his morning chores, he would eat some lunch and head back over to the Davidson farm, demanding to talk with Brian. First he needed to break the news to Terry, who was already on edge with the recent murders in the area. She was a strong woman, though, and Ron sure wouldn't want to be any killer trying to mess with her.

He took one last puff of his pipe, then snuffed it out and walked in the back door. His wife was already preparing his lunch. He stared at her for a moment without speaking, wondering how he'd gotten so lucky. A beautiful, strong-minded woman who was both smart and funny. A handful for sure, but he wouldn't have it any other way.

"You gonna come eat or stare at my butt all day?" she asked without turning around.

Even after all these years, he found himself blushing at her bluntness. He shook his head and laughed.

"You always gotta ruin a man's fantasy, huh?" Ron teased, then sat at the kitchen table, his knees producing their normal cracks of thunder.

"Your fantasy should be the ability to walk until you're in the ground. Those knees don't sound so good, hon. When are you going to hire more help and take on less of the work yourself?"

Ron waved her off and scoffed.

"Nonsense. We barely get by as it is. Hiring help would wipe out any profit we make, and I'd be working for free. I'm fine."

"Just think about it, okay? I wish I could still be out there helping you, but I can't go against the doctor's orders. The mortgage is paid off, so we don't need to make much to live a peaceful life. I'd rather have you around longer than be sitting on a pile of cash at your funeral," she said, setting a jumbo-sized sandwich in front of him—fresh roast beef with some thickly sliced cheese and homegrown lettuce. His mouth watered at the sight of it.

"I'll think about it. Spending more time with you wouldn't be such a bad thing, I s'pose."

She slapped him on the shoulder in a playful manner.

"You're damn right, it's not a bad thing. I'm sick of you working till the sun goes down and coming in when I'm ready for bed. I need someone to vent to about my daytime soaps, Ron."

He chuckled and took a bite of his sandwich. The flavor was plentiful, absorbing into his tastebuds as he mockingly rolled his eyes in ecstasy.

"*Mmm*. This really hits the spot. Thanks for lunch."

"You're welcome. What's on the agenda for the rest of today? You were out there extra early, and I know you only do that when you got plans later in the day."

Ron sighed. He had hoped to finish his sandwich before pissing her off.

"Now . . . I know you told me when I got back from the Davidson place that I shouldn't mess with them boys and their problems, but I'm telling you, Terry . . . something's wrong at that house. Why would Brian call me for help and then not even come to the door when I got there? He sounded desperate when we talked."

"Well, what did he say that made him sound that way? Maybe he just felt better by the time you got there."

"No, no. Ain't no way. It wasn't so much the words he used—although those alone were a cry for help—but the tone he spoke in. Like he was whispering and talking fast, not wanting to get caught on the phone."

Terry chewed her food, considering what he said.

"I don't know, hon. Maybe call the cops to go check on them if you're that worried. What's an old man like you going to do to help anyway?"

Ron rolled his eyes. "I ain't *that* old. And if Brian still needs help getting to a hospital, that impaired brother of his won't drive him there. Something's wrong in the noggin with that one."

Terry slapped him on the arm again and shook her head.

"Ron! Don't talk that way about anyone. It isn't the boy's fault if something's wrong with him."

"Which is exactly why I should lend a hand, Terry. I know Maggie doesn't care for me, but what kinda neighbor would I be if I didn't offer to help? Plus, she's so sick she couldn't even greet me with her typical scowl yesterday. I didn't see anyone besides Bo. So, after lunch, I'd like to head up that way, check on them, and offer to take Brian to the hospital if he still needs it. Said he fell off his horse and think's he broke his back."

"Well, please don't take too long. You know I don't like being left alone. Should I come with you?"

"No. There won't be room in the truck if he needs to lay back in the seat to help his spine. I'll be sure to stop by the house before going to the hospital, though, and let you know."

"All right then. Get to it before it gets dark, or you'll never hear the end of leaving me here alone."

"Oh, please. You'd kick any intruder's ass if they tried to mess with you," he said with a smile.

"Damn right, I would."

Ron finished his sandwich, got up from the table, then kissed her on the top of the head and rinsed his plate. He set it on the drying rack and headed toward the door.

"I'll be back soon. Love you."

"Ron . . . be safe."

He nodded as he exited the front door. He hopped in his truck with a bad feeling in his stomach.

Terry finished cleaning up the kitchen and checked the clock. Ron had only been gone ten minutes, likely just arriving at the Davidson farm, but she already wanted him back in the house. In all the years they had been married, she could count on one hand how many times she was left home alone. She was a strong woman but one who had never driven a day in her life. For whatever reason, she just never acquired her license, which was normal for the women in her family. While she felt helpless at times, it did avoid the stress of sitting behind the steering wheel. It instantly filled her insides with an uneasy ball of panic. Her father, who wasn't much of an *actual* father, died in a car accident when she was a young girl. He was driving drunk, and she happened to be sitting in the back seat. The car wrapped around a tree, and she ended up spending weeks in the hospital. Still, while she could take care of herself just fine, with the recent murders close by, she wanted her husband back before nightfall. There were plenty of hours left in the day since it was just past noon, but she knew how Ron could get to talking and lose track of time.

Once she gave the kitchen a double take, she headed to the living room with a warm cup of coffee to watch her afternoon shows. It was a simple life, one she'd grown accustomed to over the years. The love she and Ron shared was ironclad, so she hadn't batted an eye at the idea of giving up any dreams or aspirations she had as a young woman. He took care of her, and while some women might say Terry was too busy living an old lifestyle in a new world, she wouldn't have it any other way.

She sat in her recliner and grabbed the remote. Just as she clicked the television on, the rumble of an approaching vehicle pulling into their dirt driveway stole her attention from the screen. True to his word, Ron wasn't gone long. Terry set her mug on the coffee table and got to her feet, preparing to greet her husband with a kiss at the door, until she looked through the thin rectangle of glass along the door's trim and spotted an unfamiliar vehicle—a beat-up truck with rusted fenders.

"Oh hell. Where are you when I need you, Ron?"

She squinted through the textured glass, trying to make out who it could possibly be. A well-built man, his black hair slicked back in a wet ponytail, opened the driver's door and stepped out. He was of average height, and from this distance, he appeared to be in his early to mid-fifties. Terry didn't realize he could see her, but then he flashed a smile as he walked toward the porch and gave a slight wave.

She backed away from the window, her skin instantly wrapped in gooseflesh. The way he smiled . . . Terry felt the unease settle into her stomach. The man was alone, but if he wanted to have his way with her, she didn't think she'd be able to put up much of a fight.

He climbed the porch stairs, and even though she knew he was there, the rapping of his knuckles against the front door startled her. Something inside her insisted that she not answer.

At first, she planned to listen to her intuition, but then he rang the doorbell. She heard him whistle a tune she was familiar with but couldn't put a name to. Now that he was up close, she spotted a name tag on the chest of his shirt and realized he had a clipboard in one hand.

The fear turned to anger at the thought of another salesperson bugging them on the farm. Someone trying to sell them some pesticide they promised was "the newest and most effective" or attempting to pawn off animal food in bulk to "save them money." Terry learned early on in her farm life that these hucksters were a dime a dozen and never in it for the consumer, only to fill their own pockets.

She swung the door open just as the man was preparing to knock again, and he flashed that disturbing grin. The scent of stale nicotine wafted off him, and standing this close, Terry couldn't help but stare at the dark circles beneath his eyes. If someone looked quick, they'd mistake them for two black holes.

"Oh, hi there, ma'am. How're you doing today?" the man asked in a phlegmy rattle.

"Who are you, and why are you on our farm?"

She didn't have time to beat around the bush. She was missing her shows, and there were too many bad things going on in the area for her to provide this creep with any hint of hospitality.

"Well, all right then. I see you like to get right down to business. My name's Marcus, and I'm here to give the annual tax assessment of your property. May I come in?"

"Tax assessment? You assholes just came by a few months ago. Jacked up our taxes so we can barely make ends meet. What could you possibly want now?"

The man furrowed his brow but caught himself and smiled again.

"Well, once in a while, they have us come back out to a property to give a second opinion. Who knows, maybe it'll bring the cost back down?"

"That'll be the day. I'm sorry . . . Marcus, is it? You'll have to come back another time. I don't mean to be rude, but I got a million things I need to get done around the house. So if you don't mind—" She started to shut the door, but Marcus put up his hand to stop it. She noticed dirt caked beneath his fingernails.

"Ma'am, I just need a few minutes, that's all. And by the sound of your TV, you're not doing much of anything at the moment."

"How dare you stop me from shutting my own door. What I'm doing is none of your damn business. I'm done playing nice. Get the fuck off my property before I call my husband in here. He won't just come with words, he'll have his shotgun."

Terry expected the man to back off but instead, he playfully opened his eyes wide and laughed.

"Terry, your husband isn't here right now . . . we know that. Stop playing games and let me inside."

*Who does he mean by 'we'? And how does he know what my name—*

Before she could finish her thought, there was movement from the trees at the end of the driveway. Two figures stepped out of the woods wearing all-black clothing, their faces hidden behind what looked like skull masks. They stopped walking once they exited the forest, standing completely still at the tree line, staring straight ahead.

"I'm calling the cops."

Marcus pushed the door open with force, sending Terry stumbling backward. She bumped into the coffee table, sending the mug crashing onto the floor, spilling the contents and shattering. He entered the home, and over his shoulders, Terry spotted the other two figures approaching the house.

"No . . . I don't think you'll be calling anyone."

# 29

Ron pulled into the Davidsons' driveway and parked his truck. The farm was eerily silent—no rooster crowing, hens clucking, or equipment running in the fields. He shut his door and stepped up onto the wraparound porch, peeking through the window before knocking. He couldn't see anyone inside, so he rapped on the door.

"Boys! It's Ron Gould! Anyone home?"

No true farmer would be spending daylight sitting in their house, but considering Brian had told Ron he thought he broke his back, it would make sense for him to be laid up in bed. When nobody answered, he pounded again, then pressed the doorbell, which didn't ring. After a moment of waiting, Ron made a lap around the porch, looking through each window in hopes of finding one of the boys, but the place was empty.

"Well, hell. What happened at this place?" He leaned close to a window and looked into the kitchen. "Maggie! You in there?"

Nothing.

He went back around to the front and stepped down onto the driveway, glancing toward the barn. Ron doubted that either of the brothers were in there, as they likely would have heard him yelling and come to see what the commotion was. He decided to check it out anyway, stopping at his truck along the way. Something seemed off. Whatever was responsible for the uneasy feeling, he wanted to be prepared for it. He opened the passenger door and grabbed the Glock he kept in the glove box, then double-checked to make sure it was loaded.

*Don't get spooked and shoot. Last thing I need is to kill one of those boys, go off to jail, and leave Terry all alone.*

Ron headed toward the barn. He spotted pigs wandering around their pen, which eased some of his concern but not all of it. The lack of normal farmyard sounds caused an uneasy tightness in his chest. He gripped the Glock firmly and opened one of the oversized barn doors. Before walking in, he glanced down at the ground and identified a set of footprints exiting the barn and heading up toward one of the fields on the property. He also noticed another set of tracks—thin lines roughly the width of bike tires, except there were two lines a few feet apart running parallel with one another.

"Wheelchair? What the hell are these boys up to?"

He made to follow the tracks when he noticed a decaying odor festering from within the barn. His first thought was of the animals. If they had been neglected in any way, Ron would call the cops himself and have them come check the place out. He wasn't one to watch innocent livestock get treated poorly, not when he made a living himself making sure they were properly taken care of.

As he advanced deeper into the dimly lit barn, the smell became more potent. Ron slowly passed each stall, finding them empty. All except the one down at the far end, where a horse whinnied at the sight of him.

"You poor thing. They treating you all right?" he asked, walking up to the stall door. "Look at you, you're beautiful." Ron scratched the horse's neck and stared into her eyes. Something about those eyes . . . It was as if the horse was trying to warn him. He shook it off, realizing how stupid the thought was.

He started toward the back door of the barn, ready to follow those tracks, when he heard a faint buzzing. It reminded him of the time he accidentally ran over a ground nest belonging to some nasty yellowjackets and the sound they made as they angrily rocketed out of the hole to see who had the nerve to disturb their sanctuary. Only it was mid-fall in New Hampshire now, and yellowjackets were long past their season. So what the hell was making such a racket?

Ron decided to investigate the source of the noise. He double-checked the stall, making sure there wasn't anything hovering around the horse. When he determined that wasn't where the buzzing was coming from, he looked up, and it was as though just staring toward the hayloft improved his sense of hearing. The buzzing was coming from above.

"What in the hell . . ."

He approached the wooden ladder that led up to the second level. From the ground, all he could see were countless bales of hay stacked neatly along the perimeter of the wall. He tucked his gun in the back of his pants and grabbed a rung, pulling his weight up. It wasn't as easy as it used to be, and if Terry were here to watch him, she'd likely tell him to add this to the long list of reasons indicating that he needed to either retire or hire some help for the more strenuous work.

With each rung he climbed, the humming picked up in volume and the rot smell intensified. It wasn't until he was almost to the upper level that he realized it was a swarm of flies buzzing around something in the shadows of the loft. With no windows on the upper level, it was tough to see much, but Ron pulled himself up to the floor and climbed to his feet. The first thing to stand out to him was that the hayloft wasn't just used for storing hay. There were objects, relics, and odds and ends scattered about as if someone used the area for their personal storage space. The smell was unbearable, so Ron used one hand to cover his nose with his handkerchief and reached back to grab the gun with the other.

Something shifted in the shadows. He didn't see it, he *heard* it.

"Hello? That you, Bo?"

Only the flies answered, continuing to swarm around the bales of hay. Ron considered turning around and leaving, but he had to know what was causing that smell. As he left the light behind him and continued deeper into the darkness of the loft, he wished he'd brought his flashlight. He was a grown-ass man, but having the shadows engulf him, in combination with that smell and those damn flies . . . it was enough to spook even a man with the thickest of skin.

He reached the last row of hay bales, stepping around them carefully as if remaining silent mattered now that he had already announced himself. In the far corner, Ron spotted a rocking chair facing the wall. The stench and flies were coming from this corner, and even in the shadows, Ron saw a cloud of black dots buzzing around the chair.

"Holy hell."

Opening his mouth to speak allowed the rot to enter his

lungs, and Ron did all he could not to keel over and vomit. He pressed the cloth tighter to his face, but it only shielded the smell so much.

Someone was sitting in the chair, with only the round shape of their head visible.

"Hey . . . you okay?"

*Stupid question, Ron. All the dead animals you've found on your land . . . you know this smell. And you know damn well that flies love the scent of decomposition.*

Hesitantly, he stepped forward, holding the gun steady. It wasn't that he planned to shoot something that was no longer living, but if what he suspected turned out to be true, there might be more here than the dead. He knew he heard movement coming from back here. When he got close enough to the chair to touch it, he reached out with his boot and stepped on the back of one of the curved rockers, making the chair sway back and forth. The body shifted, and Ron stifled a shout. Up this close, some of the features became clearer. Long, thinning gray hair clung to the back of the head.

"Maggie?"

Ron stepped around the chair, giving a wide berth just in case. It was Maggie Davidson, all right, and she was long dead. Her eyes were open, staring through him, but they were clouded over, wrapped in a slimy substance. He shivered as if being in her line of sight would be enough to infect him.

"Jesus Christ."

A fly landed on one of her open eyes, and while it was too dark to see what it was doing, Ron knew. It was eating the rot from Maggie. Her white dress was caked in dirt, her skin hanging loosely from the bones as if she had been deflated. Who the hell would do this to her?

He needed to go back to the house and call the police, warn Terry of what he'd seen. As he went to step around her, something skittered beneath her dress and Ron jolted back, rolling his ankle and falling to the floor. A rat poked its head out of an armhole, its face smeared in blood.

Ron couldn't hold it in anymore. He leaned over and vomited, then wiped his mouth with the handkerchief. The rat disappeared beneath the dress, and Ron could hear it burrowing inside Maggie's body as the fabric shifted. He had seen enough. The pain in his ankle was minor, yet enough to cause him to wince as he got to his feet. He picked up his pace as best he could, leaving Maggie's rotting corpse behind, and headed for the ladder. As he turned and prepared to climb down, he stared back toward the corner. Her body was no longer visible from where he stood, but he couldn't take his eyes off the dark space. When he attempted to take the first step down, his foot missed the rung, and Ron felt the strange sensation of his body free-falling.

Before he even had a chance to blink, he landed on the barn floor, smacking his head. His vision fluttered in and out, then slowly faded to black.

# 30

It was rough going for Brian and Bo, but they were getting closer to the gravesite. Brian couldn't help but notice his brother acting strange—stranger than usual—the closer they got to their destination. They had to stop and take multiple breaks along the way because the wheelchair, even with Bo's abnormal strength, proved difficult to push up the hill. Brian tried to help the best he could, but his arms were getting tired after weeks of minimal physical activity, plus he had the shovel across his lap.

"Bo, what's up, man? You're acting weird."

He stopped pushing and wiped the sweat from his brow. He panted from behind Brian, then came around to face him.

"Ma told me to do it. I'm sorry, Brian."

"Do what, Bo?"

"To dig."

Brian shook his head in confusion, trying to hide the frustration boiling up inside.

"Back at the house, you said she told you not to dig . . ."

"Again. She doesn't want me to dig *again*."

Brian shook his head in confusion.

"Well, that's why we're heading up here. So let's go and stop wasting daylight, okay?"

Bo huffed and shook his head, irritated that he couldn't find the words to explain to Brian what he meant. He got behind the chair and pushed aggressively, almost sending Brian out of the seat. As they moved up the hill, Brian spotted the lone red maple tree that had become the landmark of the family cemetery. Even though it reminded him of his dead parents, he couldn't help but admire its beauty.

They were almost to the peak of the hill. It would then dip down a slight slope until the land flattened. Bo started whispering, scolding himself, "Stupid . . . You're a stupid man."

"Bo, what—"

Brian was cut short as they reached the top of the hill and the gravesite came into view. He felt his chest tighten once his eyes landed on the graves.

"What . . . what did you do?"

"Sorry, sorry! I'm sorry!"

"Calm down, man. Tell me what happened."

"I told you! Ma said it was okay to dig! I know it was wrong now, but I missed her too much. I had to see her again."

Brian felt the burning bile pumping up his throat.

In front of him, it looked as though a land mine had blown the ground apart. What was once a freshly dug grave was now a crater with piles of dirt surrounding the site. It didn't look like a hole dug up by a shovel methodically . . . more like a savage animal clawed into the earth with its paws, dead set on reaching its prey.

"Where . . . where's her body, Bo?" Brian asked. Although

he spoke the words, he didn't hear them coming from his own mouth. He was in complete shock.

Bo's eyes were glossed over, and the tears began to flow. His legs remained planted on the ground, but his upper half swayed back and forth—his go-to reaction when he got stressed. He breathed in and out in forced, heavy bursts. Brian knew he had to be careful right now. Bo was on the verge of one of his meltdowns, and there was no telling what he would do.

*On the verge? I'd say he's already in code red full fucking meltdown mode.*

"Bring me to the grave, please. I'm not mad at you," Brian said, hoping Bo couldn't hear the fear in his words. He knew his brother had become unhinged since Ma's death, but he never in a million years expected things to get to this level. Digging up their dead mother? What kind of sick fuck does something like that?

Bo closed his eyes and squeezed. Brian could only imagine what was going through his brother's head. Just when he thought Bo wouldn't go any closer to the gravesite, he grabbed the wheelchair and pushed Brian forward, grunting his way over the rough terrain. When they reached the cemetery, Brian realized something at that moment. He had never been this scared of his brother. Tying him to the bed. Talking to their mother's ghost. Digging up her grave. These were just the things Brian *knew* of since he had been injured. But he didn't have time to focus on that right now; he would worry about Bo later. Right now, they needed to retrieve what Ma sent them here for.

"Bo. I need you to listen to me right now, you understand? What you did here . . . it ain't right. You know that. I can see it in your eyes. We need to get Ma back resting peacefully in her grave, okay?"

Bo wiped a tear away and nodded.

"I was only trying to spend more time with her, Brian. I swear it. It didn't hurt nothing."

"I-I know that. But her spirit won't be at peace until she's back here. We can always talk to her. We just can't be keeping her body lying around the farm, you hear me?"

No answer.

"Bo! I need you to listen to me, damn it! When this is all done, we're bringing Ma back here. If anyone found her the way you left her, we could go to prison. They'd think we murdered her and didn't report her death. There are things beyond your grasp of understanding that *I* need to worry about. Right now, we need to dig up Dad's grave, though. Ma said there was something in the box that we'd need if the Hollow Souls ever found us. I need you to get your shit together and start shoveling. Can you do that?"

Bo squeezed his fists together so tight that his knuckles cracked. Brian thought he might have pushed too far, but as much as he knew he needed to be careful, he also knew they didn't have much time. Looking up at the sky, he figured there were only a few more hours until early evening. Hopefully they could get the hole dug before nightfall. It wouldn't be easy, but Bo clearly had no issues digging up their mother. Brian recalled seeing the dirt caked under his brother's fingernails earlier. Had he dug her up with his bare hands?

Finally, Bo pushed the chair until they reached the family cemetery. Up close, the scene was even more disturbing. Ma's coffin boards were cracked and snapped, and the lid was ripped off.

*Holy shit.*

"Bo." Brian handed his brother the shovel and watched him approach their dad's grave.

He knew losing Ma would be hard on him, and Brian's injury couldn't have helped the stress, but Bo had lost his mind. If they even made it out of this, he wasn't sure there'd be any hope for his brother. He needed proper medical help, something Ma gave up on years ago when she saw the stress it caused him. She partly blamed the doctors for his condition not improving, and once his phobia made its first appearance, she really struggled with it. She was hard on herself, and Brian had always thought it was because of Bo's condition. But now, as his brother went to work on their father's grave, he realized it was much more than that. Ma had her own secrets, and they were about to be unburied for the first time in over twenty years.

Bo continued to dig for the better part of an hour while Brian watched, wishing he could help but also thankful that he didn't need to be within arm's reach of his brother. Behind those eyes, Bo was lost. There was no telling what was going through his head, but it obviously wasn't rainbows and butterflies. With each thrust of the shovel into the earth, Bo grunted out some combination of pain and sadness, doused heavily in rage.

*Was that Ma I was smelling in the barn? Is she hidden away with the animals?*

*Of course, it was her. And I'm well aware: Bo is a problem. That this isn't something I can rein back in like she could.*

*Well, you have to try. He's your fucking brother. You can't just put him out to pasture like a lame horse.*

As Brian's conflicting thoughts fought with one another,

the shovel clanging off something metal in the ground snapped him out of it. He recalled the box Ma had set in the grave as having metal edges to help preserve it. He looked at Bo, who had stopped digging. His brother was staring into the hole, panting heavily as sweat dripped down his face.

"Can you get it out now?" Brian asked.

Bo didn't speak, only nodded as he kneeled to reach inside the hole. His arms disappeared into the grave, working the packed dirt from around the box until he could pull it free.

Brian couldn't help himself and rolled closer to the hole. He had to see down inside. As if his father's body would magically appear, even though it never made the trip to the farm when they moved. As if looking in the hole would answer all Brian's questions that he never got to ask his dad about Marcus and the Hollow Souls. For starters, why did he have to be part of it? Although his dad had told him it was because Marcus wanted Brian around for insurance, that didn't make any sense now that he was old enough to think about it more clearly.

What possible reason could a killer want with another witness around? If Marcus really wanted leverage over his dad, wouldn't abducting the girls for them be enough?

Bo finally pulled the box from the hole and set it on the ground next to them. The wood had long ago rotted but miraculously remained intact enough to protect what was inside. While Brian had no idea what to expect regarding the contents, he knew from his mother's letter that she felt what was inside was necessary to protect themselves against the Hollow Souls.

Brian vividly remembered his mom putting the box into the hole, but he couldn't recall what she'd put inside it. The memory of her intentionally turning her back while she double-checked to make sure the contents were secure still held a place in his recollection, but that was as far as it went. Now he'd find out exactly what she had gone out of her way to hide all those years ago.

"Bring it here, Bo. Let's open it together. It's what Ma would want."

His brother brought the box closer and set it next to the wheelchair, releasing the earthy aroma of something that had just seen sunlight for the first time in two decades. Brian nodded for Bo to open the box, to which his brother responded by grabbing hold of the lid and trying to pry it open. For a second, Brian worried Bo's massive hands would disintegrate the dead wood and ruin their chances of using whatever was inside. Thankfully, the top snapped open, revealing the contents within. A silk black cloth had been wrapped around an object.

"Go on now, open it up," Brian directed.

Bo rubbed the cloth fondly. Brian didn't understand why, but then it clicked. The black silk had been torn from Bo's childhood blanket, and while his memory had been spotty at best since his accident, he clearly remembered it. But was that it? A remnant from their childhood? How the hell would that help them against a group of soul-sucking monsters?

"I remember it, Brian . . . It's mine."

Tears trickled down Bo's face. Brian wanted to let his brother reminisce, but they were up against an unknown time limit.

"Is there something inside it?"

"Y-yes."

Bo carefully unwrapped the silk, revealing something the color of cream.

*Is that a bone?*

"Hand me the box and whatever that is."

Bo frowned and met his brother's eyes. He had the look of a dog protecting his favorite toy, unwilling to share. Brian was afraid if he reached out for it, Bo would snap his arm in half without hesitation. But then Bo nodded. He wrapped the bone up, put it back into the box, then handed it over. Looking inside, Brian noticed that under the item was another notebook.

He reached in and pulled out the silk, unwrapping a white shard of something. It was definitely some type of bone, and it seemed to be human.

"What the hell is this?"

It was long and narrow, the tip sharp enough that it could pierce his flesh if he tried to. Just holding it sent a tingle up his arm, a feeling unlike any he'd ever felt before. Being in its presence somehow felt important, yet Brian had no idea what he was supposed to do with it. He was expecting answers from the grave, not more questions. But then he glanced at the notebook beneath the cloth and pulled it out. The paper had aged, falling apart yet still together enough to be legible in parts.

"Thanks a lot, Ma. Couldn't you have put this in a Ziploc, at least?"

Only certain words were clear enough to make out, and all they did was confuse Brian even more. He tried to shake off the frustration and make sense of it. This notebook was Dad's.

"Shard of Asha . . ."

*What the fuck does that even mean? Did he mean Astra? No, we didn't get her until after he was dead.*

He scanned the notebook some more, squinting at the faded letters.

*Works as a talisman of sorts against the powers of Dhat. The magic of the Hollow Souls will be useless in its presence. Keep hidden and wrapped in the box surrounded by obsidian stones unless needed. The Hollow Souls can feel its presence otherwise . . . unless one was to sacrifice part of their soul to it, to protect the bone. That would only be binding as long as that person lived.*

"What is it, Brian?" Bo asked, startling him.

Brian continued skimming the pages, ignoring his brother. He read about how the Hollow Souls worshipped an entity known as Dhat. If Brian hadn't seen the Hollow Souls in action, he would have thought his dad was crazy for the things he'd written here. Even knowing some of the truth, he still wasn't so sure his dad wasn't a little off his rocker.

"It . . . it will help us against those monsters. I need to go back and read this notebook some more. I still don't know enough. I'm afraid if they show up, we won't be able to stop them."

"How do you know they're coming? They sound like the people from my dreams."

Brian knew his lack of answers was only confusing Bo more, terrifying him for that matter. Big, strong Bo, a man who could snap another human in half if he desired, but who jumped when a bee flew in his direction.

"They *are* the people from your dreams. I know they're coming because I dreamed about them too. I-I know they're close. And when Mr. Gould told you the murders were getting closer to us, it solidified my theory. Something somehow tipped them off about our location. But Ma always knew they would get here eventually. That's why she went to such measures to hide this. And bought the house in her aunt's name."

It was all coming together in Brian's mind now. The biggest hurdle was that he was still confined to a wheelchair or a bed, both places not ideal for fending off supernatural thieves that fed off fear and absorbed the souls of their victims. Brian would be damned if he was going to sit back and willingly let them have their way.

Even though he was the one who was physically handicapped, Brian still found himself more concerned about Bo and how he would handle it all. Especially the situation involving Ma and her grave. Bo truly thought he was talking to a dead woman, dug her up, and stored her body somewhere in the barn, if his senses were right.

*Stop acting like talking to a dead woman is strange. I have a bruise on my arm to prove that the nightmare about Lisa wasn't a nightmare at all. It was real. She was in the house and grabbed me.*

*That could have been me grabbing myself in my sleep, imagining she was squeezing me in the dream.*

*I know that's not right. And I need to figure out what the hell she was trying to say to me. It's part of the puzzle, along with this bone.*

"Bo, I'll ask again. Where's Ma?"

He looked down at his feet, scuffing up the loose dirt he had just shoveled out.

"Bo! Tell me, damn it. She's my mother, too, did you ever

think of that? Not some fucking stuffed animal to help comfort you."

"Stop yelling at me! She's in my safe spot, okay? I brought her there last night."

Brian closed his eyes and sighed. So, that *was* what he smelled. And that was from down on the ground, outside the barn. He could only imagine how strong the odor was inside, up in the loft.

"From now on, I need you to listen to me, okay? Stop trying to take care of me. You've done a good job up to this point, but it's my turn to take care of you. Which means I need you to do everything I tell you, no questions asked. Got it?"

"Yes, Brian."

While talking in a stern tone was a gamble, Brian hoped that years of treating his brother this way, being the one in charge, the man of the house, would resonate with him. Bo needed structure, not doubt and freedom to make his own decisions.

"Good. We need to get back to the house. We need to prepare for them. I can feel them getting close, Bo. It's why we dreamed about them. We're linked to them whether we want to be or not."

As he was being pushed back to the house, Brian realized something. If Bo was the one connected to them by way of the ritual they enacted out in the woods years ago, why was Brian sensing them as well?

# 31

When they got back to the house, daylight was fading, warning of the dreaded nightfall that Brian wasn't ready for. As they approached the back of the barn, the first thing Brian noticed was Ron Gould's truck parked in the driveway.

*Oh fuck.*

His thoughts immediately went to their dead mother stored up in the hayloft like a box of Christmas lights. The smell hit Brian as soon as they neared the front of the barn. Ron wasn't in his truck, and he was nowhere in sight. That meant, at the very least, he had smelled the foul odor wafting in the air.

"Bo, Ron Gould is here somewhere. If he found Ma . . ."

"No. No, no, no. He needs to leave Ma alone, Brian!"

"We need to find him, and if he discovered her, let me do the talking. You understand? You'll only get us in more trouble, and we have other problems to worry about right now." He couldn't believe this was something *else* they needed to worry about right now. How crazy it would look from an outsider's perspective. They remained still, listening for any sounds out of place. The pigs snorted and squealed in their pen. Astra whinnied from her stall. But there was no sign of Ron.

"We have to check the barn. Let me roll myself."

Bo complied, releasing his grip on the wheelchair, and Brian sped toward the open door. As soon as he crossed the threshold, he spotted Ron, flat on the barn floor with a pool of blood leaking from the back of his head. The old man's straw hat was a few feet away, and a Glock lay just out of reach of his unmoving hand.

*Did he fucking shoot himself in our barn?*

Brian pushed forward, careful to avoid the blood on the floor. There were no bullet wounds that he could see, and he hadn't heard a gunshot, which he surely would have, even from the gravesite. So what the hell happened? He had been so focused on checking Ron that he forgot about the rotten stench coming from above. Now that he was in the center of the barn, his nostrils stung, his eyes watered. It was unbearable and surely the reason Ron came in here.

A sudden fear that maybe the Hollow Souls had already arrived and did this to him crossed Brian's mind, and he scanned the barn for any sign of them. This wasn't their modus operandi, though. In the time Brian spent with his dad, learning what they were all about, they didn't waste a soul. They were fucking scavengers and would suck every last drop from the body before they moved on.

Brian leaned down close to the old man, afraid to touch him, but then he spotted his chest moving. He was alive.

"Ron! Can you hear me?"

His neighbor groaned, wincing in pain. Nightfall crept in,

leaving very little light in the barn, but Brian saw Ron's eyelids flutter. Finally, he came to and attempted to sit up.

"Easy does it. What the hell happened to you?" Brian asked.

As the fog faded from Ron's eyes, he glanced first at Brian, then over his shoulder to Bo, who stood in the open doorway.

"Get the hell away from me, you freaks!"

Ron attempted to crab-walk away from Brian, but he was too weak to move.

"Please . . . I can explain everything. It's not what it looks like," Brian said, trying to remain calm, hoping it would rub off on Ron.

"Oh yeah? What it *looks like* is you kids killed your ma and kept her up here like some fucking trophy. That's what it looks like. I'm gonna call the cops. Now get the hell away from me," Ron said, wincing. He pushed himself to his feet and his knees cracked like two whips.

Bo started to come in, but Brian held up his hand, telling his brother to wait.

"Fine, if you want to call the cops, just hear us out first. Please. That up there"—he pointed to the hayloft—"is my crazy brother trying to stay close to our ma. She died of cancer. While I was laid up in bed, Bo dug her up because he missed her. You know my brother isn't all right in the head, but he's not a damn killer. That much I can tell you. But as fucked-up as that is, it's not our biggest problem, Mr. Gould."

Ron stared up at the dark corner of the loft through fearful eyes. Brian couldn't even imagine what he saw up there. Or what happened to him.

"Son, I'll only say this once. Holding a dead body hostage

like that, whether it's your mother or not, is sick and twisted. Even though she hated my guts, her soul deserves a proper burial. Something ain't right here. You boys are hiding something . . . and not just your dead ma."

"You mentioned her soul, Mr. Gould. I also overheard you talking with Bo about the murders nearby. You mentioned they were getting closer to us and to be careful."

"That's right. So are you about to tell me you been killing people? Is that what this is? Your giant brother going around murdering innocent elderly folk?" Ron asked, his eyes moving to the gun on the floor.

"No, just please listen. Ma's death has nothing to do with the murders, and neither does Bo. At least not the killing part of it. What I need to tell you might take a few, so I think you should sit down and listen. That head injury looks rough. What the hell happened to you anyway?"

Ron touched the back of his head and yanked his hand away.

"After I saw her up there, a goddamn rat came crawling out of her insides. Then when I tried to hurry down the ladder, I lost my grip and fell off. Christ, it's almost evening! I need to get back to Terry."

The thought of rats burrowing inside his dead mother's stomach sent a wave of nausea rolling through Brian, leaving his head spinning. Barn rats drove Ma nuts. She had set out plenty of traps and poison to keep them at bay, and now they were getting the last laugh. He was tempted to go up there and shoot all the fuckers, but the thought of seeing her rotting corpse intensified the dread pulling at his heart.

"I haven't seen her. I just found out Bo put her up there. I-

I can't even imagine what she must look like. I'm sorry you had to see that."

"And I'm sorry I had to inform you what they were doing to her body. But I still don't trust you two. I'd like you to tell me what the hell's going on and give me one good reason not to leave here and call the police," Ron said, then covered his nose and mouth with a handkerchief and continued. "Listen, kid, can we take this conversation out of the barn? This smell is giving me a headache."

Brian nodded and they headed out the door. As Bo moved out of their way, Brian noticed Mr. Gould giving his brother the side-eye as he picked up his hat and Glock, not taking his eyes off Bo as he passed him. Brian didn't blame him. None of this was normal. And what he was about to hear would only further complicate things. They went to the wraparound porch, where Bo lifted the wheelchair up, then Ron and Bo sat in the wicker chairs that Brian would often relax in after a long day's work on the farm.

"So, what is it you need to tell me that can help any of this make sense?" Ron asked.

"I'm not so sure anything could explain the things you've already seen. But I wanted to talk about the murders and why I think we're in danger."

"I'm listening."

"First, let me grab my dad's notebook. It'll help put some of the pieces together," Brian said.

"Your dad? Wasn't he dead when y'all moved out here?"

"Yes. And there's a reason we moved out to the middle of nowhere. Bo, hand me the box."

The old man continued to stare daggers at the younger brother, waiting for any sudden movements.

"Okay. I don't think we have much time. This notebook explains so much but first, let me tell you the gist of all this. When Bo and I were kids, our dad got involved with some bad people. They weren't just your average thugs or criminals, though. They . . . had certain powers. They forced my dad into working for them, bringing them victims that they could have their way with—"

"Like some sex trafficking? Your pops was into that sort of thing?" Ron interrupted, lifting his upper lip in a snarl.

"No, no. Nothing like that. But I'm afraid it really wasn't any better. These people call themselves the Hollow Souls. Call them a cult, a gang, whatever you want. But they are pure fucking evil. They suck the souls from the living, feeding off the very essence of life. I know how ridiculous that sounds, believe me. If I hadn't seen it firsthand, I wouldn't have believed such a thing was even possible."

"Yeah, I thought your brother was the one with the head injury, not you. What is this crazy witchcraft stuff? Why should I believe it?"

Brian sighed. Apparently, the CliffsNotes version of this story wasn't going to be enough to convince Mr. Gould of the danger they were in.

"My dad would bring these girls to an abandoned house out of town near where we grew up, and the Hollow Souls would drain the life from them one by one. I found this out one day when I was forced to go with him. I witnessed a girl being dragged through the front door screaming, never to come back out. These people, the Hollow Souls, they're led by a man named Marcus. He made a deal with my dad that if he helped Marcus with some jobs, he'd make Bo the best baseball player this state had ever seen. My dad wanted nothing more than to see us succeed and make a living doing something we loved.

"So, he said yes to Marcus without even knowing what he was getting himself into. And then he changed. The more he was forced to help them, the more agitated he became. He and Ma would fight all the time, and she'd accuse him of cheating and being on drugs. And I always thought that's what she believed, that she only knew a little about the Hollow Souls—enough to move us out here in isolation to hide from them."

"Just a minute. Are you telling me that these murders are related to this story? This . . . group is on some killing spree looking for you guys?" Ron asked, pulling his pipe out of his chest pocket and lighting it.

*Just tell him what he needs to know. No need to explain how Bo got injured or what my part in all of it was.*

"Yes. When my dad died, Ma buried a box up at a gravesite on the hill. His body's not here, but we made a memorial. What I didn't know until today was what the box contained. And that they want it. We've been living like we're in witness protection for more than half our lives, and now it appears they've finally found us, Ron.

"In their eyes, my dad never fulfilled his duty to them before he died, and he stole the object they worship. Instead of trying to make things right with them, Ma took us and ran. It's why she was so standoffish with you and anyone from the outside who tried to be friendly. We couldn't afford to let anyone get close to us."

"Whether it's from hitting my head in the fall or trying to make sense of what you're saying, my brain's scrambled right now. None of this makes a lick of sense, Brian. Until this afternoon, the craziest thing I ever saw was a coyote drinking the blood from one of my cow's throats like some fucking werewolf. Then I come here and find your dead mother, you in a wheelchair, and am fed a story about a group of soul-eating killers that your dad worked for when you were kids, who are hunting you down to get something he stole from them. You couldn't make that story make sense no matter how you tell it. Yet somehow, part of me wants to believe you. What is it you think these people want?"

Brian grabbed the box and opened it, then pulled out the black silk and unraveled it. He held up The Shard of Asha, and for the first time, he noticed there were intricate designs carved into the bone. They were hard to make out with the sun sinking below the trees, but they appeared almost tribal. Ancient. Something that belonged to another world.

Ron cleared his throat to get Brian's attention.

"I can feel it, you know. I can't explain it, but being in its presence . . . I believe everything you just said."

Brian felt it, too, and he wasn't sure why he hadn't at the gravesite, but just holding it in his hands sent a radiating warmth through him. Almost like it was healing him.

He felt a jolt travel through his entire body, something that started out as pain and transitioned to euphoria. It was almost orgasmic. Something was happening to him. The sensation remained for what felt like minutes, but when it faded, Brian's entire body thrummed. He could feel something changing inside him. He looked down at his feet and wiggled his toes. It was the first time he'd been able to do so since the injury. He needed to test it, take it another step further.

Brian stood up from the wheelchair, and Bo jumped to his feet to try and stop him.

"No! Sit back down, Brian."

Only it didn't matter what demands his brother shouted. The Shard of Asha was in control. The warmth extended through his core, down to his legs. He stepped forward. Took another step. *Holy shit . . . it's healing me.*

"This . . . This is what they want, Ron. My spine was shattered. There's no reason imaginable that I should be able to stand right now, let alone take a step without falling on my face. Oh my God."

Brian began to cry. He never thought he'd walk again. Bo stared at him with his mouth agape, amazed at the miracle transpiring.

"I need you to tell me the rest, son. What are these people capable of?"

"It's all in here—my dad's notebook. He stole the shard from them, trying to escape their grasp. He knew it was leverage over them . . . only he died before we got to escape as a family. But this book will tell us everything."

Brian opened the cover and began to read aloud.

## 32

"Dhat is no mere ghost or demon; it is an ancient force, older than the trees and mountains themselves. It is a void that consumes endlessly, feeding on the essence of the living—their souls. Those who succumb to its call, the Hollow Souls, wear its mark upon their faces: skull masks, grotesque and unholy, carved from human remains.

"The masks are not merely decoration. They are vessels, infused with Dhat's power, allowing the wearers to consume the souls of their victims. This act strengthens Dhat's hold on the Hollow Souls and spreads its influence like a cancer. The screams of the victims can be heard when the masks are near because the skulls trap those souls inside. With every soul devoured, they grow more powerful, more unstoppable. They are no longer men or women but empty vessels, slaves to the void.

"There's a way to fight Dhat, but it demands a price no one should take lightly. The Shard of Asha—an ancient fragment of bone—is the only thing I know that can sever the

Hollow Souls' connection to their master. The shard itself is lifeless until it is infused with a part of a living soul. This sacrifice awakens its power, turning it into a weapon capable of repelling Dhat's influence.

"But this is no small act. Whoever chooses to transfer a part of their soul to the shard will find themselves diminished. The process leaves them weakened, and the body cannot sustain this condition for long. Illness will take hold, then death will follow. The shard becomes a lifeline to others, but it comes at the ultimate cost. I will give it my soul to protect my family. I got us into this situation, and I'll get us out of it.

"The shard's power can also be extended to others. By infusing a fragment of a soul into another living being—a man, a child, even an animal—the bone can create guardians capable of withstanding Dhat's influence. But this, too, comes with consequences. The giver's body will fail them. They may last months, perhaps years, but the end is always the same. Death follows such a gift, relentless and certain. The shard's power is finite. It must not be wasted, for once it's used, it needs time to recharge before it can be used again. Another soul must be given to do this.

"I'm sorry I couldn't do more. I'm sorry I put this burden on my family. But they're stronger than they know. They have to be.

"I'm writing this for Maggie and the boys. Because if I somehow fail, they need to know the truth. For if the day ever comes when they must confront Marcus and the Hollow Souls, they need to be prepared.

"Had I known the stakes when I first got involved, I never would have done it. What they did to my boys . . . I'll never forgive myself. And I know Maggie has her suspicions. She's questioned me and my motives, accused me of many things that I wish were true instead. I wish I had cheated. I wish I had done drugs. At least in those situations, I would be the one who suffered most. I'm afraid if I don't take down the Hollow Souls, the entire family will suffer for my mistakes."

## 33

Brian's grip on the notebook tightened. He was unable to read anymore. After going weeks without being able to walk, then regaining that ability just moments ago, he found his legs turning to rubber, threatening to lose functionality again. There was so much information to unpack and little time to do it. When he forced himself to pry his eyes from the notebook, he noticed both Mr. Gould and Bo staring at him, waiting for more.

"I-I need a minute," he said, then ran off the porch and threw up in the shrubs.

Suddenly, his nightmare came back to him—what Lisa was trying to tell him with her unhinged jaws. She told him: the skulls held the power; it was in their mask. But that wasn't the biggest thing eating at Brian. Something he had tried to push to the back of his mind all these years was forcing itself forward.

It wasn't just Bo that the Hollow Souls changed with their ritual. They had changed Brian as well. He thought back to the day Marcus and his dad dragged Lisa into that abandoned house, her eyes desperately begging Brian for help. He thought of the other nightmare that had occurred many times since he was a boy, where he followed his dad into that house, discovering not just Lisa but a number of young girls in cages, their souls being slowly drained as if they were a food source. In that dream, he thought he saw the Hollow Souls injecting Bo with the power of Dhat. But it wasn't just Bo, after all. The second figure, the one he couldn't see in the dream, was him. They had done something to him while he was in the truck waiting for his dad, and when he woke up, he had no idea that he had been through something so horrific. And then Brian recalled watching his brother in the woods behind the outfield fence, thrashing around, eyes rolling back in his head as the Hollow Souls chanted in their ancient tongue.

"How . . ."

*How could I have forgotten that all this time? How could I be so stupid? And The Shard of Asha, it just healed me. Which means someone sacrificed a piece of their soul to give the shard power. It wasn't Dad. But Ma knew all along. She sacrificed part of her soul to the shard, and because of it, she got sick. And died.*

*She died protecting me and Bo.*

*But* how*? How did she know how to use the shard? When did she give a part of her soul? If she did it before burying the box, that means she went years before getting sick. Still, there was no other time she could have done it. She went years holding that secret within herself, years knowing she was going to die for it. And I just wasted it on myself when I could have healed Bo's head injury. We would need another soul to do that.*

Brian took a deep breath. He needed to force the shock

away because the Hollow Souls were close. He could feel them. With The Shard of Asha now exposed and used, it would become a beacon for the evil bastards. That's if they didn't already know where to go. When he made it back to the porch, Ron was staring off into the sky, exhaling smoke from his pipe. He had the look of someone who just found out there really were monsters under his bed. Bo sat in the other chair, hugging himself from the cold, rocking back and forth.

"Bo. Did any of this make sense to you? Do you understand what I just read?"

His brother nodded, squinting his eyes like he was trying to prevent the tears from flowing. Brian doubted that he got all the facts, but Bo understood enough to know that the bone they dug up was powerful, and that it could take down the group that was responsible for all the pain their family had suffered.

"Ron. I don't expect you to stick around after all the shit you've seen and heard here tonight. I just hope you understand now what we've been through."

The old man let out a half chuckle, but his eyes showed the laugh was anything but humorous.

"Son, I can't sit here and say I make sense of all this. I'd be lying if I did. And you boys need to get your poor mother back in her grave. Nobody should be violated like that. But like I said before, I believe you. I've never really thought we were alone on this planet. I'm a God-fearing man, so I hope you understand that this is all far beyond anything an old fella like me could expect to have thrown their way at this stage of life. I need to get back to my wife. She's probably scared shitless, wondering why I've been gone so long. She'd drive up here herself to check on me if she knew how to operate a vehicle."

"I understand. So you won't call the cops on us?" Brian asked, holding out hope.

Ron glanced over at Bo, obviously still not convinced he was innocent in all this.

"I reckon I can hold off. But let me ask you this: if you know these evil bastards are coming, why hang around and wait? I understand that earlier, you were stuck in bed and your brother wouldn't drive, but you're all healed up now. Isn't that a sign to get the hell out of here before the shit hits the fan?"

Brian knew he was right. But he also knew what he had to do. For Dad, for Ma, for Bo. He also knew that they could only run from Marcus for so long before he found them again.

"That would be the smart thing, I know that. The thing is, after realizing what Ma did for us, giving part of her soul to protect us on this farm, it just feels like running is the wrong thing to do. We've been hiding for over twenty years now. They ruined my dad. Turned him into a puppet who had no choice but to do as they said. They did something to me and Bo, too, somehow linking us to them for the rest of our lives.

"No . . . we need to end these monsters. They didn't just leave our family for dead, they made Ma suffer for years. And they killed countless victims just to feed whatever the hell this Dhat is. Bo and I will be here waiting when they come."

Ron nodded in appreciation.

"I'd do the same, son. Say, it's pretty late. Do you mind if I call the wife from your phone before I head back home? Let her know I'm okay?"

Brian sighed, looking at Bo. He looked dejected. As if the

poor guy knew he was the reason things were more difficult for them because of the way he was.

"Don't have a phone. Because of Bo's condition. The phone I called you on earlier was a prepaid cell Ma and I kept hidden for emergencies. When Bo found me talking to you on it, he destroyed it."

"I don't envy this balancing act you got going on at this farm. Well, I wish you the best. And if you change your mind, you can always come to our place and we can call the authorities together. Have them come arrest these people and put them away for life."

"I appreciate your understanding, Ron. Most people wouldn't think twice before calling the cops. This whole situation is fucked, and I just want it to end. The authorities won't do any good against the Hollow Souls, though. That much I can promise you. If we ran, they'd follow. We've just been putting off the inevitable for years," Brian said, glancing up at the sky. "It's getting pretty late, so we better get to preparing."

Ron stepped down onto the driveway and as he got to his truck, he turned back to face them.

"Be careful, boys."

Brian nodded and watched as Mr. Gould drove off, leaving a cloud of dust as he headed back down the long, narrow driveway toward the main road.

"Bo, you okay?"

He shook his head violently. Brian felt awful for his brother, but they were in this together. The only difference was that he didn't suffer from permanent brain damage, something The Shard of Asha couldn't fix without sacrificing another soul.

*Neither would Bo if I hadn't bashed his skull in with that buried rage inside me.*

*I was trying to protect the family. I wasn't thinking.*

*Keep telling yourself that. You were always jealous of the attention Bo got, and the first chance you had to take it out on him, you went for it.*

That was it. All these years, Brian knew it was that built-up jealousy that led to the attack on Bo. He could hide behind the statement that he was protecting his family all he wanted, but that wasn't the whole truth.

As Brian opened the front door to head inside, two tiny red dots lit up the dark forest at the end of the driveway. Ron had stopped, braking as if he realized he had forgotten something at the last second.

"What the hell's he doing?"

They watched as he put his truck into reverse and sped back up the driveway, bouncing off the potholes along the way. When he made it back to the house, his door opened before he even killed the engine, and he had a shotgun in his hand. Brian thought for a second that he was going to kill them, having a change of heart and thinking they were the threat. But there was panic in the old man's eyes.

"Boys, there's someone coming. Through the woods. Get back in the house, now!"

# 34

The three of them ran inside and Brian locked the door behind him. The house was dark, too dark to see more than a few feet in any direction, but maybe that was a good thing. If they could hide from Marcus and his followers, maybe they could actually gain the upper hand.

"What did you see, Ron?" Brian asked.

"Figures . . . walking through the woods, crouching low. I couldn't make out what they looked like, but there was more than one of 'em."

"Did they see you?"

"I don't know. I don't think so. I slammed on the brakes as soon as I spotted movement, but my exhaust is loud. I can't imagine they didn't at least hear me."

"Damn it. Bo, we need weapons to defend ourselves. The Shard of Asha will only work if we get the chance to use it. They'll do everything they can to stop us. Ron, what's your plan?"

"Well, I can't exactly drive by them and give a thumbs-up,

can I? I got my 12 gauge here and my Glock. Do you have any firearms?"

Ma didn't dare keep any in the house due to Bo's episodes. After she shot Dad, the police confiscated the gun for evidence, and she never got another. Even with the looming threat of the Hollow Souls possibly finding them someday, she didn't think it was worth the risk of Bo going on a rampage if he snapped.

"No. We got tools—an axe, chainsaw. Bo, grab the bat you keep in your room."

"The one I hit balls to the moon with?"

Brian couldn't help but smile. "Yeah, buddy. The one you 'hit balls to the moon with.'"

Bo ran into the darkness toward his bedroom, leaving Brian and Mr. Gould together.

"Ron, this isn't your fight, man. These people are dangerous. This will only end with death. Either them or us."

"Ha. Believe me, I know I coulda kept driving by them. But what kind of man does that? What you read to me . . . that's bigger than any of us. These things belong in hell. They need to be stopped, or they'll just keep killing. Here, take the pistol. I'll keep the shotgun."

Brian had a sudden newfound respect for the old man. He wished they had more of a relationship over the years, and that Ma had gotten a chance to know Ron outside of their uncomfortable business exchanges that were necessary for the sustainability of both farms.

"Thank you. For everything. For trusting us and this insane story and situation. For having our back when we don't even really know each other well. It means a lot."

"That bone, you can feel its power. Makes believing all

this a hell of a lot easier, kid," Ron said, then moved the curtain to look out the window. "Now what's the plan? They're clearly gonna try to sneak up through the woods and get the jump on us. I don't think they saw me, but like I said, if they didn't hear my truck, I'd be shocked."

"I don't think that matters. They know we're home. And I'm pretty sure they know Bo and I can sense them. Whatever they did to us when we were kids, it linked us to them. The closer they get . . . it's like my whole body feels it. It must be how they narrowed down where to look for us after Ma died. She gave some of her soul to hide us, but when she died, that protection vanished," Brian said. He sighed and thought for a second. "I think we keep the house dark. Stay together and wait them out. If we spread out, it'll be easier for them to get rid of us one by one."

"Agreed. So we wait here with the front door in view. The first sign of it opening, I blast a hole through their asses."

"Marcus is smarter than that. He'll have a plan, and I can guarantee you it won't be just coming through the front door by force. He'll try to get in our heads, compel us to make stupid decisions. No matter what he says, don't listen. It's part of the game for him. Like the more he scares people, the more enjoyable the souls are to devour."

Ron nodded.

Bo came back to the living room with his bat in hand. He was panting, and even in the darkness, Brian saw how wide-eyed he was. The poor guy was terrified. Brian recalled the range of emotions forced on Bo in just a few short weeks. Sadness from their mother's death. Guilt for the injury he brought on Brian. Rage upon learning the truth. Confusion about how to take care of Brian after his injury. And now abject terror, coursing through his entire body as the Hollow Souls approached.

"Bo . . . take a deep breath, buddy. We got this. Just listen to me, okay? And remember, it's just like with the bullies when we were kids. We defend ourselves when we need to, and this is one of those times. Got it? These people are the reason our lives are the way they are. They caused this."

"I'm scared, Brian."

"I know, buddy. Me too. Stay close to me and do as I say."

Bo nodded.

Brian sat on the couch with the pistol while Ron remained in the shadows, shotgun at the ready. Through all of it, Brian cared about the safety of his brother. It was a chance for him to right his wrongs, try to make up for the mistakes he'd made as a child that caused Bo's suffering. Brian told Bo to wait in the corner, ready to strike when needed.

"Guys, they might come in a few minutes or a few hours. Knowing Marcus, he'll take his time, playing the mind games he loves to play. Remember, go for the masks; it's what holds their power. If we can get them off, I can try and use the shard to drain them of their strength. It's the only way to end Marcus for good," Brian whispered.

Ron nodded, and Brian hoped that Bo was listening from the corner. After all of this, there should have been a better plan in place than hiding and waiting for them.

*Traps should have been set. Distractions created.*

*Anything is better than allowing the monsters to come to us at full strength.*

*I was in a fucking wheelchair. What the hell was I supposed to do? I didn't even know The Shard of Asha existed until a few hours ago. And now they're already here.*

Time trickled away. Seconds felt like minutes. Minutes like hours. It got to the point where Brian started to wonder if maybe the old man was seeing things. Maybe it was just a damn postman down the road putting bills in the Davidson mailbox.

As much as he wanted to believe that, Brian knew it wasn't true. He knew it was really the Hollow Souls here to claim what they had been seeking for two decades. He could sense them. And that connection was getting stronger.

The whispers of the trapped souls were getting louder.

Just when he was ready to get up and check the windows, he heard something on the front steps.

*Creeeak.*

And then the warped silhouette of someone moving across the porch, gliding silently past the windows.

Brian looked at Ron.

"They're here."

# 35

After the first shadow passed by, a few minutes lapsed with no sign of movement. Brian wondered what Marcus was up to. His mind went to things he could have done to help their chances. Did he lock the back door? It was something they usually left unlocked, thanks to living alone in the woods. What about the windows? If it had been summer, there would be a high likelihood that they were open to let in the cool evening air. Thankfully, with autumn wrapping its claws around New England, Brian had done some of the winter preparation before he fell off Astra.

*Astra. They better not do anything to her!*

It was too quiet. There were no approaching footsteps, no doors or windows being tested. Brian heard Bo breathing heavily from the shadows, and it took all he had not to yell out to his brother that it would be okay, to just take a deep breath.

A squeal cut through the night, followed by another, from somewhere on the farm close enough that Brian could hear every excruciating cry. He realized it was the pigs. The sick fucks were slaughtering them one by one, which meant Marcus likely planned to go down the line, taking the lives of every living thing on the farm before he moved on to the inside of the house.

"Fuck," he whispered. "Ron, they're killing our animals. If they get my horse . . ."

"You told me they want you to come out. They're testing you, Brian. Don't cave," Ron said.

"Astra means everything to me. I'll die before I let them butcher her," Brian insisted, then moved toward the front door.

Ron stormed after him, grabbing him by the shoulder.

"No! I get it, kid. I really do. I'd be devastated if they got to my horses. But I can't let you put all our lives on the line right now. If we're going to try and stop them, we need to be smart about it. What if we go upstairs? Is there a window where we can get a good view of the barn? Maybe open fire if we get a clean shot?"

"What're you going to do? Snipe them with a fucking shotgun? Throw shit at them from the windows? I need to go out there, Ron."

"No. I can't let you do that. I'm a pretty damn good shot, but you're right. The shotgun won't do much good from that range, but still . . . I trust my shot. Let's go upstairs and see if we can find them out there. Trust me, kid. You're not thinking with a straight head right now."

*SQUEEEAL!*

"He's killing all of them. We need to stop them!"

"Son, no damn animal is worth your life!"

Brian closed his eyes and punched the wall, trying to hold in the frustration and failing miserably. Meanwhile, Bo began to groan in the corner, whispering something to himself. It hadn't even been ten minutes and Marcus was already getting inside their heads.

A dark blotch appeared outside one of the porch windows on the side of the house. It was hard to tell with the way the moon hit it, but Brian thought it must be the big guy. He motioned for Ron to look. They might not even have time to make it upstairs before the Hollow Souls infiltrated the house.

"Bo, come here. We need to change our plan," Brian whispered.

Bo stepped forward, gripping the bat more like someone holding it for the first time than someone who had been one of the best players in the state as a kid. Brian motioned for them to go upstairs, and the three of them climbed quietly. When they reached the second-floor hall, Brian spoke, "I think Ron's right. Getting an advantage up here is a better choice than staying downstairs. There's only one way up here, and we can be ready for them. Plus, we can look out the windows to see where they come from. I still say we don't split up, though. We stay together, travel from room to room."

"Agreed. We see one of them climbing the stairs, they get a shotgun blast to the face," Ron said.

"The masks hold the essence of Dhat, according to my dad's notebook. If we can get the masks off, we can stop them. Once we get them off, I can use the Shard of . . ." Brian trailed off. "Fuck! I can't let them find the bone. I left it downstairs on the couch."

"You can't really be considering going back down there, kid."

"Please, go check the windows in that bedroom right there

—they overlook the porch. I need that bone, Ron. If they get it . . . we're fucking dead."

The old man pushed past Bo, who stood in the hall like a confused child awaiting instruction. Brian stopped at the top of the stairs.

"I don't see them. But the porch roof is blocking half the driveway."

"Fuck it," Brian said, then bolted down the stairs two at a time, almost tripping over his feet in the process. He turned a dark corner toward the living room and sprinted down the hall, careful not to trip over anything that Bo had left out in his weeks of caring for him. When Brian reached the living room, he ran to the black cloth and swiped it up, feeling the weight of the bone in his grasp. He turned to head back toward the stairs.

*Thump!*

The sound came from the porch.

Brian eyed the closest window but only saw inky darkness below the bottom of the blinds.

*Thump!*

This time, the sound had moved around the side of the house, toward the back door. It was as if Marcus was toying with them, playing a game of cat and mouse before deciding it was time to enter the home. The back door rattled, pulling Brian's attention in that direction. He walked quietly into the hall, carrying the pistol in one hand and The Shard of Asha in the other. Even with his light steps, the old farmhouse groaned beneath his weight.

"Little pig, little pig, let us in . . ."

Brian almost dropped the gun, catching it at the last second. It was muffled through the wall, but he'd recognize

Marcus's rattling smoker's voice anywhere. It was coming from a different location than the thumping. They were surrounding the house, blocking all exits. He looked around, trying to determine his next step. He needed to get back upstairs to Bo and Ron.

*Thump!*

"There's a lot of blood out here, Brian. I wouldn't want to shed even more. Give us what we came for."

Brian tried taking a deep breath, but nothing came. Panic had taken over, pressing on his chest like a cinder block. He found his arm shaking as he squeezed the gun, aiming straight ahead. The hall was dark, but his eyes had adjusted enough to see where he was going. The thump came again, and it sounded like the back door was beginning to crack. He took off toward the stairs, then heard the front door.

*Click.*

Marcus had picked the lock.

Brian wanted to yell to Ron, alert him to get ready to fire, but he didn't want to give away his location. The problem was that to get to the stairs, he would have to go past the back door. Whoever was trying to break through would see him. Instead, Brian pulled open the pantry door and stepped inside. The room was big enough to walk in because this was where they canned and stored their vegetables for the winter season. He carefully shut the door and waited, his heart thrumming in his chest.

*BAM!*

The back door slammed against the kitchen wall, echoing through the house like a stick of dynamite. In the confines of the pitch-black pantry, Brian couldn't see anything except a sliver of light from the moonlight hitting the hall, creeping beneath the bottom of the door. He watched that space, waiting for shadows to pass. The Hollow Souls possessed the ability to sense The Shard of Asha, but Brian just hoped they couldn't pinpoint its exact location. They knew it was on the farm. Did they know it was right around the corner, hiding in the pantry?

The floorboards creaked.

A shadow passed by the door, a shade of black engulfing a lighter shade of black, and then it was gone. Just like when Bo moved through the house while Brian was strapped to Ma's bed, every little sound stood out. He knew at least two of the intruders were inside, and more likely, all three. He needed to cause a distraction to save the others. If Ron was forced to fire, he might hit one of the Hollow Souls, but the others would be on him before he had a chance to fire again. They were fast when they needed to be. Brian remembered how quickly they moved in the woods the day they infused their evil into Bo.

*Bo!*

After everything his poor brother had been through, Brian couldn't let them hurt Bo. They had done enough to him—and their family—already. When the sounds faded, Brian risked cracking the door open, peering out into the hall. There was no sign of Marcus or the others, so he stepped out quietly. When the shadow had passed the door, it moved to the right, toward the stairs. Brian followed, hoping he could catch whoever it was off guard. His limbs wobbled, but so much adrenaline pumped through him that he thought he might pass out.

Something moved behind him.

Brian spun around, coming face-to-face with a skull.

"Hello, Brian."

Marcus struck him, sending him stumbling backward. The punch had the impact of a sledgehammer, transmitting a radiating pain through Brian's cheek. He aimed the gun and fired before he had his shot lined up, but the bullet still connected, lodging into Marcus's shoulder. All it did was make the right side of Marcus's upper body jerk back slightly as he continued to step toward Brian.

"You stupid shit," Marcus said, spitting the words like venom.

Brian continued to back away toward the stairs, keeping his eyes locked on the Hollow Souls' leader. The skull was so white it almost glowed in the dark space. Two black craters where eyes used to reside hid most of Marcus's *actual* eyes, but his irises sparked off a blue glow, piercing into Brian with sinister intent.

*Don't look into his eyes. Remember what Dad had said: Marcus can persuade any person if they make eye contact.*

"I'm going to need you to give me The Shard of Asha. It belongs to us. Your daddy took something that wasn't his. He thought he was smart enough to stop us. Stupid fuck. You know how easy it was to convince him to work for me? To bring me those sweet little ladies to feed to Dhat? Your dad was a weak man, kid. And the apple doesn't fall far from the tree.

"Did you know the only reason he had us do the ritual with you was to prove it wouldn't hurt your brother? Can you imagine that? Your own dad willing to sacrifice you to protect his favorite kid. How's that make you feel?"

Brian gritted his teeth, squeezing the gun in his hand. He wanted to shoot him again. To blow Marcus's fucking head clean off. He prepared to do just that, but when he raised the gun, he caught movement to his right coming from the mudroom. He risked a quick glance over, spotting the female member of the Hollow Souls. The dead snakes dangled from her skull mask, their black skin glistening in the moonlight that bled in from the mudroom window. Marcus swatted the gun from Brian's hand and it went skittering across the floor.

Brian knew it would be difficult to defend himself against Marcus one-on-one, but being cornered by two of them made it virtually impossible. He turned and ran down the rest of the hall, climbing the stairs quickly until he reached the second floor.

"You're making this more difficult than it needs to be. Just give it to us, and we'll be on our way!" Marcus yelled from below.

The door to Brian's bedroom was still shut. He attempted to turn the doorknob, only to find it locked.

"Let me in! It's me!"

Rushed footsteps approached from inside the room and Ron's face appeared as the door swung open.

"Get in!"

There was no point in being quiet now. The Hollow Souls knew where Brian was and they had him exactly where they wanted him. Ron slammed the door shut, locked it again, then motioned for Bo to move toward a dresser against the wall.

"Put some of that muscle to use, kid. Push that thing against the door."

Bo looked to his brother for confirmation and Brian nodded. The dresser was heavy, but it wouldn't hold for long. Still, it might buy them some time. Bo slid it across the floor, creating a loud scraping sound of wood on wood. Brian ran to the window, looking for a possible way to escape.

"What was that shot? Did you hit one of them?" Ron asked.

"Yeah . . . but it didn't faze him. You would have thought I hit him with a damn spitball. He knocked the gun out of my hands, so I don't have a weapon anymore. There are three of them. I saw two in the house. I'm not sure where the third is. I don't see him out here," Brian said, still staring out the window.

"Ain't no way in hell my old ass can climb out that window and off the porch roof, if that's what you're thinking," Ron said.

"I know this sounds ridiculous at this point, but I still think our best bet is waiting them out in here. We have the shotgun. One shot to the head and they'll know they can't just mosey on up here and take us."

"So, what then? We call their bluff and wait here? You said so yourself, they won't leave until they have what they want. Eventually, we'll need to eat something, go to the bathroom. And I need to get back to my wife, who's probably worried sick about me."

Brian wished they had more time to strategize, but it was too late for that. Marcus was always one step ahead. Brian didn't know what to expect, but he knew the wily leader wouldn't waste much time waiting downstairs.

"Bo, how're you doing, buddy?" Brian asked.

"I'm scared. The skeleton people are here. Those masks . . . they make my skin burn. I remember what they did to me, Brian. They made my body hurt so bad."

"I know. And that's why we need to get those masks off

them. If one of them comes after you, do whatever you can to get the mask off and destroy it. Okay?"

Bo hesitantly nodded.

Something was wrong, though. Too much time had passed without any noise from downstairs. Brian checked out the window again, finding no sign of them. The silence was disrupted by a crackling sound at the base of the stairs. Brian heard it before he smelled it.

*Fire.*

"Shit, they're smoking us out! Ron, I know you said you can't climb out the window but now might be a good time to try."

Smoke forced its way beneath the door, rolling in like a low cloud. They wouldn't have long before the entire room was filled, and they suffocated.

*Why didn't I consider this a possibility? This was a terrible plan. How did they start a fire that fast?*

Brian shook those thoughts and ran to the window, forcing it open. The brisk fall air blew in, helping to spread the polluted cloud now engulfing the room.

"Come on! Let's go. Bo and I can climb out first and help you, Ron."

"No offense, son, but you were in a damn wheelchair an hour ago. I can't say I trust you to help my overweight ass get down there."

"Then fucking jump! I don't care. But we need to go now. Come on, Bo."

"I'm scared."

"I know you're fucking scared! You keep saying it! Come on!"

Bo flinched.

"I'm sorry. I know that came across mean. I'm just stressed right now. And I'm sorry to you, too, Ron, but they're burning our damn house down, and if we don't get out soon, we're going to burn with it."

Bo scanned the room, tears flooding his eyes, "Our home . . . All Ma's things!"

Brian wanted to comfort him, but there wasn't time. He clutched The Shard of Asha and climbed out the window, stepping down onto the roof of the porch which was a few feet farther down than he anticipated. When he had his feet planted safely, he turned back to help Bo out . . .

. . . and felt panic clamp down on his lungs.

The fire had entered the room, licking along the doorframe, climbing the wall, and spreading to the ceiling. Their house was burning down.

## 36

By the time Bo made it out the window, Ron was glistening in sweat, coughing so violently that Brian thought the old man might have a heart attack. He grabbed the shotgun, then he and Bo helped their neighbor through the window. Ron wasn't nearly as nimble, straining to crouch low enough and climb through without falling over in the process.

The whole house was going up in flames. Their entire life after escaping the Hollow Souls, hoping for a fresh start . . . gone, just like that. But no matter how long they remained hidden from Marcus, Brian knew that someday it would come to this. As they carefully moved along the edge of the roof, the bones of the house cracked and popped inside. Even if they made it out of this alive, everything would be lost.

They made it to the far end of the roof, where Brian glanced over the edge, trying to find the safest spot to jump. While it wouldn't feel great, the area where Ma had planted the most bushes seemed like the best bet. With the way the night was trending, Brian pictured one of the rhododendron bushes impaling him on his jump down.

*That would be an honorable way to go.*
*Like I deserve anything better.*

"Over here, guys. We jump down into those bushes, soften the landing. Then we need to catch them off guard, get the masks off."

"And then what? You don't think they're waiting for us? You saw what was happening in there. They know there's no way we're going down those stairs to get out. We won't be catching anyone off guard, kid."

"If you want to stay up here, be my guest. Bo, let's go."

He hesitated, his eyes darting back and forth between Ron and Brian. His brother won out, and Bo approached the edge with him. They had to move quickly before the Hollow Souls found them.

"Will it hurt?" Bo asked.

"Maybe. But I can promise it won't hurt as much as burning to death. I'll go first to show you it's okay. Sound good?"

Bo nodded, squeezing his bat like it was his protector. Ron stood behind Bo shaking his head, muttering under his breath.

Brian prepared to jump, then stopped himself. He couldn't risk The Shard of Asha getting damaged in the fall.

"Hold this until I'm landed. Then I'll have you drop it down to me. We're only about ten feet up, Bo. It can't kill us. We'll be okay."

He handed the silk-wrapped bone to Bo, hesitant to let it out of his sight. Then he turned back toward the ground, locating the bush that he planned on aiming for. The flames had reached the window, forcing their way out and latching onto the exterior of the house.

Brian crouched, then jumped over the side, feeling a momentary sensation of free fall in his stomach before hitting the bush directly. A jagged branch aiming skyward scraped up the side of his leg. He maneuvered himself so he landed hard on his side, trying to avoid landing directly on his feet and snapping his ankles. The cut stung, but it could have been a hell of a lot worse.

There wasn't time to check himself over. He got to his feet and looked up at Bo, who stared down at him, the terror obvious on his face like someone who was about to jump to certain death. Brian lifted his hand up, motioning for Bo to drop the bone shard. He tossed it, almost throwing it over his brother's head, but thankfully, he caught it on its way by.

"Come on, Bo. We need to hurry. Jump down," Brian said, wanting to whisper but saying it loud enough for his brother to hear.

Bo's massive figure gave off an orange hue as the flames expanded behind him. The heat radiated off the home, creating a wave of blurry space between them. Even with the obstruction, his wide eyes stood out.

"Bo, jump!"

Finally, his brother dropped over the side, but unlike Brian, he missed most of the bush, landing awkwardly, his knee buckled. He cried out, landing face-first onto the ground. Brian ran to him, trying to help him up.

"We have to help Ron, let's go."

"My knee . . . It hurts bad, Brian."

"Can you stand on it?"

Bo grimaced as he stood and put weight on his leg. Brian

helped him out of the bushes and then looked up, ready to instruct his neighbor to jump next. Ron held his shotgun, preparing to leap, but that wasn't what Brian focused on. Behind him, the female member of the Hollow Souls stalked toward the old man. The blaze eating away at the house roared, drowning out any other sounds, allowing her to sneak up on him undetected.

"Watch out!" Brian yelled.

Ron turned just in time for her to reach up and squeeze his throat. He dropped the shotgun, which slid down the shingles and fell off the roof. Brian was helpless. All he could do was watch as the woman with snakes for hair continued to force the life out of the old man. Ron gasped, clutching at her black denim jacket as her eyes shimmered bright blue beneath the skull.

Brian realized there was no hope for Mr. Gould. He had to get Bo out of the open before Marcus found them. He wasn't even sure what to do with The Shard of Asha. All he knew was: it was the one thing that could rob the Hollow Souls of their powers. He just hoped that once they got the masks off—*if* they did—the mystical bone would do the work itself, similar to how it healed his legs.

"Bo, come. We need to go!"

He hesitated, watching Ron struggle with the woman above. Brian was losing patience. He pulled his brother by the arm toward the barn. The sky was dark but the fire lit it up like an eternal night-light. For the first time since they had come out of the house, Brian observed the yard. His eyes followed the chaos until they locked on the pigpen. It was one thing hearing them die, but it was another to see them all slaughtered across the mud like a war zone at the end of a surprise ambush.

Seeing the pigs reminded him that he hadn't checked on Astra yet. As if he didn't have enough motivation to get to the barn. Finally, Bo felt the urgency of his brother's plea and forced his eyes off the roof. Brian placed his brother's arm over his shoulder and helped him limp along. When they rounded the side of the house, the barn came into view. Brian's heart pumped so hard he heard it thrumming in his ears.

The doors were open.

Ron's vision blurred. This girl appeared small and weak but holy hell, was she strong. She had her hand wrapped so tightly around his throat that he thought his windpipe might tear. He needed to do something soon, or he was going to choke to death.

He removed one of his hands from the woman and reached into his chest pocket, feeling around. His hand landed on his pipe, and he clutched it tightly. The Medusa-looking bitch loosened her grip just a fraction and Ron took advantage, stepping back and driving the narrow end of the pipe into her right eye. An unnatural, guttural scream escaped her. Like an animal being disemboweled while alive. When her mouth opened, Ron saw she had no tongue. It looked like it had been ripped from her mouth, only a small nub remained. She let go of Ron to grab at her face, and he could have sworn he saw the snakes thrashing around as if they were feeling the same pain she was. Beneath her hand, the pipe hung from her eye, firmly planted into her socket. He had been through a lot with that pipe over the years, but he never expected it to save his life.

*Can't wait to tell Terry about this one. Bet she won't argue with me about smoking ever again.*

Ron inhaled deeply, taking in oxygen his lungs had been deprived of. Once he had his bearings back, he rushed at the woman, pushing her toward the edge of the roof. They collided, then both fell over the side, smashing onto the ground. The wind was knocked out of him, forcing Ron to once again gasp for breath. He turned to face the woman, only to find that she wasn't moving. Her mask was cracked, revealing part of her mouth. There was no way she was dead; the fall wasn't high enough. But she appeared unconscious, and that bought him some time to try and get to Brian and Bo —wherever they were. Ron crawled through the bushes, realizing how badly his body had been damaged from the fall. After hitting his head earlier in the barn, then hitting it again just now, he knew he definitely had a concussion. His brain was scrambled, trying to instruct him on what to do, but his body didn't want to listen. Each movement drained him of a little more energy. Eventually, he stopped. He needed to rest. He attempted a look back at the girl, but his vision faded, and then he passed out.

## 37

The barn door was open. Brian couldn't bring himself to walk forward, but he needed to know. He hadn't seen Marcus since the altercation in the house, and he hadn't seen the giant man at all since the Hollow Souls arrived. The only thing left in the barn . . . was Astra. At least the only thing *living*. Ma continued to sit in her rocker in the hayloft, rotting away while the rats and maggots consumed her. He struggled to get past the thought of going into the barn and not only possibly discovering that Astra had been harmed, but also willingly entering a space where the stench of his mother saturated the air.

"Be ready, Bo. They're in here, waiting for us."

"How do you know?"

"I can feel it. Can't you? Can't you hear the voices in your head?"

"I-I thought that was the chickens, Brian. I'm so sorry," Bo said, furrowing his brow.

"Oh, Bo. It's not your fault. It would confuse anyone to hear those sounds. Let's go save Astra."

Brian strode forward, prepared for the worst. When he entered the barn, the light from the fire behind him no longer lit his path well enough to see with any clarity. It was dark, with only thin beams of moonlight poking through the gaps in the wall of the loft above. He listened for Astra—a whinny, snort, anything—but only silence greeted him. His eyes gravitated toward her stall in the back, which appeared to be shut. From where Brian stood, the wall blocked the inside of her stall. Bo remained a few paces behind him, gripping his bat.

Something moved above them in the darkness of the loft. Brian realized how vulnerable he was with no gun or weapon and was relieved to find a pitchfork leaning against the wall next to the tractor attachments.

*A gun didn't stop Marcus. The tool used to clean up horse shit isn't going to do any better.*

He took another step forward. Only a few more feet and he'd discover the fate of his beloved horse. Why wasn't she making any sounds? She was full of personality—that was one of the traits Brian loved most about her. If she sensed him coming, she would never just remain silent. Maybe she really was depressed, like he feared. But that wasn't it. Something was wrong. He could feel it in his bones.

Finally, he reached the stall and peered inside. Astra remained upright, facing the wall.

"Thank God, Astra girl."

"Don't go thanking your God yet, Bry."

Marcus stepped out from the shadows in the corner of Astra's stall, holding a long butcher knife in hand. The cream-colored skull with the symbols of Dhat glowing on the forehead wrapped around his face, hiding his features. All except a set of piercing blue eyes.

"You got a pretty horse here, Bry. Now, I don't think you cared about those piggies out there too much, but I know how much you *love* this horse. I can smell the fear wafting out of your pores while you stare at this blade, knowing that I could gut her in seconds. Give me the bone, or I'll slice her from throat to asshole."

*Don't look into his eyes.*

The more he told himself that, the more his attention focused on the glowing blue orbs resting inside the skull.

"We both know damn well that whether I give you the shard or not, you'll try to kill us all. Why should I listen to you?"

Marcus laughed and moved closer.

"You're dumber than your daddy was, boy."

He raised the blade, ready to cut into Astra, and Brian could no longer keep up with the tough guy act.

"No! Stop. Please!"

"You know . . . they say the soul of a horse is majestic. That they're one of the most spiritual animals walking the planet. I bet her soul would taste . . . *wonderful.*"

"Please! I'll give it to you! Just stop!" Brian exclaimed, finding it difficult to breathe. When Marcus lowered the knife, he took a deep breath and continued. "Why do you do this? Why kill innocent people? My dad was a good man. He said you sought him out, not the other way around. At least tell me *why.*"

Even while saying it, Brian realized how dumb he sounded. Giving Marcus The Shard of Asha would seal their fate. He'd have what he needed, and he'd kill every living thing on the farm before leaving. It didn't matter why Marcus did it. Yet Brian needed to know. He needed to have a reason for why his once-happy family crumbled in the span of weeks after his dad met Marcus.

"Your daddy used to ask me why we did what we did. In the end, he was selfish like the rest of the world, too worried about making sure his own family benefited, even at the expense of others. But I never told him why, so I suppose I might as well tell you since you got a bit of us inside you now.

"Back in seventy-eight, I was stationed in Pakistan. We were there to aid them, believe it or not. Gotta love it when the Soviets can bring two enemies together, am I right? Anyway, we weren't active combat, per se, just there to provide supplies and help train, more or less. But that didn't stop some blood from being shed. I was wounded, left for dead by my own team. Then one of the Pakistani soldiers I helped train came to my rescue. His name was Imran. Good, young kid. He realized traditional medicine wouldn't save me, so he told me about Dhat and that he knew a man in one of the local villages who studied folklore and might be able to help me. I thought Imran sounded like a crazy motherfucker, but I was desperate, could feel the life draining out of me. Every culture has its own version of the boogeyman, and Dhat was that for this village.

"But what most people feared, this old man that Imran brought me to, worshipped. Imran told him how I helped him and his fellow soldiers, which in turn, helped the village. That's what convinced the folklorist to use The Shard of Asha on me. He taught me their ways, how to speak to Dhat. Even said it was an evil entity or some syndrome that people came down with when they lost their desire to live. The rest of the village feared Dhat. They just didn't know it like we did—like

*I did*—and didn't understand the true meaning of the deity that is Dhat and how to use its powers as strength. The only problem was that the old man didn't want to part ways with the shard after he healed me. I didn't like that so much. He couldn't have had much longer to live anyway, so I did him a favor by taking his soul," Marcus said, then winked one of his glowing blue eyes.

"So, you view me much like those villagers viewed Dhat—as a monster that sucked souls from the living. But when my people, my fellow fucking soldiers, left me for dead, Dhat was there for me."

"Understand, Bry, I'll do whatever it takes to get The Shard of Asha back. You love this horse, but it pales in comparison to what that bone means to me."

Marcus petted Astra, and Brian felt every muscle in his body tighten.

"But . . . I know this horse isn't the only thing in this barn that you boys love."

*What is he talking about?*

Marcus looked up at the ceiling in the stall and laughed again. The floorboards above vibrated as thundering steps moved across the hayloft, sending dust motes floating down into the darkness.

"You're some sick fucks keeping your dead mama up there like that. Too bad I couldn't give her a proper send-off before she died after the shit she pulled on us. But she's got some company up there now, so your dumb oaf of a brother doesn't have to worry."

Before Brian could stop him, Bo backed away from the stall, limping toward the ladder.

"Bo, stop! They want to get in our heads. Don't listen to them."

"I'd say we're already in your heads, kid. Your mother's already dead. Don't make me add your horse to the tally."

Brian was stuck. He wanted to stop Bo from climbing to the loft, knowing the giant of a man Marcus had up there waiting for him in the dark. He knew if he followed his brother, Astra was as good as dead, and that Marcus would follow right behind to finish him off as well. There was no stopping Bo, not when it came to Ma. Brian turned back to face Marcus and stumbled backward as the skull mask was now mere inches from his face.

Marcus forced the stall door open, driving it into Brian's stomach and sending him to the floor. He stepped out of the stall. Astra lashed around frantically, whinnying as she tried to break her lead free from the wall. Marcus ignored her and closed in on Brian.

The pain shooting through his abdomen burned his insides. He tried to get to his feet, but Marcus lifted his foot and shoved it onto Brian's face, sending him back down. Through the open barn doors, Brian could see that the fire had completely engulfed his home. There was nothing left except for the charred carcass of the house, with flames that reached for the sky, growing and stretching for the barn. The dark structure was quickly illuminated as the fire spread toward them. Brian stared at the image of Marcus, his skull mask and blue eyes towering over him with a background summoned straight from hell.

"Give me the damn shard, Brian."

He winced, grabbing at his stomach with one hand,

clutching The Shard of Asha with the other. As Marcus approached him, Brian noticed movement at the barn doors. He assumed it was Bo, but his brother was already climbing the ladder to the loft. It was Ron Gould, hobbling along, his shotgun hung loosely in one hand. He lifted the weapon, aiming at Marcus's back.

*Holy shit, he's going to do it. Shoot him!*

The old man steadied his aim, preparing to take the shot.

And then another figure appeared behind Ron—the woman with the snake hair.

"Look out!" Brian yelled.

Both Ron and Marcus turned as the woman swiped at the shotgun. A deafening blast exploded through the barn, followed by a hole splintering through the ceiling. Brian took advantage of the distraction, grabbing the pitchfork and driving it into Marcus's midsection. The tines impaled flesh for a few inches before meeting resistance. Marcus turned back to Brian in shock, the blue spark in his eyes fluttering.

"You—"

Brian forced the tool deeper, pushing through the restriction until the tines were all the way in. Blood spattered from Marcus's mouth, spraying Brian in the face. He didn't care. Instead, he twisted until the metal twisted no more. He let go of the handle and reached for the skull mask. But when he met Marcus's glare, he backed up.

The Hollow Souls' leader was smiling, his bloody mouth inside the skull turned up in that sinister grin that had haunted Brian since childhood. The faded blue eyes sparked back to life, and Marcus grabbed hold of the pitchfork, pulling it out. Blood spouted from the fresh wound, but Marcus showed no indication of concern. Brian charged, but Marcus swung the handle of the tool, striking Brian on the side of the face. He flew into one of the empty stalls to his right, smashing off the wall and landing on the floor, unable to move.

# 38

Bo reached the top of the hayloft, panting for breath as he set the bat down on the floor. While the bottom level had some light provided by the glow from the house fire, the loft remained dark, blocked off from the rest of the world. He couldn't let anything happen to Ma. Not after everything she had been through to protect them.

The first thing he noticed was the smell. She needed to be cleaned as soon as this was over. He wanted to remember her telltale scent that he grew up smelling. Her shampoo, the cinnamon hard candies she was always sucking on. This . . . this wasn't what she would want people to remember.

He reminded himself of why he was up here: to look for the intruder who threatened her. The thought of it twisted his insides, and he grabbed the bat and walked toward the back where he had placed Ma to rest—his happy place. There was a support wall that blocked the back corner where her rocking chair sat, with row after row of hay bales stacked almost to the ceiling. Bo didn't hear anyone moving, not Ma or the Hollow Soul. He paused and listened closely. Something scampered from the shadows, out of sight. As he raised the bat, prepared to strike, another movement flashed from the opposite side of the loft, coming at him from behind a stack of hay.

A huge man wearing a skull mask and a long black jacket stormed toward him. His arms were chiseled, tensing up beneath the fabric as he prepared to strike. It was one of the skeleton people from his dreams.

Bo was well over six feet, but this monster towered over him. As the man lifted his arms, Bo remembered he had the baseball bat. He swung the metal into the giant's midsection, the bat clanking off something beneath his coat. The man grunted, but it only slowed him down for a second. Bo tried to swing again, and the man caught the bat with his massive hand, tossing it away with ease. Then he was on Bo, grabbing him by the throat, forcing him back against the dividing wall. The wood cracked but didn't give, so the man rammed him into it again. Bales of hay toppled to the floor around them.

Bo didn't want to hurt anyone, but this man was trying to kill him. And Ma warned him about these people. Whether Brian thought she really talked to him or not, Bo knew the truth. Ma was watching over her sons—her soul was all around them. He couldn't let the skeleton people win.

As the monster tugged Bo away from the wall, preparing to slam him against it once more, Bo drove his fist into the man's wrist as hard as he could, hearing the bone *crunch* on impact. The man howled beneath his mask, but it quickly turned into a growl. The monster used his remaining good hand and drove Bo into the dividing wall again, splitting the wood down the middle. Both men fell through to the other side, landing hard on a pile of jagged boards. Stacks of hay bales collapsed on top of them.

Panic sprouted up through Bo's chest and into his throat as he attempted to see through the countless rectangles of hay that now covered him. He couldn't find the skull-man, who could be anywhere. Coming for him. Or worse, doing something to Ma.

Bo pushed up through the hay, getting pricked and poked along the way. It was like swimming through a pool of dry grass. Finally, he broke the surface, taking in large gasps of air. He blinked away the stray strands poking into his eyes.

When he cleared them enough, he looked up and spotted Ma sitting in her rocker, head hanging to the side, her throat chewed out. The tail of a rat thrashed from side to side within her exposed windpipe, feasting on her.

"Ma!"

He tossed bales of hay left and right, stepping through the piles to get to her corpse. He was so distracted by her that he didn't notice the movement beneath a pile behind him.

As he reached Ma, the big man shot out of the sea of rustic green and brown, grabbing hold of Bo's ankle. He tried to kick the hand loose, but the man's grip was ironclad. Fingers squeezed into his skin, sending stabbing pain through his joint. All Bo could think about was saving his mother from the rats, and this man was doing everything he could to prevent it.

The monster squeezed until his fingers penetrated the skin, sinking deeper into the flesh, all the way to his knuckles. Bo's leg felt like it was on fire. He yelled, as much in frustration as in pain, and then stomped down on the skull-man's hand with his other foot. Finally, the grip loosened, which allowed Bo to pull free, but not until the skin tore away from his bone as the man's fingers tried to cling to his ankle.

"Let. Me. Go!" Bo shouted.

He backed away from the skull-man, inching closer to his mother. Behind the giant, the orange glow had started to light the loft as the fire spread to the barn. The man's silhouette was enormous. For the first time, Bo noticed that the skull didn't have a lower jaw attached to it, that it was the man's actual mouth showing beneath.

Looking at the skull with its orange hue, Bo remembered what his brother told him earlier. *If one of them comes after you, do whatever you can to get the mask off and destroy it.* But the skull-man wasn't going to make it easy. Still, the only way he could save Ma from the fire and the rats was to get rid of this behemoth first.

The two giants marched toward each other as the rodents chittered, swarming around them to protect their food source. Bo collided with the skull-man, throwing a fist, aiming for his exposed mouth. The punch connected, whipping the man's head to the side. Both of the skull-man's hands appeared to be broken, dangling lazily from each arm. It should have been enough to stop this monster from attacking, yet it appeared to agitate him more than anything. His eyes glowed a fiery blue as he refocused to stare at Bo, who threw another punch.

This time, the henchman moved just enough so Bo's fist collided with the skull mask; his knuckles cracked on impact. He tried to shake off the pain and punch again, but the monster was ready this time. He reared back and headbutted Bo on the nose, instantly breaking it. He stumbled back a few feet, and the giant charged, spearing his shoulder into Bo's ribs as both men went airborne toward Ma's corpse. They landed a few feet from her, and the rats squealed in anger as they scattered beneath the hay spread across the floor. The skull-man mounted Bo, then repeatedly elbowed him in the face, each strike connecting with the force of a cement block.

Stars scattered through Bo's vision, and with each hit, he felt himself giving in to the darkness that surrounded his peripheral vision. The titan threw another elbow, connecting with his already broken nose, which snapped his head to the side. His eyes locked on Ma, who he felt watching him, *judging* him. *Did her eyes just move?* As the giant raised his arm again, prepared to strike with the killing blow, Bo shoved his thumbs into the blue eyes, gouging as far as they would go. The skull-man's mouth opened wide to scream, and Bo realized that he didn't have a tongue. It was just a mouth filled with uneven teeth, which blocked the black hole behind. Bo pushed his thumbs in deeper.

When the Hollow Soul screamed again, Bo pulled his fingers out, swiping at the mask. He wrapped his hand around the skull's teeth and pulled up, yanking it free. The man's face was hideous, with dark circles pressing so deep into the top of his cheeks that it was a wonder his face hadn't caved in. The pruney skin gave off a decaying stench that matched Ma's body. Years of wearing the skull had apparently reshaped the man's face beneath, taking on the appearance of the skeleton. He opened his tongueless mouth and let out a guttural cry as the blue spark in his eyes faded.

Bo struck him in the face, sending his towering frame to the rodent-infested floor. The rats—which had continuously attempted resuming their meal—smelled a new, *fresher* source of food. The odor of the big man's face attracted them, and they shifted their attention, scurrying toward him. They bit and clawed, climbing up his arms and legs until they covered his face, digging and scraping into the pruney flesh. He screamed, swatting at them with his broken hands.

Bo backed away in a crab-walk, bumping into his mother's chair. His eyes were glued to the horrific scene of rats feasting on a living person. Just when Bo thought they were going to conquer the skull-man and devour him into an actual skeleton, the giant turned to his stomach and pushed up with his elbows, getting to his feet. The rats didn't even register that their new victim had moved, digging their way up his legs, burrowing beneath his jacket and shirt. The sound of them clawing at his midsection was nauseating, but not nearly as sickening as the pained cries coming from the man. Bo could no longer see his face, just a ball of rats clinging to his loose skin, digging in.

The skull-man stumbled through the hay, swatting at the vermin to no avail. As he neared the edge of the loft, Bo saw his opportunity. He got to his feet, quickly checking to make sure Ma was still watching, then paced toward the giant. He was now only five feet from the edge, but he dropped to his knees, tearing off two rats at the same time and tossing them over the side. For a brief second, his blue eyes shone through, and Bo ran at him.

The behemoth's scream was cut short as another rat filled the empty space, and Bo collided with him, sending him tumbling back to the edge. He tried to regain his balance, but he swayed backward as the rats continued to devour his face. Bo spotted the baseball bat on the floor amid the hay and grabbed it.

With the Hollow Soul unable to see what was coming, Bo reared back and swung the bat as hard as he could. The metal connected with the skull-man's temple, sending him to the floor below. Bo ran to the edge of the loft and peered over, witnessing him landing on the round hay rake attachment. The sharp tips stabbed through his chest, spraying blood all around him. The giant tried to lift his head, but it flopped back down as blood pooled in his mouth and dribbled down his shredded face. The remaining blue of his eyes faded to black, and his body stopped moving.

Bo just killed a man. His chest tightened. Even though he knew it was the right thing to do, he felt awful. The flames had spread across the barn floor, working their way toward the first stall. The entire farmhouse was up in flames, and the barn was about to be right there with it. They had to get out.

"Ma!"

Bo wasn't leaving the barn until he got his mother out safely. He gave one last look at the dead man below and turned back to Ma. He'd kill every damn rat if he had to.

## 39

Brian opened his eyes to a throbbing pain on the side of his face and a bright orange glow surrounding him. He looked around and realized he was in an empty stall, tied to the wall with one of the horse leads. Both of his hands were bunched together above his head. He tried to pull them free, only to be met with searing pain as the thick rope pressed into his skin.

"You're not going anywhere, Chief. Thanks for getting this back to me, though," Marcus said as he came into view holding The Shard of Asha. "Sorry about your house. Suppose it won't do you much good once you and your stupid brother are dead anyway."

"Fuck you."

"Fuck me? Listen, kid. I really liked you. Your daddy was a loser, and your brother's slow in the head, but you? I saw potential. I don't say that lightly. There's a reason I've had the same two followers all these years. They dedicated their lives to me. To Dhat. I thought you might be next in line. Clearly, I was wrong. So while your house burns down, and I kill everyone and everything you care about, remember that. It wasn't personal . . . until you made it personal."

"I'm going to kill you. I'm going to end your pathetic little group."

"Tough talk from a guy who's bound to the wall. I'm going to enjoy draining the soul from your body. But first, I'm going to make you watch while I take your horse, your brother, and the old man. Hang tight, the show's about to begin."

The flames danced around the barn, spreading by the second. Marcus, the orange glow intensifying the features of his skull mask, didn't seem to care. He disappeared from the stall. As soon as he was out of sight, Brian went to work on his hands again. He pulled, he twisted, ignoring the rope sliding across his raw skin.

Astra whinnied from her stall, loud enough to let Brian know it wasn't just a normal attempt to communicate. She was scared. The fire crackled and popped, eating away at the aged wood like it was a light snack. Where was Bo? Where was Mr. Gould? The last he saw of Ron was the snake woman attacking him. They struggled in the doorway, that area now engulfed in flames. And Bo? He had climbed to the hayloft to go after the big man.

Something slammed near the farm equipment. Brian tried to move forward to get a look, but the lead rope only reached a few feet. He wasn't sure if it was Ron or Bo, but the loud commotion likely meant something had happened to one of them. Brian understood that if he didn't escape his current situation, they were all going to die.

## The Devil's in the Next Room

While Bo and the big man clashed above, Ron had climbed to his feet, reaching for his shotgun, but the snake woman wouldn't allow it. She kicked the gun out of reach and then kicked him. Her foot landed squarely on his ribs, and he felt a snap upon impact. She stared down at him through her cracked mask. Her blue eye now pulsated, almost blinding him. Even with her face covered, he knew she was enraged. She kicked him in the ribs again. He rolled onto his back, wheezing for air. As he prepared for death, he thought of Terry and how he wished she had tried just a little bit harder to stop him from coming here. He didn't want to die without saying how sorry he was for not listening, for not minding his own business and letting the Davidson family deal with their troubles.

Ron was a good twenty feet from the fiery doors, but he still felt the heat radiating through the interior. The snake woman prepared to kick him a third time when a massive object came flying down from the loft. It took a second, but Ron realized it was the third member of the Hollow Souls—the titan that Ron hadn't gotten a good look at until this moment. The hay rake attachment impaled him through the back, ripping up through his chest. The fire lit his facial features as he lifted his head in shock, and Ron thought he was one of the ugliest sons of bitches he'd ever seen.

The snake woman turned to see what caused the commotion, and Ron took advantage. He crawled to the shotgun, shocked to actually reach it without her stopping him this time. As he rolled onto his back, ready to fire, the snake woman returned her focus to him. This time, Ron didn't miss. He pulled the trigger, watching as the right side of her head exploded. The skull mask shattered, falling to the floor in pieces. The woman let out half a scream, her mouth opening wide, then she collapsed and went limp.

Ron fell back, letting his head hit the floor as he took a few shallow breaths. Two of the killers were now dead. There was one left.

As if the thought of the Hollow Souls' leader conjured him from the depths of hell, when Ron sat up, he saw Marcus coming toward him from the stall where he had untied Astra, intending to bring the horse out and slit her throat in front of Brian. The man was so focused on the commotion from the gunshot that he forgot to shut the stall door. Ron had just enough time to see the horse exiting the stall behind Marcus before he reached down and grabbed the old man by the shirt, lifting him off the ground with ease.

Everything happened so fast. The crash over by the farm equipment, the gunshot blasting through the barn, and Marcus speeding back past the stall Brian was held captive in. He had been ready to give up only seconds before but found a new sense of purpose. He forced himself to his feet and turned toward the wall to get a better look at the knot holding his wrists together. Marcus did a far superior job than Bo had done at making sure he couldn't escape. Still, he couldn't give up. Not after everything these monsters had done to their family. He needed to redeem himself to Ma, to Bo, even to Dad, who died because he was trying to help the family.

Brian's heart sank when a sound behind him let him know he wasn't alone. He turned expecting to find Marcus, but instead stared back at Astra. She wasn't hurt. At least not yet.

"Come here, girl," Brian whispered, clicking his tongue.

Astra entered the stall silently, as though she knew making any noise would alert Marcus that she was moving. She approached Brian cautiously, and all he wanted to do was reach out and pet her. He looked into her eyes, and there was something in them that he had never noticed before. He was hit with a bout of lightheadedness, leaning against the wall to stop himself from falling over. As he stared into her eyes, watching the blue shimmer behind the enlarged black pupils, he understood the reason for their change to such a unique color years ago. From reading about The Shard of Asha and Dhat, he knew a part of someone's soul could be transferred to the bone, and not just to the shard, but to other living creatures. It was how the Hollow Souls had transferred some of their strength to Bo in the woods.

It was also how Ma had transferred part of her soul to Astra. They were Ma's eyes.

"Ma . . . why?"

The horse nudged him with her nose, and Brian stared at her as tears poured down his face. She nudged him again, and he understood that she was trying to get him to look toward the wall, just out of reach. At first, he didn't know what she was going on about, but then he saw it. With a flickering flame lighting up the wall briefly, Brian spotted a nail protruding out of the support beam. They used to hang extra leads from it, but in the dark, it was easy to miss. There was no way in hell Marcus would have tied him up in that stall if he had seen it.

If Brian could just reach the nail, he could attempt to cut through the rope before Marcus came back. The barn was starting to fill with smoke, making it difficult to see. Brian pulled at the rope, praying it reached the nail. To his surprise, it did, with a few inches to spare.

*Thank God.*

He went to work, forcing the nail between two loops of the lead, then aggressively rubbed the rope back and forth. It only took a few passes to start tearing the fibers, sending up loose threads of the rope resembling frizzy strands of hair. His wrists burned, but he fought through it, trying to limit taking too many deep breaths as the smoke thickened. He thought of Bo up in the loft where the smoke rose, likely creating an intolerable environment.

The first bind ripped. Astra stood by his side while he continued sawing the rope, and then a second bind released. Brian wiggled his hands and finally got them free, dropping the lead to the ground. He turned, shaking the numbness from his arms, and leaned his forehead on Astra's nose.

"Thank you."

Now it was time to stop Marcus, or die trying.

# 40

As soon as he exited the stall, Brian realized just how bad the fire had spread. At this point, there was no escaping through the main doors. If they were going to escape, they would have to go through the back exit, which so far hadn't ignited. But that would change fast because all the hay above was in the rear of the loft, and once that lit, goodbye barn.

Through the smoke, he spotted the outline of Marcus holding Ron. He approached quietly, not that he needed to with the roaring sound of the flames. A charred board dropped from the ceiling, landing a few feet in front of Brian. He jumped back with a start, then looked up to make sure there was no more falling timber on the way down. It was pointless. Anything a few feet above him was a dense cloud of smoke.

*I need to get Bo. He's going to die up there. If he hasn't already.*

*I've failed him again.*

He couldn't allow himself to get caught up in those

thoughts. Not right now. He needed to take care of Marcus first. As he got closer, he heard his voice.

"Your wife suffered dearly, old man. She had spunk, but I made sure to drain that along with her soul. Now it's time for you to join her."

Ron didn't respond but instead let out a violent cough as the smoke suffocated him. It appeared that Marcus was somehow immune to the smoke. Before Brian could reach him, Marcus started the ritual. Ron's eyes expanded wide, wide enough for Brian to see the fear through the smoldering cloud. Marcus gripped the old man's mouth, forcing his jaws to spread. Ron screamed as Marcus stretched it beyond its normal capacity. Brian had to do something or Ron was going to die. His neighbor's cheeks clung to his jawbone, sucking inward as his soul was depleted. Brian moved, and once he got closer, he spotted The Shard of Asha stuffed in the back pocket of Marcus's jeans.

Ron gargled on something, fighting for breath.

Brian picked up the shotgun from the floor and swung it at the back of Marcus's head. The butt snapped upon impact with his skull, and Ron dropped to the floor. Brian quickly reached out and grabbed the shard from Marcus's pants as he stumbled, turning to see what had struck him. The smoke hid most of the skull, but the blue eyes burned through the cloud, locking on Brian.

"You son of a bitch."

Marcus lunged at Brian but didn't see The Shard of Asha in his hand. As the Hollow Souls' leader reached him, Brian drove the sharp tip of the bone into Marcus's chest. His entire body went stiff as glowing blue lines appeared beneath his skin. Brian tore the skull mask off his face to reveal a look of shock. Marcus had no idea that Brian had grabbed the shard, and now it was too late. Unlike the pitchfork earlier, there would be no ripping this free and living to tell about it.

The Shard of Asha suddenly lit up, the intricate symbols Brian had noticed earlier now pulsated as the light traveled through Marcus and into the bone. Marcus swayed, trying to remain on his feet. His skin rippled, his face caving in. Brian backed away, rubbing at his stinging eyes as smoke coated his corneas. Marcus tried to step forward but dropped to one knee. He pulled at the shard, trying to dislodge it from his chest. This time, he didn't possess the strength to do it. He fell to his side, grasping at the bone, choking on blood.

Brian continued to back up until he bumped into something. He spun around expecting one of the Hollow Souls but was relieved to find Astra. He tried to hug her, but the horse pushed past him.

*What the hell is she doing?*

As Marcus clung to the shard, fighting for his life, Astra stopped when she reached his body. Brian wasn't sure what she was doing, but then she whinnied, reared up on her hind legs, and drove her front hooves into Marcus's face. His body stopped moving. Astra backed away, leaving a bloody mess in her wake. His face was gone, replaced by a pulpy pile of gore.

Brian remained frozen in shock. His body wanted to give up and drop to the floor, just go to sleep and never wake up. The smoke was so thick, draining the limited energy he had left. Then half of the loft collapsed behind him; the flames had reached the peak of the ceiling. Floorboards dropped from above, crashing into the stalls in a fiery explosion.

*Bo!*

Brian stepped over Marcus's dead body and ran for the ladder, but he had a feeling he was already too late. Ron gasped from the floor, reaching for the sky. The last thing Brian wanted to do was stop and check on him, but the old man had put his life on the line to stand his ground with the two brothers. Brian owed it to him.

"Can you move, Ron?"

"I . . . I can't feel my face."

Brian leaned and grabbed Ron by the shirt, shaking him.

"Snap out of it, man! Can you move? We need to get out of here, but we can't go through the front door. I'm not sure I can drag you all the way to the back, especially across the collapsed boards."

It was pointless. Ron was dazed, hardly able to even lift his head. While he was lucky to still be alive, Marcus had drained some of his soul, weakening him to the point that he was as sick as Ma right before she died. Brian had to decide whether to leave him here until he got back from checking on Bo or to help him out of the barn first.

Astra snorted behind him. He realized she was trying to talk to him again. Ma's soul was still in there somewhere. Brian bent at the knees, struggling to pull Ron up. The old man was much heavier than he looked, but finally Brian got him to his feet. Ron swayed, and if he let go, Brian knew his neighbor would collapse again. There was no way he could get Ron up onto Astra's back by himself. Just then, his horse kneeled like a trained professional, dropping her front legs low.

He pushed Ron's dead weight over the back of the horse

horizontally, careful to make sure he didn't drop off the other side. When he felt it was safe, he backed away and clicked his tongue. Astra stood to her full height and turned around, heading through the cloud of smoke toward the back door. Brian didn't wait to see if they made it out. He ran to the ladder, which somehow still hadn't caught fire, and climbed rung by rung until he reached the top. With his upper half above the loft floor, he tried to see the back where Bo kept all his private stuff.

"Bo! Are you okay? We need to go!"

The smoke was even thicker up here, making it so Brian couldn't even see a foot in front of him. The floor was a maze of flames and broken boards. Dead rats lay scattered everywhere, their bodies charred to a crisp.

There was no sign of Bo.

Brian climbed all the way up and walked toward the back corner, covering his mouth with his shirt to try and stop some of the smoke from infiltrating his lungs. He crouched as low as he could, but it didn't make a difference. The smoke was thick from floor to ceiling. And many of the rafters were burning. Brian stepped over flames that tried to latch onto him like venomous fangs. The deeper he went, the more he realized how much of a lost cause it was. There was no way anyone could possibly survive these conditions. Any wrong step and his foot would fall through the floor, likely taking him with it.

When he reached the back corner, a wall of hay had caught fire, creating an impossible impasse. He had to turn around. Then he spotted movement behind the fire, coming from the corner.

"Bo! Can you hear me?"

"Brian!"

He sped forward to the fire, finally seeing his brother behind the flames. Bo sat next to Ma's rocker, hugging his knees with her corpse spread across his lap.

"We need to go! Now! I need you to run through, Bo!"

The fire was ferocious, sounding more like a running waterfall than flames.

"I can't leave Ma! I need to get her out of here, Brian!"

"It's too late! She's already gone! Please, Bo. You're going to die if we don't get you out of here now!"

Brian thought of all the times he had failed Bo over the years. From the jealousy he felt every time the crowd cheered for him at baseball games, to the attention he stole from their parents. None of it was his brother's fault. Brian tried to make up for it in later years, going above and beyond to take care of Ma and Bo, sacrificing a normal life to make sure he lived comfortably with his condition. But he knew deep down he did it out of guilt. Every time he had a chance to do the right thing, he failed Bo. He wasn't about to do it again.

He looked for the weakest spot in the fire, and without hesitation, he sprinted through, rolling to the floor to put out the flames rising up his pant leg. When he sat up, he stifled a scream. Ma's ravaged body had been torn to shreds by the rats. Her eyes were gone. Her throat and stomach were open wide, displaying what little remains she had left. Brian leaned over and vomited. Then the smell hit him. With the fire heating it up like an oven, the rot was severe, causing his eyes to water. Yet Bo just sat there, rocking with her like he was singing her a lullaby.

"Bo, she's gone, bud. We have to get out of here now. Please, come with me."

"I can't leave her. She'd never leave us, Brian. Help me get her out!"

"You're not thinking logically. She's dead! You need to see that. If we don't leave the barn, we'll be dead along with her."

"Then that's what I want. I want to be with her."

Brian closed his eyes and squeezed out tears. He couldn't just leave Bo for dead. He had to try. He got to his feet and pulled on his brother's arm. At first, he thought Bo was going to allow it, but then he shoved Brian in the chest, sending him stumbling onto his backside close to the wall of flames.

"Bo! What the fuck are you doing? Ma's spirit is still with us. It's not in her body anymore. She . . . she's in Astra! I saw it with my own eyes. I'll show you!"

Bo looked at him, confused. Then he shook his head as if he'd caught Brian trying to trick him again, just like he had so many times when they were younger.

"No! She's right here. I can see her. I can touch her. And I won't leave her, Brian. You can't make me."

"*Please*," Brian whispered, more to himself than Bo.

And then he understood. Bo was too far gone. The loss of their mother was what sent him over the edge, and there was no coming back. If he stayed another minute longer, he was going to die. Even if Bo survived, what were the odds he would be able to live without being institutionalized?

"Just go! Ma wants you to get out alive. She told me so. I'll be okay here, Brian. I promise."

Brian noticed a single tear slide down his brother's cheek as he continued rocking back and forth.

He had to go. He got to his feet.

"I love you, Bo. I'm so sorry. For everything."

"I love you too."

A piece of the wall collapsed between them, the flames swirling up to reach the ceiling. Brian was never going to see his brother again. He turned and found a weak point in the fire, then jumped through. The hair on his arms singed and his lungs burned, but he made it. When he reached the ladder, he saw that the bottom few rungs had finally caught fire as the flames worked their way up. Brian climbed down the first few, getting to where he felt comfortable jumping, then fell the rest of the way. He weaved through the debris, avoiding the biggest flames, losing oxygen by the second. It was a miracle he had even lasted this long with how much smoke filled the space. He ran past what was left of Marcus's body as the flames melted through his skin.

Once he saw the back door, relief flooded him, and he picked up the pace until he fell through the opening onto the grass beyond. He crawled far enough away from the barn, listening to the structure cave in on itself, knowing Bo was still inside. His heart ached. Everyone he ever loved was now dead. And in a way, every single one of those deaths was on his hands. He wished he could've stopped his dad from talking to Marcus that first time, preventing them from ever learning of the Hollow Souls.

Something crunched behind him, and he turned to find Astra walking toward him from the tall grass, looking as majestic as ever. Ron was no longer on her back, but Brian had no doubt that she saved the old man. He got to his feet and embraced the horse.

"I'm so sorry, Ma. He wouldn't listen."

Astra nudged him with her head as if to say, "It's okay. You tried."

The Hollow Souls were no more. Neither was the Davidson farm nor the Davidson family. After all they had been through, Brian couldn't help but feel he had the hollowest soul of all.

After many excruciating hours of watching firefighters do their job and answering police questions, Brian finally motivated himself to sift through the carcass of what was once their barn. As he approached the charred heap, he saw Ron strapped to a stretcher, receiving medical treatment near an ambulance. Before he went to the barn, he wanted to see how Mr. Gould was doing.

As he got closer, he realized how bad the old man looked. An oxygen mask covered much of his face, but his eyes were bloodshot, his skin an unhealthy off-white that was covered in soot.

"Hey, Ron. How you holding up?"

His neighbor pulled down the oxygen mask, and a male EMT with a stern look stepped up.

"Hey, hey. Leave that on, sir. You need all the oxygen you can get right now."

"Just a sec. I survived this shitshow, I can survive another minute without a mask."

The EMT shook his head and went back to whatever he was doing in the back of the ambulance.

"I see you still got your charming personality," Brian said, forcing a smile.

"I'll be okay. At least as far as recovering physically. Mentally . . . They took my Terry, Brian. Those sons of bitches killed her. Over the last forty years, I haven't gone a day being away from her for more than a few hours."

Brian didn't know what to say. While he himself had lost his entire family through all this, Ron was never supposed to be involved. He tried to help and lost his wife because of it.

"I'm so sorry, Ron. I owe you my life. If there's anything I can do, anything at all . . ."

"We got rid of them. That's all I would have asked. And please don't feel guilty about what happened to Terry or me. You were just a boy when all this started. There was no way for you to avoid this. I can see the guilt in your eyes. We all have our demons, kid. But you have a good heart. Plus, those evil bastards would have stopped by my farm whether I helped you or not. At least by being here, I got to avenge my wife, you know?"

Brian nodded, but he thought it would take a very long time to unburden the guilt inside him. Mr. Gould didn't know the whole story.

"Thank you, Ron. Make sure these people take care of you. I have something I need to do."

"If he wants us to take care of him, he can start by putting the mask back on," the EMT said from the ambulance.

Ron chuckled and pulled it back over his face, then gave his neighbor a slight wave. Brian turned back toward the rubble that was still smoking, emitting the smell of a bonfire rendered impotent after being doused by a thousand gallons of water. As he got closer to the mess, a firefighter approached him.

"I wouldn't go in there, man. The fire's out, but that shit would still burn you if you touched it."

"I'll be careful. There's something I need to do."

The firefighter didn't look thrilled, but he didn't push it either. Brian stepped through the rubble carefully, avoiding the smoking timber as best he could. He knew if the police saw him going through evidence, they would likely put a stop to it, but they were over by their cruisers, taking a breather from the unhealthy air hovering over what used to be the farmhouse and barn. Brian made it back to the area where Astra's stall used to be, then crouched near a pile of blackened boards.

This was where Marcus died.

Brian made sure nobody was looking in his direction and moved some of the debris with his boot. It didn't take long for him to find what he was looking for. The Shard of Asha remained white in a pile of darkness. He reached for it but pulled his hand back when he felt the heat radiating off it. He took off his button-up shirt and wrapped it around the bone. He pulled it close to him, allowing the warmth from it to make up for the fact that he was now only wearing a T-shirt on the chilly autumn night.

He walked toward the back area of the barn and climbed out that way to avoid the crowd of cops and firefighters. When he reached the spot where he had rested while waiting for help to arrive, he spotted Astra roaming in the tall grass. Brian decided in that moment that he would bury the relic just like Ma did to protect the family. Marcus was dead, and he would make sure that nobody ever found the shard again.

All the tack was destroyed by the fire, but that wouldn't stop Brian from riding his horse.

He climbed up on Astra and wrapped his arms around her neck, then clicked his tongue. She took off slowly toward the family cemetery, where Brian could bury The Shard of Asha and his family's secrets once more.

**THE END**

September 1, 2024—February 17, 2025

# Acknowledgments

There are many thanks I want to give for this book. First, as always, I want to thank my wife and kids. With each new book, project, etc., I'm finding that my writing blocks for an hour or so at night aren't cutting it anymore. I've started squeezing in more writing time on the weekends when my family isn't sleeping, and besides my six-year-old daughter continuously coming up to my keyboard and typing so she can see letters fly across the screen, they tend to leave me alone when I ask.

Next, I want to thank the team that helped this project come to life. Christian Bentulan knocked it out of the park with the cover art. Any time I post about the book, I get multiple compliments on the cover. My editor, Danielle Yaeger, continues to be the perfect editor for my work. She catches many things I miss, beyond just your typical copy edit fixes. For example, I haven't owned a horse since I was a kid, so the terminology was erased from my brain years ago, but she let me know exactly how wrong I was with some descriptions. She works efficiently, is very available for any questions, and someone I depend on a lot. I also want to thank my beta readers, Ali Jane Sweet and Heather Ann Larson. Again, these two caught so many things for me to fix, big and small, that helped this novel improve significantly.

Steven Pajak worked his magic with the interior formatting, making sure the inside is just as beautiful as the outside of the book. Thank you to all my ARC readers for taking the time to read the book early and leaving advance reviews to help make sure this book gets some early attention. As always, thanks to my crew of author friends for keeping me sane and providing feedback along the way. Nick, Felix, Gage, Lynch, and Jay. I talk to these guys every single day and learn from them as much as I laugh with them.

Thank you to my patrons who continue to support me and my journey as an author. I hope the content I provide you makes it all worth it! Lastly, thank you to all of you readers who continue to read every book I release into the world. It means more than you know. Oh, one last thank you I almost forgot. Thanks to my *A* key for having enough fight to finish this book. It's on its last life, but we made it. On to the next one!

# A SPECIAL THANK YOU TO MY PATRON MEMBERS

Alicia Toothman
Crystal Evans
Janeth Acevedo
Julia Terry
Leanne Meyer
Liz Wallace
Mari Pittelman
Mary Trujillo
Megan Stevens
Meredith Livingston
Montez Oudenaarden
Paige French
Sophia McIntyre

Steven Jeczala
Trina Thompson
Aaron Masters
Gage Greenwood
Molly Mix
Nancy Crowley
Stephanie Winegeart
TripleAre
Andrea Wright
April Butler
Jay Bower
Megan Stockton
Tyler Shields

# About the Author

John Durgin is a proud active HWA member and lifelong horror fan. Growing up in New Hampshire, he discovered Stephen King much younger than most probably should have, reading *IT* before he reached high school—and knew from that moment on he wanted to write horror. He had his first story accepted in the summer of 2021. His debut novel, *The Cursed Among Us* was released June 3, 2022, and went on to become an Amazon bestseller. Next up, his sophomore novel titled *Inside The Devil's Nest*, released in January of 2023, followed by his debut collection, *Sleeping In The Fire* in June of 2023. In 2024 he released two more novels, starting with *Kosa* which released to stellar reviews, and *Consumed by Evil* through Crystal Lake Publishing in November 2024.

www.johndurginauthor.com

facebook.com/John_Durgin_Author
x.com/jdurgin1084
instagram.com/durginpencildrawings
tiktok.com/@johndurgin_author

# Want a signed copy of John's books?

Want a signed copy of John's books? Visit his online shop for swag, signed books, and more!

**ONLINE SHOP**

OTHER WORKS BY JOHN DURGIN

*The Cursed Among Us (Book 1 of the Newport Curse series)*

*Inside The Devil's Nest*

*Sleeping in the Fire: A Collection of 9 Horrifying Tales*

*Blank Space*

*Kosa*

*Consumed By Evil (Book 2 of the Newport Curse series)*

*What Swallows The Light- Suffocating Skies (Dark Tide book 19)*

**Coming soon from John**

*The Envelope-* **August 2025**

*Conjuring The Demon (Book 3 of the Newport Curse series)* **November 2025**

*Yule (Mid-grade horror novel)-* **December 2025**

Printed in Dunstable, United Kingdom